ANY WITCH WAY

A WITCH IN WOLF WOOD, BOOK 3

LINDSAY BUROKER

Copyright © 2021 by Lindsay Buroker

All rights reserved.

No part of this book may be reproduced in any form or by any electronic or mechanical means, including information storage and retrieval systems, without written permission from the author, except for the use of brief quotations in a book review.

ACKNOWLEDGMENTS

Thank you, good reader, for following along with my latest series. When I originally thought up Morgen and Amar's story, I only planned to write one book. But one is never enough for those of us who adore series and tend to fall in love with our characters and want to spend more time with them.

So, now we have three books, and I must confess that as I get this manuscript ready to publish, I'm already outlining a fourth. I hope you enjoy *Any Witch Way* and don't mind a few more adventures!

Before you jump in, please allow me to thank my editor, Shelley Holloway, and my beta readers, Sarah Engelke, Rue Silver, and Cindy Wilkinson. Thank you, as well, to my cover designer, Jesh Art Studio, and my narrator for the audiobooks, Vivienne Leheny.

1

"An almond-milk latte and a vegan blueberry scone, please."

As Morgen Keller stuck her debit card in the reader, she tried not to think about her dwindling savings account and the dearth of programming jobs in the tiny town of Bellrock, Washington. Unfortunately, her new hobbies of sassing werewolves, learning about her witch heritage, and organizing Grandma's old farmhouse didn't pay. It was also unlikely she would get rich from her latest endeavor of compulsively entering information on every incantation, spell component, and quirky occult item she could find into a custom database.

"Vegan? I can't imagine you and the werewolf dine out together often." Phoebe Aetos, owner of the Crystal Parlor and the only witch in town willing to talk to Morgen, stepped up to the counter, the hem of her blue boho dress swishing around her ankles. "Black coffee."

"Amar likes baked goods." Morgen almost added *and Girl Scout cookies,* but he'd been a little shy about admitting a love for those, no doubt due to their unmanly nature. She felt as if he'd shared a secret when he'd showed her his stash of shortbread, and she smiled at the memory. "I don't think he cares if the baker uses butter or coconut oil."

"I guess I imagine werewolves craving their scones jammed with meat."

"That's an empanada, not a scone, and I'm sure he likes them."

The teenager taking orders curled her lip at this talk of meat pastries in her vegan bakery, but she filled the orders without comment. In Bellrock, the Timber Wolf restaurant filled the meat needs of the populace, even wheeling the beef trolley out to diners so they could select a raw slab. Morgen occasionally had nightmares about the place, admittedly more because she'd been attacked by werewolves in the parking lot than due to the carnivore-centered offerings, but that trolley always seemed to roll through the dreams.

"I'll bet." Once they had their drinks, Phoebe led the way to a table, frowning out the window as a burly man in overalls and a tank top strolled past out front.

Morgen recognized him but didn't say anything.

"Thanks for joining me here," Phoebe said. "There's something I need to talk to you about."

Morgen withdrew her scone from a brown bag that promised it was made from recycled paper. "Is it that you're so delighted by the inventory-management system and web shop that I set up for your store that you feel compelled to pay me for my time?"

"No, that isn't it."

"I was afraid of that." Morgen smiled and took a bite of her scone, but she was uneasy. The message that Phoebe had sent to her, courtesy of her familiar Zeke, had been terse and nonexplanatory. The raven, who'd squawked loudly at Lucky for five minutes from the barn roof, had been much more verbose, but Morgen wasn't ornithologically fluent. "Any chance you'd be willing to come up to the house and teach me how to set wards to protect the property?"

Morgen watched Phoebe's face, wishing she was better at guessing people's thoughts. Phoebe had been giving her magic lessons in exchange for the computer help, but lately, she hadn't been willing to teach Morgen anything that would be useful for defending herself or the property she'd inherited. Phoebe had tightly limited what she was willing to share since Nora, a witch in the town's coven, had tried to burn down the farmhouse while siccing werewolves at Morgen and Amar. It wasn't entirely Morgen's fault that Nora had crashed her gyrocopter and died, but Morgen *had* been doing everything she could to defend her home at the time.

Phoebe sipped from her cup. "I'm afraid I need to terminate our mentor-mentee relationship."

A piece of scone stuck in Morgen's throat. She'd been afraid Phoebe would distance herself from her, but it still came as a blow.

"Any particular reason?"

"The coven believes you're dangerous and shouldn't be taught. I do appreciate you helping me bring my store into the twenty-first century, especially since I've started getting orders from around the world, but you've decided to start making talismans for the werewolves, talismans that prevent us from using our magic on them—using our magic to *defend* against them..." Phoebe spread her hand, palm toward the ceiling.

Outside, another fit man ambled past, tools hanging from a belt that only partially succeeded in keeping his jeans properly anchored on his slim hips. Phoebe frowned out at him, then turned a suspicious eye on Morgen.

Since Morgen was trying to pretend the men—the Lobo werewolves—weren't out there, she didn't acknowledge it. "I've only made talismans for Amar and the vet, Dr. Valderas. They're both lone wolves. It seemed like they could use the protection."

"It seemed like you should make them impervious to our magic, you mean?"

"I understand the witches wanting to be able to defend themselves—trust me." Morgen touched her chest. "But it's not right to be able to control werewolves, to turn them into mindless *zombies* doing your bidding." Morgen lowered her voice. "Olivia used Amar to *kill* someone."

"That's his side of the story."

"It's the *truth*."

"Were you there? Did you witness it?"

"No," Morgen said reluctantly, "but I believe him."

"Of course you do. He's warming your bed at night with his big furry body." Phoebe made a disgusted face into her coffee cup.

Heat flushed Morgen's cheeks. "He's *not* doing that. And his body isn't furry when he's naked and human. He looks like a normal man."

A normal, six-and-a-half-foot-tall man with powerful muscles, a lean frame, and the piercing blue eyes of the wolf that he could turn into at night. She'd occasionally thought that his shaggy, gray-flecked black hair, goatee, and mustache made him look like a creature of the wild—or a prehistoric hunter chiseled out of a glacier in the Alps—but somewhere along the way, she'd started finding that sexy. Appealing. *Hot*.

They'd kissed twice before the battle at the house, but Amar hadn't approached her with his sultry bedroom eyes since then, and she'd been too uncertain of his feelings to approach *him*. Besides, as a shy introvert and someone who'd rarely initiated sex, even with her ex-husband, such brazenness was even more awkward than calling strangers on the phone. But she'd lain awake more than a few nights, wishing he *would* come warm her bed.

Morgen glanced toward the blue sixties truck parked along the curb across the street. Amar remained where he'd said he would wait, leaning against the door in his jeans and leather vest, the powerful muscles she'd been imagining nicely displayed by his crossed-arm posture. He was gazing through the coffee-shop window at her, unabashedly watching her meeting with Phoebe. *Protecting* her, as he'd promised he would. Her cheeks flared even warmer, though there was no way he could know what she'd been thinking about.

"Are you *sure* you're not having sex with him?" Still frowning, Phoebe followed her gaze, though Morgen didn't think she could see Amar from her seat. "Your familiarity with him naked speaks volumes."

"He's a werewolf. He's naked every time he shifts out of his wolf form. If you're around when he does that, you happen to see... *things*."

"I'm certain. Listen, Morgen. Who you sleep with is none of my business, but the witches and werewolves have been butting heads since long before you came to Bellrock. *We're* from here." Phoebe pointed at herself. "Those brutes are the invaders who came to this area and made trouble. We've been defending the townspeople from them, and what you're doing... It removes our ability to stop them and effectively protect others."

"You have the ability to protect people and combat enemies with all kinds of magic. You don't need to be able to *control* the werewolves. And like I said, I'm not giving them *all* talismans."

After her unpleasant run-ins with the Loup pack, Morgen had no interest in helping them in any way.

"Just the horde of Lobos that's been congregating at your house these past few weeks?" Phoebe asked.

"They're not congregating. They're remodeling." Morgen leaned back in her seat. "They're contractors, and I'm in need of mouse-proof baseboards and a laundry-room ceiling that doesn't leak."

Among many, *many* other repairs and improvements that Amar's pack had been working on. Grandma had inherited the house from *her* grandmother, and it was well over a hundred years old. More than once, Morgen had seen sparks when she flipped a light switch.

"Contractors, of course. That explains why they're milling around outside the bakery like your bodyguards." Phoebe pointed a thumb toward the window as the first werewolf who'd walked by passed in front of it again, glancing in while pretending not to glance in.

"That's Eduardo, the tile guy. The other one is José Antonio. He does decks and drywall and is, I hear, a fabulous chef and grillmaster. Elk balls are his specialty."

"They're neither tiling, drywalling, nor grilling right now. Why are they here?"

"They heard the scones were good." Morgen smiled and raised hers.

"Morgen... be careful. The coven isn't vengeful and—aside from a few... rabble-rousers—doesn't bother anyone, but they may make an exception if you flagrantly take actions that proclaim yourself an enemy."

Morgen lowered the scone. "That's not what I'm doing. I don't *want* to be anyone's enemy. I just want to figure out a way to pay the taxes on Grandma's property so I can keep it in the family and... I want to learn about my heritage. That's why it means a lot to me that you are—were—" she winced, "—willing to teach me. How can I convince you and the other witches that I don't want to be against them? I'd rather be *with* them."

Before coming up to Bellrock, Morgen hadn't believed in witches, at least not witches who could genuinely conjure up magic, and if she'd known there was a coven, she wouldn't have wanted to be a part of it, but now... Now, she was learning about her heritage and that she had the ability to cast spells and craft magical items, the same as her grandmother had. She hated the idea of being ostracized by the only people who knew what she was going through. She'd spent a lot of her life being an outsider and not fitting in, but that didn't mean she'd ever grown to like it.

"You can't be with us if you're with them." This time, Phoebe didn't look out at any of the werewolves, but it was clear who she meant. "Shoo them away from your home, and don't make any more talismans for them."

Morgen couldn't keep the bleakness from her expression. The Lobos were looking out for her and remodeling the house solely because they wanted talismans similar to the one she'd made for Amar. They all resented being susceptible to witch control—understandably so—and hoped that by doing things for her, she would help them.

And she *wanted* to help them. It was wrong for the witches to be able to control them. By giving the Lobos what they wanted, she believed she would be doing the right thing.

Not that she was able to make them talismans right now. She needed more of the magical silver necklaces that could act as receptacles for the special resin she would make. She'd gotten the first two from Wendy, but Morgen hadn't spoken to her since the young witch had learned of her sister Nora's death, and Morgen highly doubted that she would want to make anything for her now.

"I don't know if that'll be enough for the coven to want to take you in," Phoebe continued, "or stop pressuring me to avoid you, but it would be a start. Honestly, I'd like to keep teaching you, Morgen. You're a fast study, and I genuinely appreciate the help you've given me with the Crystal Parlor. Last month, I was wondering if I'd ever be able to catch up on my lease payments—the only reason my landlord hasn't kicked me out is he's afraid I'll put a hex on him—but now, it looks like I'll be able to get fully out of debt by this fall."

For the first time, Phoebe lost her frown and reached over and patted Morgen's hand. "I understand that as Gwen's granddaughter, you probably don't care much about appeasing others, but you'll be much happier with your own kind, and I'd like to see you accepted into the coven."

"Maybe I can show them that I can be a valuable member of your community. Did I tell you about the big database and software application I'm building? I've been putting all the information on recipes, spells, components, and much more from Grandma's books onto my laptop. I'm working on a phone-app version too. Any witch will be able to quickly find what they're looking for without having to dig through old handwritten grimoires without indexes or glossaries." Morgen shuddered, remembering the confusing books she'd waded through. Half of them were more like diaries than organized resources.

Phoebe drew her hand back. "You're making… an app? Of all of Gwen's collected books of arcane knowledge? For anyone to download? Morgen, those are the secrets of our people, of those of us who have witch blood. You can't put them out there for any bumbling mundane to download."

"I wasn't going to put it in the app store. I thought it could be useful for other witches here in the community."

"I don't think the witches of Bellrock are ready to embrace that kind of technology. On average, we're not the youngest and most modern group of people." Phoebe waved at her graying brown curls.

"You just said that you're turning a profit in your store now that *you've* embraced technology."

"I know, but I'm a businesswoman, and I need to do that. Most of the others are retired librarians, clerks, clairvoyants, massage therapists, and the like. Some of them can barely *work* their phones and prefer sending messages through their familiars."

Morgen didn't point out that Phoebe *also* sent messages that way.

"I'm sure you mean well," Phoebe said, her face and tone still vaguely mortified, "but if you want to be one of us and belong, get rid of the werewolves. Don't interact with them, don't let them loiter around your house—or *you*—and for goodness' sake, don't make any more talismans for them. If you insist on doing that... I don't know what the coven will do."

2

As Morgen was about to walk out of the coffee shop, her phone dinged with a text.

Phoebe had already left. Morgen had waited a few minutes, not wanting a witch witness if Amar, Eduardo, and José Antonio converged on her as soon as she stepped outside. Even though she'd denied it, the werewolves, Amar included, *had* come along to act as her bodyguards. Until she made them talismans, they had a vested interest in keeping her alive.

The number that popped up was local but not one Morgen recognized. *Will you meet me at the Back Alley Pub?*

Who is this? Morgen texted back.

She hadn't yet been in Bellrock's only pub and hadn't planned to change that. From driving by, she knew it was a block off Main Street and always had no fewer than ten motorcycles parked out front. It seemed like the kind of place where the Loups might be partial owners—supposedly, they had a stake in the Timber Wolf and other establishments in town—and they had to hate her more than ever since she'd fought with Amar against them.

Wendy.

Morgen blinked. Nineteen-year-old, jewelry-making Wendy was hanging out at a pub?

I have a warning for you, Wendy added.

I don't suppose you'd like to meet at my house instead? I made cookies this morning. Assuming her werewolf construction team hadn't devoured them all while she'd been gone. Morgen had intended to give them some, figuring she should feed them treats since they were working for free, and had left several batches out on cooling racks, but she'd hidden a dozen on top of the refrigerator, hoping to keep those for herself. Why she thought she could hide things from men who had noses like bloodhounds, even when they were in human form, she didn't know, but she kept trying.

Your house is full of scary werewolves. And aren't you already in town?

Morgen grimaced at this admission that Wendy knew where she was. Had Phoebe told her? Or could the witches in the coven track her every move? A depressing thought.

Yeah. Morgen couldn't blame Wendy for finding the werewolves alarming, not when Amar had torn the extra tire off her van when she'd visited. *I'll head over.*

Morgen went back to the cashier to order more scones. After having a hand in her sister's death, she would be delusional to believe Wendy would help her—especially to make talismans for werewolves—but if Morgen could talk her into selling her some more receptacles, she wouldn't have to find another witch jeweler.

"Four scones, please." Morgen glanced over her shoulder, spotted Eduardo gazing through the window at her, and amended her order. "Make that eight."

One was probably supposed to feed bodyguards as well as construction workers.

When Morgen stepped out of the bakery, not only Eduardo but José Antonio appeared, the burly men walking to either side of her as she headed for the truck. Amar continued to lean there, his arms folded over his chest, as he watched them approach. No, as he watched *her*. His focus was singular and intent, and she wondered what he was thinking. Probably not about their kisses and bed warming.

Lucky, who'd insisted on riding along, stuck his furry head out the open window of the truck and wagged his tail at her approach. Morgen reached into her bag and pulled out the scones, handing one to each of the men, and breaking off a piece for Lucky. He chomped it down happily, leaving crumbs all over the bench of Amar's truck. Fortunately, Amar didn't notice, or maybe he didn't care. The sixty-year-old vehicle lacked anything resembling carpet or upholstery, unless the torn vinyl bench seat counted, and she'd seen him clean it out by directing a hose inside.

"A witch came by," Amar said, as the other two men sampled their scones.

"Not the one I came to talk to, I presume?"

"Another one. They're keeping tabs on you."

"It's a good thing we're here to protect her," Eduardo said around a mouthful of scone.

"No witch would *dare* cross us." José Antonio rubbed away a blueberry smudge on his stubbled chin.

Morgen decided not to say that the Loups were probably the reason the witches were keeping tabs on her. She didn't want to appear unappreciative.

Lucky stuck his head out the window and leaned over Amar's shoulder. The dog had chomped down his piece quickly, and his nostrils twitched as he sniffed the scone she'd given to Amar.

He growled like the wolf he could turn into, and Lucky pulled his head back and lay obediently on the seat. Amar took a chomp out of the scone, chewed a few bites, and made a face.

"These are dry," he said.

"Well, they're vegan. And gluten-free, too, I think." Morgen thought they were good, but she'd also come to accept that baked goods without the usual core ingredients tasted different from the norm.

Amar's forehead furrowed.

"Using different flour and removing butter and eggs makes things challenging for the baker," she added.

"I like mine." Eduardo pointed to Amar's. "If you don't want it—"

Amar glared at him and took another bite. He must not have found it *that* unpalatable. "My mother used to bake with lard."

"To the delight of everyone's arteries, I'm sure," Morgen said before remembering that his mother was not only dead but might have been killed violently. He'd only told her part of the story of how he'd been taken in by the Lobo wolf pack long ago. "I'm sorry. I'm sure you miss her."

He grunted and got in the truck, waving for Lucky to scoot over. "Back to work."

José Antonio and Eduardo hopped in the back, wedging themselves between stacks of lumber they'd picked up earlier. Morgen felt weird about sitting up front with her dog while they had to ride in the open, especially since the mist was threatening to turn into rain, but not so weird that she insisted they share the bench with her and Amar. She didn't want to be squished between werewolves.

"I need to stop at the Back Alley Pub on the way," Morgen said as she got in.

"Why? The Loups own that place. It's not for witches."

Ugh, she'd been afraid of that. What if Wendy hadn't been the one to send that text? What if it had been one of the Loups trying to lure Morgen over for some nefarious reason?

"Wendy wants me to meet her there." Morgen showed him the text, more because she wanted him to see the number than read the message. If it belonged to a Loup, he might recognize it.

"She's one of the sisters who lit the barn on fire, tortured me, and stole all of the magical moss in Wolf Wood. Naturally, you should meet her wherever she wishes."

"She also made the necklace you're wearing." Morgen pointed to the talisman that hung on a silver chain around his neck, the murky dark-red medallion resting next to an animal fang that he wore on a leather thong.

Amar lifted his chin. "It is an *amulet*. Or *talisman*. Or *chain*. Not a *necklace*."

"Because your new hobby is reading the thesaurus? Or because necklaces sound girlie and your ego won't allow you to wear anything called that?"

"A powerful talisman capable of keeping witches from taking over your mind must have a powerful name."

"So, ego."

Amar squinted at her.

She smiled. "Back Alley, please."

He hadn't started the truck yet, and he didn't do so now.

"It's better than having to drive all the way to the campground to meet her. We're wanted felons there, you'll remember." Morgen flicked a finger toward the area behind the bench seat; he'd tossed the parking ticket they'd received on their last visit back there, and she didn't think he'd hosed it out of the truck yet.

Amar kept frowning grumpily, perhaps envisioning Loups leaping out at them as soon as they entered the pub.

"Like I said, Wendy is the jeweler who made your *manly* silver chain. I don't know if she'll agree to make more, since the witches are unhappy with me for crafting the first talismans, but it would be ideal if I could talk her into it. Hence my bribe." Morgen held up the bag holding more scones.

"You believe inferior *butter-less* baked goods will convince her to go against the wishes of the coven?" Maybe Amar had also heard that the witches weren't pleased about her efforts on behalf of the werewolves.

"If you think it'll help, we can stop at the Grocery Expedition for lard to slather on them." She waved across the street toward the quaint six-aisle grocery store with the lofty name.

"You are a strange woman." Amar finally turned the key in the ignition, and the engine started with the smoothness of a malfunctioning rocket careening out of orbit.

"I'm fortunate you like that in a lady." Morgen smiled, suspecting it was true, even if he hadn't admitted it.

"I like a *lady* who makes me talismans and defends my honor to those who would besmirch it." Amar nodded firmly at her, his gaze a little less forbidding as a hint of a smile curved his lips.

Morgen thought about saying that it wouldn't be inappropriate for him to kiss her after admitting such things, but with her dog between them and two werewolves peering through the back window, it wasn't the ideal time for romance.

At the rumble of the engine, Lucky sat up and looked through the windshield. There were noseprints on the rearview mirror that Morgen was certain Amar hadn't left there. She pulled down the sleeve of her hoodie and used it to wipe the mirror. Lucky licked her cheek.

"Yeah, I know it was you," she said.

Her dog had stopped glowing a couple of weeks earlier, but the rest of the spell hadn't worn off, leaving Lucky, and Zorro the owl, her familiars. From time to time, they gave her visions. Zorro grasped when something might be useful for her to know about and shared the relevant imagery, such as people sneaking into Wolf Wood to harvest the magical things that grew there. On the other hand, Lucky shared visions with her whenever something excited him. It might be someone knocking at the door when she wasn't home, but it might also be a chipmunk chittering at him from a tree branch. For *hours*.

Before Phoebe had broken things off, Morgen had been contemplating asking her how to *un*-familiar Lucky. It probably wasn't as easy as un-friending someone on a social-media site. No doubt, it involved another ritual that required chanting while prancing nude around a fire.

It only took a minute to drive from one end of Main Street to the other and navigate a block over to the Back Alley. Even though it was morning, the sign hanging on the blue metal doors was flipped to *open*, and motorcycles were parked in a row out front. Apparently, it was never too early to start swilling beer. Though maybe they had an espresso machine inside. Morgen smirked, imagining leather-jacket-wearing Harley riders sipping from tiny demitasse cups.

"Huh." Amar pointed across the street.

Wendy's white pop-up camper van, its sides painted with cartoon frogs, was parked between two RVs.

"I thought you were being lured into a trap," he said.

"I'm way too smart for that," Morgen said, even though she'd been thinking the same thing.

Amar eyed her. "It could *still* be a trap. She could be tied up in the back, and that message could have been sent by brutes using her phone."

Morgen wished she could scoff, but Wendy's own sisters had kidnapped her before to keep her from warning Morgen about a plot afoot.

"Then let's hope brutes like scones."

Amar made a face, suggesting *he* hadn't, but he'd also eaten the whole thing, so who knew. From what she'd noticed, the werewolves all worked so hard that they were usually ravenous and willing to eat anything.

"Here." Amar shifted and pulled a rolled-up clump of bills out of his pocket. He held it out in offering.

"Uh? Aren't I supposed to have sex with you before you pay me with a wad of cash?"

"Only if you're moonlighting as a prostitute. Offer it to the witch in exchange for more chains that you can turn into talismans. I want the pack to be protected, and you know it's what they want too." Amar pointed his thumb toward the men in the truck bed.

"I do know that, and I've been concerned about what will happen if I'm not able to make talismans for them." Morgen imagined vengeful werewolves rampaging through the house and pulling out freshly installed flooring, light fixtures, and sink faucets. "According to the formula in Grandma's book, the talisman works better if I *care* for the person I'm making it for. When I was making yours, it didn't seem to work at all until I thought... caring thoughts."

She glanced at him, flustered by her admission, however roundabout, that she cared for him.

"It would mean more that you care about me if you hadn't also made one for Dr. Valderas, a man you'd met only twice when you made it."

"He fixed up Zorro after he was injured, remember, and examined Lucky's strange glow on short notice. How can a person *not* care for the vet who looks after her familiars?"

When he heard his name, Lucky thwapped his tail on the seat.

"You're not going in," Morgen told him.

That got her another lick on the cheek and more hopeful tail wagging.

"It's a pub, not a park. There's nothing in there for you."

Not that Lucky wouldn't happily go from drinking person to drinking person, trying to finagle pats and ear rubs out of them.

Amar shook his head and parked behind the RVs. He got out and told the others to wait in the truck bed unless they heard a fight. Morgen left the window partway down for Lucky and joined Amar to cross the street.

"I haven't kissed Dr. Valderas in the root cellar," she said quietly, hoping Amar didn't truly think she felt the same way toward both of them. "Or anywhere else."

"I know." He looked at her as they walked toward the pub entrance. "I would have been forced to eviscerate him if I'd smelled his scent on you."

Morgen might have found such a statement horrifying, but she knew he was joking. "That's how it works in the wolf world?"

"Yes."

"I wasn't sure you cared since, ah, you haven't been that demonstrative lately."

"Others have been around," he said cryptically.

"You're inhibited by the presence of the rest of your pack? Or... is it Maria?"

Pedro and Maria hadn't been at the house as often as the rest of the Lobos—they handled the administrative duties of running the small construction company—but Morgen remembered the way Maria had gazed admiringly at Amar when he'd been on the roof putting out fires. For someone who was presumably happily mated to the Lobo pack leader, she'd been checking Amar out thoroughly. And the fact that Amar had a portrait of her in the glove compartment of his truck suggested that he still had feelings for her. He'd avoided answering Morgen when she'd asked about that.

"I am not inhibited by her or them, but you are a witch."

"I know that, but..." They'd reached the door to the Back Alley, but Morgen stopped him with a hand on his forearm. "I thought you didn't mind that so much, since I'm not... You don't think I'm like the rest of them, right? Does it really matter that I can speak incantations and make magic happen? Because of blood I didn't ask for? A month ago, I didn't know anything about any of this."

A month ago, she hadn't believed in magic. Even if someone had convinced her that it and witches were real, she wouldn't have thought anything of it. She certainly wouldn't have desired to *become* a witch. But since she'd discovered she had this strange gift, she'd liked exploring it and learning to do things that few people could do. All the lore was intriguing as well, all the obscure information she could categorize and slot into her database. It appealed to her desire to organize and improve. And maybe it all made her feel a little special. A little less bland and forgettable to the rest of the world.

Amar gazed down at her hand on his arm, and Morgen almost pulled it back, feeling presumptuous. But he rested his hand on hers.

"You are different," he agreed. "*I* know this."

"But the others don't? Is that the problem? And you're afraid of what they'll think?"

Amar sighed. "I thought I did not care what the pack thinks—what *anyone* thinks. Not anymore. But working with them these last few weeks... I've enjoyed the camaraderie." He lowered his voice. "Not being an outcast."

"But if they thought you had a relationship with me, that would change things?"

"You are a witch. They do not hate you, as they do the others, but... you are what you are. Someone who can manipulate magic. Manipulate us."

"Ah." Morgen wasn't sure she understood what difference that made, especially now that she'd made him that talisman. Even if she'd wanted to, she couldn't control him. "So, we can't be... anything?" Her voice cracked a little, and she rolled her eyes, disgusted at herself. She was forty, not fourteen. She shouldn't feel this emotional about being rejected by a guy, a guy she'd never even wanted a relationship with.

Amar took her hand and pulled her into the alcove that held

the doors. He put his back against the wall and drew her into his arms so that the men in the truck wouldn't be able to see them.

Morgen started to say he didn't need to prove anything to her, but he dropped his mouth onto hers and kissed her with an intensity that surprised her. She'd never been the type of person to wantonly engage in public displays of affection, and she hadn't dated anyone who had been either. This flummoxed her, and if anyone had been on the sidewalk, she might have pushed him away, but when her hands went to his chest, it was only to slide them up to grip his hard shoulders.

Maybe she should have been disgruntled that he didn't want his pack to know that they had a relationship, that she was an embarrassment to werewolf-kind, but it was hard to muster any indignity when she enjoyed being pressed against Amar's chest. In seconds, he assuaged her concerns that he'd changed his mind and wasn't interested in her. In seconds, he also made her forget where they were and why they'd come.

Until the door opened and someone blurted, "What the hell?"

3

AMAR BROKE THE KISS AND GLARED OVER MORGEN'S SHOULDER AT the speaker.

She tried to turn and look at the man who'd walked out the front door, but Amar's arm tightened protectively around her, and she found her cheek mashed to his pecs. He growled, the rumble that reverberated through his chest convincingly lupine.

"Isn't it a little early for making out in an alley with your female, Lobo?" a voice with a Canadian accent asked.

Morgen's fear that this might be a trap returned, though the Loup sounded surprised to find them there.

"It's an alcove, not an alley, and isn't it a little early to stink of beer and have pork rinds mashed in your beard?" Amar shifted around Morgen so that her back was to the wall and he stood between her and the Loup.

Morgen didn't recognize the man or the voice, but he might have been one of the wolves who'd attacked them at the house. More than a dozen of the Loup pack members had shown up for that.

"Never too early to munch on something delicious." The

bearded man peered around Amar's shoulder at Morgen. In plaid flannel and jeans, he looked more like a lumberjack than the other neatly trimmed and luxury-brand-wearing Loups she'd met, but the gold monogrammed belt buckle was suitably pretentious. "Though I prefer my snacks younger and blonder." He smirked at Morgen.

Amar growled again and bent his knees, coiling like a cobra to spring.

"Easy, Lobo. You're alone here, and I am not." The man glanced through the open door.

"Lucien wasn't alone either when we fought," Amar said. "How's his shoulder?"

The Loup squinted at him. "It was a shallow wound. He healed fine." His nostrils twitched and he sniffed as he peered out of the alcove. He must have caught the scents of Eduardo and José Antonio. "You better take your female and your pack and leave. The bartender won't serve your kind. I know him well."

"I wouldn't drink the same swill as you Loups if he paid me."

Morgen patted Amar on the back of the shoulder. Even though she understood the bad blood between the two packs, bad blood she suspected the witches had fomented over the years, she didn't think it was a good idea for him to intentionally pick a fight. Who knew how many Loups were loitering inside? Those motorcycles might all belong to them.

"I wonder why your pack cast you out," the Loup said. "It's a mystery."

He sneered at them and walked away, heading in the opposite direction from the truck and the other Lobos. Only when he turned a corner and was out of sight did Amar relax, though a disgruntled scowl remained on his face.

"The real mystery is why his pack hasn't cast *him* out, right?" Morgen patted his shoulder again and smiled, hoping to lighten his mood or at least lessen his scowl. If he wore that face when they walked up to Wendy, she might shriek and run out the back door.

"They're all like that. He only insulted you because he knew it would annoy me."

"It's all right. I've heard worse." Maybe it would have been more correct to say she'd received insults that hit closer to home. "I think I told you my ex-husband said he divorced me because I'm cold and aloof."

Something she needed to let go of, but it was hard. Her ex hadn't been the only one to say such things, and a big part of her couldn't help but believe they were true.

"You are not cold. And a woman should not be overly *available*. Some of the female homeowners that my pack has worked for threw themselves at them when their husbands were not home. It was unseemly."

"Yeah." Morgen decided not to ask if the werewolves had availed themselves of the offerings. Occasional comments they'd made here and there led her to believe that at least some of them had few qualms about satisfying the urges of female homeowners.

"You do not even *look* at Pedro and the others." Amar smiled smugly and rested a hand on her hip, as if he had kissing in mind again. "There is only one man who you would let kiss you against the wall outside a bar."

"True, but technically, I'd be more into the couch in the privacy of my house."

"Your house is not very private." Amar lifted his hand to her face and brushed her cheek with his thumb.

She wanted to close her eyes and lean into his touch. If not for their alley—alcove—location, she might have.

"They should be done soon, and then it'll be just us again, right?" Morgen asked. "Maybe then we could try the couch." Or her bedroom?

"They are talking about adding landscaping, a deck, and a gazebo."

"They must really want those talismans," she said.

"They do." Amar traced his fingers down her jaw to her neck, making her body tingle as she wondered if his hand would stray lower. "If you care about me," he added, "and about how I care about them and want them to be protected, would that be enough to make the spell work?"

"I'm not sure. If we get the necklaces, I can try." Morgen pointed to the door; they ought to go inside and find Wendy, not dally out here longer.

"The manly chains."

"Of course."

His face softened, and he bent close. To kiss her?

Thoughts of going inside disappeared as she hoped he would, but instead, he brushed his lips against her ear and whispered, "If you grow lonely at night, come to me in the woods. There is privacy to be found."

"On a bed of ferns? That doesn't sound quite as posh as the couch." Though she could understand why he might hesitate to join her there or even in her room when several of his pack mates were crashed out on the porch or in their truck. The Lobos had been working long days, and it was common for some of them to spend the night, especially if they intended to change into wolves to hunt in the nearby woods.

"I will ensure you do not notice any discomfort." Amar kissed her cheek and squeezed her butt before letting her go.

"Considerate," she whispered, needing a moment to remember her quest.

He stepped back and held the door open for her.

Wendy. Right.

Amar's smile was a little too knowing—and smug again—when Morgen straightened her clothes and took a deep breath before walking in. Well, she'd wanted to alleviate his scowl. She'd managed that.

They walked into a pungent cloud of marijuana smoke. That quashed her thoughts of dalliances on fern beds. The lighting was dim, with the only windows shuttered, and most of the voices laughing and talking belonged to men. Led Zeppelin played on what would optimistically be called a *vintage jukebox,* but what Morgen was inclined to label as a piece of junk.

If not for the frog camper van out front, she wouldn't have believed Wendy would come into such a place. Nor would Morgen have expected to find such a seedy bar in Bellrock. Hadn't smoking in public establishments been outlawed in Washington decades earlier?

She'd taken no more than three steps when the bottom of her shoe caught on a sticky patch of floor. All manner of stains proliferated on the tacky green vinyl.

A faint but familiar chittering sounded over the conversations, and Morgen turned toward a corner full of pinball machines and arcade games that might have been state-of-the-art in the early eighties. A familiar ferret was perched atop one, chattering and squeaking at the player below. Wendy, only her shoulder-length brown hair visible from Morgen's perspective, hunkered over the joystick of a Frogger game—her infatuation with amphibians ran deep.

A coffee-and-cream-colored drink in an ice-cube-filled glass balanced on the control panel. Given the dubiousness of the establishment, Morgen suspected the beverage had a kick from more than caffeine.

Two skeezy-looking guys in their forties, with cigarettes dangling from their lips, were watching Wendy play. Or watching *her.* One nudged his buddy and made an ass-squeezing gesture in the air with his hand. His buddy nodded and smirked.

"Are those werewolves?" Morgen whispered, fantasizing about

clobbering both of them. Wendy was only nineteen. She shouldn't have been in the pub, or drinking anything stronger than coffee, but even so, those guys should have been doing something less creepy and more productive with their lives.

"No," Amar replied, not bothering to whisper as he studied the pub with a disdainful sneer.

"So you can kick their asses without repercussions?"

"Do you want me to?"

"Yes."

Amar took a step forward, as if he would actually do it.

Morgen grabbed his arm. "I was kidding." Sort of. "But thank you. I always wanted my very own Brute Squad."

She weaved between tables, giving the air-gropers a wide berth, and headed for the gaming corner. The ferret saw her coming and rose up to give Wendy a warning squeak. That warning might have been more about Amar than Morgen, for the ferret promptly flopped over and played dead.

"I see his classic move hasn't changed in the past few weeks," Morgen said as Wendy let an alligator eat her frog and turned around.

She was cute in a floral dress, sandals, and denim jacket, but her eyes were bloodshot and a little unfocused. She swayed, grabbed the edge of the console for support, and almost knocked over her drink before apologizing to it. Had she been there all night? Or started in early?

"Whatcha drinking?" Morgen asked, hoping wisdom had kicked in at some point and it *was* something nonalcoholic.

"A Dublin Iced Coffee."

"I'm going to assume anything that came out of Ireland contains more than caffeine."

"It's beer and coffee." Morgen eyed the glass. "And some other things."

"Uh huh. I'd ask if you're old enough to drink, but I'm sure you're not. I'd ask why the bartender *served* you a drink, but since they don't enforce the smoking law, why bother carding minors?"

"I told you to come so I could give you a warning. Not get a lecture." Wendy swayed again.

Morgen reached out and steadied her. She was aware of Amar looming behind her with his arms crossed, but he didn't comment or interfere. He was watching the crowd and the door like a protective bodyguard. The Brute Squad indeed. She almost reached back and patted him on the stomach, but that seemed overly familiar in public, never mind that they'd been kissing on the threshold to the pub minutes earlier.

"I think what you need is a nap," Morgen said. "Do you have anywhere to go besides your van?"

"No. Olivia kicked me out." Wendy gripped the glass and lifted it to her mouth. "So, I'm here pondering what I'm going to do with my life."

"Is that what she suggested you do?" Morgen took the glass from her and set it on a table out of reach.

"No. All she said was that I was disobedient, ill-considered, and a bad sister." Wendy shook her head. "Nora's dead."

Morgen hesitated, the memory of the twenty-something witch in the gyrocopter springing to mind. It was hard for her to feel guilty about causing the woman's death—it hadn't been intentional—given that Nora had been trying to burn down the house at the time. And she'd commanded all those werewolves to attack Amar.

"I know," Morgen said quietly, wondering if Wendy knew she'd been partially responsible. She must. Olivia would have tried to put all the blame on Morgen. What was surprising was that Wendy had called her here and was talking to her. Unless Amar was right and this was a trap. "I'm sorry."

"I don't know what to do. I mean, I want to go to school for graphic design and get hired to make digital art for video games, but I don't have enough money for that. I can't even afford to stay in the campground."

Morgen wondered if Wendy had an artistic knack, or if it was only her love for gaming that made the idea of such a career intrigue her. Morgen could use someone with an eye for design to work on the interface for her software, but it wasn't as if she had money to throw around for hiring people.

"You didn't make enough from the magical moss you stole from Wolf Wood?" Amar asked coolly.

Morgen winced, not wanting to accuse Wendy of anything, not when she was the only person Morgen knew who could make the magical receptacles needed for the talisman ritual. But Morgen couldn't ask her to do that now, not when she was drunk and tired and mourning her sister's death.

Wendy shook her head. "Olivia and Calista took that somewhere and maybe already sold it. They didn't give me a cut." She shrugged. "I didn't want it anyway. I knew it belonged to the woods—to you."

A sneeze came from the top of the arcade game. A ferret sneeze. Three more followed, ruining the familiar's attempt to play dead. As if the ferret knew that, as soon as he finished, he stood on all fours, then flopped over even more dramatically on the flat surface. His limp tail dangled over the side.

"It's dusty up there," Wendy said.

"Cleaning doesn't seem to be a priority here." An idea popped into Morgen's head. "Why don't you bring your van up to my place and stay there until you figure out what you want to do?" She sensed Amar glaring at the back of her head but smiled and pressed on. "There's plenty of room, and you can use one of the bathrooms in the house."

Normally, privacy-loving Morgen wouldn't dream of inviting anyone to stay with her, but since the house was already overrun with werewolf contractors, did it matter if more guests showed up?

Besides, if Wendy slept in her van, it wouldn't be that much of an invasion of privacy. Morgen rarely used the downstairs bathroom, and Amar had been sleeping in the barn—or maybe the woods—instead of in the house, so he didn't use it either.

Wendy drew back at the offer, her bloodshot eyes growing fearful as she glanced at Amar. "There are werewolves all over up there. That's what I heard. Not just..." She threw another glance at Amar.

"They won't be there that much longer." Morgen hoped. "And they won't bother you." Could she truly guarantee that? Some of the Lobos seemed overly sexed, and Wendy was a pretty, young woman. "Just put some magical booby traps around your van—sort of like the one that blew me across the campground. I *know* you can take care of yourself."

"I don't think it's a good idea. Why would you even want me there? I helped my sisters..." Wendy waved vaguely.

Morgen thought about mentioning the jewelry she needed, and offering to pay her for it with Amar's wad of bills, but if Wendy feared werewolves, she might not want to aid and abet Morgen in armoring them with talismans. Just because Wendy hadn't objected out loud when she'd seen Amar's talisman, made from the necklace that Morgen had taken from her van, didn't mean she approved.

"I could use your help," Morgen said.

Wendy didn't seem the type to be suspicious by nature, but for the first time, she frowned and eyed Morgen warily. "For what?"

Was she anticipating a jewelry request?

Though it made her feel dishonest, Morgen said, "I'm building some software and eventually a phone app, and a graphic designer would be helpful. I'm horrible at making things pretty."

"An app?"

"For witch stuff." Morgen drew her phone and showed Wendy an early version she'd loaded onto it. "It's basically all text right now, with some pictures I took of ingredients in Grandma's root cellar, because that's what I can do. But for anyone to want to use it, the interface would need to be a lot cleaner and, ideally, aesthetically pleasing."

Wendy's eyebrows lifted, the suspicion fading as she poked around in the app. "That's a neat idea, but I'm not a trained designer yet. That's why I want to go to school for it."

"Did you paint the mural on your van?" Morgen wouldn't call the art breathtaking, but as far as cartoon frogs went, it was cute and serviceable.

"Yes. A couple of years ago when I first got it. I've gotten better since then. But I've mostly worked with real paints and pencils, not tablets."

"You can learn anything online. We can find you some tutorials. While you're staying at the house." Morgen turned and smiled at Amar, who had indeed been glowering at the back of her head. "The werewolves won't bother her, right?"

More sneezes came from the top of the game machine.

"Your owl will eat her ferret," Amar said.

"He's still with Dr. Valderas, relaxing in a quiet spot while the bones in his wing heal." She'd visited him a few times, and Zorro had sent her visions whenever someone he deemed interesting arrived in the vet's office. It had usually been someone delivering food or a client with a furry pet that an owl considered to be food. "Even when he returns, he'll be too busy molting in the barn to hunt for ferrets."

"I'm sure he can do both," Amar grumbled dourly. He hadn't answered her question about the werewolves.

Well, Morgen believed she was right and that Wendy could take care of herself.

"I'll think about it." Wendy handed back Morgen's phone, though her gaze lingered on the app. "Are you going to charge for it?"

"I was planning on sharing it for free with the witches in Bellrock." To get them to like me, Morgen thought but didn't add. It sounded goofy. And maybe manipulative. But she had to do *something*. "If their libraries are all like my grandmother's was... they could use something to make searching for information easier."

Wendy shook her head. "They won't take anything from you. That's why I asked you to come. To warn you. They're having a meeting in three nights, and you're the topic of discussion."

"Lovely."

"I think they're going to band together and give you an ultimatum. Leave Bellrock or else."

"Or else what?"

"I don't know, and I doubt you want to know either."

4

Morgen's phone rang as Amar drove the truck back to Wolf Wood. It was her sister, and Morgen answered right away. In the past few weeks, she'd only received a few text updates from Sian, the terse messages saying little more than that she was alive and recovering from the Dengue Fever. A week earlier, they'd let her out of the hospital in Borneo, but Morgen didn't know if she'd been allowed to return to her camp—her mosquito-infested camp—where she studied orangutans in the wild. Her sister was the most private of Morgen's siblings, if not the most private person she knew.

"Hey, Sian. What's up?"

On the seat between her and Amar, Lucky flapped his tail. He didn't quite understand phones and always assumed cheerful greetings were for him. Morgen petted him as her sister answered.

"I'm alive, my temperature is normal, and my nose and gums are no longer bleeding."

"So, you're ready to run marathons."

"I'm not even ready to walk to the mailbox."

"Do they have mailboxes in Borneo?"

"Of course. There's even an underwater mailbox off Layang Layang Island."

"Underwater?"

"It's forty meters deep. You have to scuba dive to it."

"I'm beginning to see why you lack the energy to reach it."

"I called to make a request," Sian said.

"Not because you adore me and long to hear my voice, huh?"

"I need to return to the US for... a time," Sian said, ignoring the question. "The fever hit me hard, and it may be some weeks before I'm able to go back to work."

"I'm sorry. That must annoy you. You're more of a workaholic than I am."

"I prefer projects to keep me busy, yes. You may recall that I placed my belongings in storage before I left, since I had plans to be gone for three years. I don't currently have a domicile in the state. Or in the country. Caden offered to let me stay with them, but his wife works from home, and they have children."

"And you, being even more of a seclusion-loving introvert than I, find the idea of passels of people in the house unappealing?"

Amar turned the truck off the paved road and onto Pothole Lane, as Morgen had started thinking of the mile-long dirt driveway that led up to the house.

"I do," Sian said. "I called to ask if you're still in Bellrock and if your apartment in Shoreline is available? I would, of course, pay you rent while I'm staying there."

"I'm not running an AirBnB. You don't have to pay me."

The part of Morgen that kept tabs on her savings being depleted admitted that some extra cash would be nice and that maybe she *should* charge her sister, but she couldn't do that to a family member. Even if it would help with the bills. She'd been debating moving her belongings up here so that she wouldn't have to continue to pay rent on an apartment she wasn't using, but given how many enemies she'd made in Bellrock, and the dearth of jobs in her field—in *all* fields—she didn't know how long she would be able to stay. But if she left, who would watch over Wolf Wood? Amar?

"Though I have not seen it," Sian said, "I trust you would not have selected an apartment in a complex teaming with children, adjacent to a freeway, or next to a construction site."

"It's in a small complex in a quiet residential neighborhood, but... you could come up here for a few weeks. To stay at Grandma's old house." Morgen couldn't believe she was inviting *another* person to visit, but she'd been worried about Sian and wanted to see her. And, she admitted to herself, she wanted Sian to see the root cellar, the werewolves, *and* the witches, so she would stop implying that Morgen had lost her mind.

Sian hesitated. She couldn't find the offer *that* unappealing, could she? Morgen knew her older sister well enough to know she would prefer her own place rather than sharing a house, but it had been more than two years since they'd seen each other. Surely, Sian had some vague interest in catching up with Morgen.

"I do remember it being quiet and peaceful up there," Sian said. "A good place to catch up on reading."

"Absolutely." Morgen ignored the long look Amar gave her. By the time Sian got home, the werewolves might be done with their noisy remodeling work. She would tell them she appreciated their help but did *not* need a gazebo or a deck. "When are you coming? Do you want me to pick you up from the airport?"

"That is not necessary. It's a long drive from SeaTac to Bellrock. I do not wish to inconvenience you."

"Right. You should pay two hundred dollars for a taxi ride instead." Since they were both mature women in their forties, Morgen resisted the urge to roll her eyes at her sister's tendency toward independence and refusing help. No doubt, whichever nurse had cared for her in the hospital had found her a tedious and recalcitrant patient.

"It is unlikely the shuttle will be that expensive. I may also be able to get a flight into the Bellingham airport. I will consider this and keep you apprised of my travel plans."

"Good. Keep me apprised of when you want me to pick you up too. I'll bring Amar. I know you've wanted to meet a werewolf."

"Goodbye," Sian said without acknowledging the rest.

"It's possible she *doesn't* want to meet you," Morgen said to the second long look that Amar shared with her.

"She is another loner?"

"The women in our family trend that way. Except for my cousin Zoe, but she takes after her dad. He's Greek, and I understand they're a very passionate and garrulous people. She'd be excited to meet hunky handyman werewolves."

"Handyman?" That earned her an indignant eyebrow twitch.

"Sorry, I like alliteration. Hunky contractor werewolves didn't have as nice a ring."

"You will invite this cousin to the house too?" Amar sounded disapproving.

"I wasn't planning on it. Are you bothered by all the people around? I know you prefer your privacy too."

"I do. I will be pleased when the pack finishes and leaves."

"Do you mind that I invited Wendy? It was a spur-of-the-minute idea, but I should have asked you."

"She is one of the ones who tortured me and burned the barn. A lot of my furniture and art pieces were too damaged to salvage. I lost months' worth of work."

Morgen suspected that irked him more than the torture, though he had plenty of reason to resent the witch sisters for both.

"I know," Morgen said, "but Wendy wasn't the ringleader. I'm beginning to believe that she didn't want to go along with her sisters but was too young and maybe too afraid to stand up to them."

"Should she show up, I will refrain from perforating any more of her tires."

"And will you refrain from perforating *her* too?"

"As long as she doesn't attack me first."

They rounded the last bend in the long driveway, and the house and barn came into view, along with nine or ten Lobos. The men were staring at the sky instead of working. Dread crept into Morgen's gut, and Wendy's warning popped into her mind. The sky was gray, and it took her a moment to pick out what the men were looking at. Seagulls.

Dozens and dozens of the white-and-gray birds were flapping around over the hilltop, circling like vultures. Since the water of Rosario Strait wasn't far away, it was common to see them, but not *flocks* of them and not loitering over the house. There weren't even any appealing power lines up here for them to perch on.

Something crunched under the truck's tire as Amar parked, and Morgen frowned as she spotted brown and white objects all over the driveway, the lawn, and even the roof of the house. The seagulls were dropping things. Trash? Dead animals? Morgen couldn't quite tell.

An object struck the windshield, somehow clattering and splatting at the same time. Morgen flinched as Lucky surged to his feet and barked. It rolled onto the hood, a giant clam with a huge peach-colored body hanging out. It took Morgen a moment to identify it as a geoduck.

A chunk of brown kelp splatted onto the windshield next.

"What is going on?" Amar growled over Lucky's barking.

Morgen slumped back on the seat. "I think the witches are delivering their ultimatum."

"What is it? Leave the area or be pelted by sushi?"

"I have a feeling it's worse than that," Morgen said glumly.

5

Seaweed, clams, geoducks, kelp, and more beach debris than Morgen could name littered the driveway, the house, and the lawn by the time the seagulls left. It was unclear if they'd departed because they ran out of ammo or if the werewolves had scared them off.

After one big gray gull had dropped kelp on Fernando, one of the crew's carpenters, he'd turned himself into a human artillery weapon, launching pieces of scrap wood from around the sawhorses where he'd been cutting lumber. He'd knocked three seagulls out of the sky. After that, the rest had fled, all save one that landed atop the barn and stared down at Morgen with beady eyes.

"That one might be someone's familiar," she said.

If it had been Phoebe's raven, also known as Lucky's nemesis, he might have barked at it, but he didn't seem to notice the seagull. He was too busy running around and sniffing all the sea debris. He nosed a geoduck onto its side, then plucked it up in his teeth and trotted off to find a private spot to play with it. Or maybe eat it.

Morgen's stomach turned at the idea, though she knew people did cook them for human consumption.

"Not vegetarian people," she muttered, though it wasn't anything she would have eaten even before she'd adopted that diet.

Amar stood next to her, but he didn't comment, other than to look over at one of the werewolves. José Antonio had found a bucket and was whistling as he wandered about, picking up clams and geoducks.

"José Antonio isn't disturbed by the witches' warning," Amar noted. "He's probably deciding what sauce is best to baste seafood with before barbecuing."

"I can't imagine any sauce would make a geoduck taste good."

"We'll find out when he breaks out his grill tonight."

"*You* might. My palate and I are going to let it remain a mystery."

The remaining seagull flew down from the roof toward them.

Amar stepped in front of Morgen, as if to protect her from a strafing run. But the seagull wasn't attacking. It clutched something in its talons and dropped it as it soared past a few feet above their heads, wingbeats stirring the air. A little scroll tube. Amar caught it and handed it to Morgen as the seagull flapped off.

She tugged open the cap and slid out a rolled-up note.

"'It is forbidden for witches to harm other witches, and you have killed one of the coven,'" she read aloud. "'You have one week to leave Wolf Wood and Bellrock forever, or we will destroy your ancestral home, whether you are in it or not. The werewolves will not be able to protect you. It is not our way to take such measures, but you leave us no choice.'"

It was signed by the Sisters of the Trillium Moon, but it looked like the same calligraphy that had been used on the letter she'd received from Calista, the warning to watch her back. Wendy had said the coven was going to meet in three nights to discuss

Morgen. If they'd already decided what to do about her, they wouldn't *need* to have a meeting. Maybe this note and these seagulls were all Calista's doing, and she was acting without the coven's support.

"The werewolves *will* be able to protect you," Amar said, growling again. He met her eyes. "*I* will protect you."

"I appreciate that. You're a good ally."

"Yes." His eyelids lowered halfway, making her think of their kiss outside the pub.

Unfortunately, with two new houseguests arriving soon, it would be even harder to find the privacy they both preferred for intimate moments. She thought of Amar's invitation for her to come find him in the woods at night, but she would likely get lost or break her ankle tripping over a root. A make-out session under trees dripping rainwater didn't sound that appealing.

Still, the fact that he seemed to *want* to be with her titillated her. Maybe it would be worth a late-night forest trek to spend romantic time with him.

A truck rumbled up the driveway, and Amar looked away.

Pedro and Maria sat in the cab, and the bed was full of lumber and drywall supplies. The pair climbed out and lifted their hands in greeting, Pedro now recovered enough from his shoulder injury to move his arm freely. As usual, Maria radiated beauty even though she was dressed in baggy work pants, wore no makeup, and had her raven hair pulled back in an unassuming ponytail.

The whole pack knew she was Pedro's mate, but several of the men gazed wistfully at her as she lowered the tailgate and helped him unload wood. Amar walked over to help them. To help *her*?

Morgen tamped down the jealousy threatening to rear up. He hadn't given any indication that he wanted to leave his budding relationship with her to pursue his brother's girl, and as far as Morgen knew, Pedro and Maria were still an item. Besides—she looked down at the note—she had bigger problems to worry about.

A twinge of dizziness came over her, a sensation she recognized as a vision coming on from one of her familiars. Since Lucky was noshing on a raw geoduck, she hoped it wasn't from him.

But it was Dr. Valderas's office that formed before her eyes, a view from the perch where Zorro spent much of his recuperative time. Sometimes, he was in a cage, when other patients were arriving for treatment, but more often, he was free to hop about as much as he could with the bum wing.

Valderas must not have had any appointments that morning for the owl was free. No sooner had Morgen had the thought than the vet stepped into Zorro's view, heading through the waiting area to the small foyer to answer the door. After opening it, Valderas didn't step aside or invite the visitor in. He seemed to speak, though Morgen never heard sound in these visions. She only saw what Zorro or Lucky saw.

Valderas backed up, his eyes wary, his jaw set. He looked like he wanted to close the door on his visitor, but a woman stepped inside, using one hand to keep it open and resting the other on his chest. She smiled up at him, and Morgen sucked in an alarmed breath. It was Wendy's older sister, Olivia. Olivia, who'd led the torture session on Amar and who'd probably coerced their other sister Nora into attacking Morgen's house.

A fox trotted into the room with her. Her familiar.

It peered around and focused on Zorro.

The vision tilted and wobbled as Zorro shifted on his perch, no doubt unnerved by the arrival of a predator. A predator that sat on its haunches and stared up at him.

Concern flooded Morgen. She feared that Olivia had learned Zorro was there and had intentionally brought her fox to attack him. *Again*. Even though Morgen hadn't witnessed it or received a vision, she was certain the fox had been the one to injure Zorro in the first place.

Valderas shook his head as he spoke to Olivia. He removed her hand from his chest and stepped back. He was focused on her and seemed oblivious to the fox.

On his perch, Zorro kept shifting uneasily from foot to foot. A hint of nausea came over Morgen as the view he shared tilted back and forth, making her feel like she was on the deck of a ship in rough seas. She wanted to rush down to the vet's office to protect the owl, but until the vision relinquished her, she couldn't do anything. Other than the nausea, she was barely aware of her own body or the world around her.

Olivia ignored Valderas's coolness and what was clearly a request that she leave. Instead, she smiled and unbuttoned her shirt part way, revealing a lacy royal-blue bra with her breasts attempting to spill out of it. What the hell kind of vet visit was this?

The fox circled them, neither person paying attention to it, and headed into the office where Zorro was alone and without a way to defend himself. His perch was more than five feet above the floor, but Morgen wagered a fox could jump that high.

"Get that beast out of there," she whispered harshly.

Could she manage to dial Valderas while the vision held her in its grip? She dug into her pocket for her phone.

With her blouse unbuttoned, Olivia sashayed toward Valderas. He lifted a hand toward her. She gripped it and kissed his fingers. He jerked his hand away and thrust his arm toward the door. She frowned, propped her fists on her hips, and recited something. The werewolf-control incantation?

Valderas sneered and pulled out the silver chain—and the talisman Morgen had made—from under his shirt. He shook his head, saying something that might have been, "No more," but

Zorro's focus was on the fox, and Morgen wasn't a lip-reader anyway.

She barely caught a glimpse of the fury and indignation in Olivia's eyes before Zorro tilted his head downward. The fox was creeping closer to him.

Morgen struggled to see her phone screen with the vision overlaying it.

"Amar," she said, hoping he was close enough to hear. "Dial the vet, please. It's important."

The fox sprang for the owl's perch. Morgen's vision shifted abruptly as Zorro leaped from it. He flew around the room, wings beating wildly as the fox jumped from chair to desktop to bookcase in an attempt to catch him.

Morgen's stomach lurched as the nausea intensified, and she dropped to her knees, her phone tumbling from her fingers. Zorro flew into the waiting area and tried to escape out the door, but Olivia, eyes wild, slammed it shut.

Morgen couldn't see Valderas but cried, "Stop him!" as Zorro's vision tilted left and right, and the contents of her stomach threatened to come up. "Amar!" she rasped, though she didn't know what she wanted him to do. *Valderas* was the one who needed to do something.

Zorro flew toward a room that Morgen hadn't seen before, but his wing clipped the door frame, and he lurched sideways, crashing into a bank of cabinets. He hit the floor, and Morgen cried out, "No!"

There was no way the fox would fail to catch him now.

"It's ringing," came Amar's distant voice. "He's not answering."

"He—" Morgen lost the battle with her stomach and threw up. Damn it.

The vision dissipated, and terror clutched her heart as her stomach heaved up her breakfast. Did that mean Zorro was too injured to keep sharing his vision? Or that he'd been... killed?

Morgen lurched back and dragged her sleeve across her face, tears threatening. The poor owl had gotten nothing but trouble since flying out of the woods to answer her call.

A hand came to rest on her shoulder. Amar.

"He answered." He offered her the phone.

Morgen accepted it with a shaking hand as she looked blearily at the screen.

"Dr. Valderas?" she rasped, dreading a report that her owl lay dead at the vet's feet.

"Ms. Keller?" he asked formally.

"I saw a vision from Zorro," she said, though he'd sounded so calm that she wondered if somehow she'd imagined everything. But no. She'd had numerous visions from Zorro and Lucky. By now, she knew what they felt like and knew that they'd truly happened. Although... Lucky had once shared something with her that had happened in the past. Maybe the fox and Olivia had come to the vet's office the day before. "Is he all right?"

"He will be, yes. We had a little mishap." Valderas paused. "The owl shared a vision with you? You saw..."

"That witch and her fox attack him. Yes. And you. I mean, try to, you know, with you." Morgen rolled her eyes at her awkwardness. Magically force him to have sex with her. Those were the words she'd wanted, though she worried less about that than the attack on Zorro. "The fox didn't get him?"

"No. I stopped him in time. I grabbed him by the tail and threw him out. I was also able to throw *Ms. Braybrooke* out." Valderas's voice had lost its formality, and he sounded relieved. "It was the first time," he admitted quietly. "She uttered that dreadful incantation. I sensed that your talisman helped me."

"I'm glad." Morgen slumped from her knees to her butt, though she grew aware of the vomit in the grass and scooted away from it.

"As am I. She will not be able to control me and use me as her *patsy* anymore. None of them will."

"Do a lot of them do that? Uh, the witches?" Morgen pictured Valderas's face in her mind. His *handsome* face. She could see why a woman would be drawn to him, but the idea of one or more of the witches using their power to force him to have sex with them was despicable.

"The two eldest sisters did, yes. A *bonding* event for them. I wasn't displeased to hear of Nora's death."

Morgen rubbed her still-shaking hand over her face, disturbed by more than the fox's attack now.

"Watch out for Olivia and Calista," Valderas warned her. "They have similar tastes and think their power puts them above the law." His tone turned bitter. "In this town, it does."

"Yeah."

"I'm going to give the owl a more thorough exam to ensure he wasn't hurt, but I don't think he was. Given how effectively he evaded the fox within the confines of my house, he should be about ready to return to the wilds. I'd give him another two days to recuperate, as there are even more dangers out there. Do you want to come pick him up then? Or shall I set him free? Given your apparent link, I trust he can find you again."

"I'm sure he can—he's drawn to Amar's furniture in the barn—but I can come by to get him, and you can give me an invoice. I want to pay you for taking care of him."

"That's not necessary. This talisman is worth far more than its weight in gold. I'll treat any of your pets or familiars forevermore, and I refuse to accept payment."

Morgen wanted to object, but with her bank reserves dwindling, she couldn't muster the will for it. "Thank you, Dr. Valderas."

"You are welcome."

She hung up and grew aware of Amar at her side, which was

nice, and Maria crouching in front of her, which was less nice. Even though Maria was frowning and looked concerned, all Morgen could feel was mortified to know that the beautiful werewolf woman—not to mention all of the other werewolves in the area—had witnessed her throwing up in the driveway. Worse, Morgen had made a mess on her shirt. It was hard to aim when one was clutched in the midst of an erratic vision sent by a flying owl.

"Are you all right?" Maria asked.

"Fabulous." Morgen scraped damp hair out of her eyes and thought about smiling, but who knew what might be stuck to her teeth. "I'm going to wash and change clothes. In case you were thinking about getting a familiar, I'd advise against it. They're a lot of drama."

Lucky ran past, his tail whipping back and forth as he chased a garter snake through the grass. Morgen hoped he wouldn't share any visions of the hunt with her.

"A *lot* of drama," she reiterated.

6

Two days later, Morgen was adding photographs of powders, tinctures, and dried herbs to her burgeoning database when a familiar camper van drove up to the house. She grabbed her laptop and hurried outside, wanting to greet Wendy before any of the werewolves ambled over to check out—and possibly hit on—the visitor.

"Hey, Wendy." Morgen lifted a hand as the van rolled to a stop and the driver-side window descended.

She checked on the werewolves. Amar was helping two of the Lobos nail boards onto the new deck that Morgen hadn't asked for but was getting. The framework for it had appeared almost overnight, nobody consulting her on whether she wanted such a structure. Maybe it was assumed that all homeowners desired decks.

Amar glanced over at the van's arrival but nothing more. His gaze lingered on the empty stump in front of the barn where he worked on his chainsaw art. It hadn't seen any use since the pack started renovating the house. As far as Morgen could tell, Amar had been helping them full-time. She hoped it wasn't because he felt obligated to work on the house as a repayment for the talisman.

"Hi, Morgen." Wendy bit her lip and peered at the deck builders and two other werewolves who were attaching new siding to the house. Was that recognition in her eyes? Morgen hoped she hadn't had any run-ins with the Lobos. "Uhm, do they spend the night?"

"Not usually." Compelled to honesty, Morgen added, "I guess that's not entirely true. Some of them work late, then crash in their truck or on the porch."

Something that had kept her from going out to look for Amar the last couple of nights, despite his invitation. She didn't want to run into any *other* werewolves who might be wandering the property. What would she say if she did? Amar had implied that he didn't want the pack to know he was dating her—if that was indeed what they were doing. She didn't know if sitting on the steps and eating Girl Scout cookies with him or stealing a kiss outside a pub counted as *dating.*

"Oh." Still biting her lip, Wendy glanced back down the driveway, as if she were already contemplating fleeing.

"They won't bother you," Morgen said firmly.

She believed that was true, but she would walk out and whack them with her staff if it wasn't.

Wendy wrinkled her nose dubiously.

"You can park over there if you want. I don't have a septic hookup for RVs, but like I said, you can use the bathroom inside. And if you want electricity, I can run a power cord from the outlet there to your van. Or you can stay in the house if you want. Do you want to see the full software for my program? So far, there's a lot more on the desktop version than the app. We could discuss ideas for making the interface for both better." Morgen held up the laptop, thinking a project might distract Wendy from her werewolf concerns.

It had been successfully distracting *her* from her witch concerns, though she was aware of time ticking down toward Calista's deadline. Her ultimatum. Somehow, it was much easier to work on a project than to think about how to deal with belligerent enemies. Besides, it was possible some of the witches in the coven might see the value in her app. Might see the value in *her*.

"I'm not sure I know enough to help you," Wendy said, "but I could take a look and maybe draw some ideas on paper. I was thinking about your program and that it would be neat if, in addition to lore and photos, you could put in videos of crafters teaching other crafters how to do things. Like when I learned jewelry making, my aunt Beatrice gave me some tips, but after she passed, I stumbled through learning on my own. Videos would have been really helpful."

"It would be simple to add instructional videos if witches would be willing to let me record them and give us consent to use them." Morgen resisted the urge to ask if Wendy would do a video teaching interested parties how to craft magical receptacles for talismans. *She* would be such an interested party. If she could learn how to make the jewelry herself, she wouldn't have to rely upon anyone else.

"I'm not sure how many would. Some of the older witches like to teach and pass on their knowledge, but they can be picky about who it goes to. *I* would be happy to share." Wendy smiled. "I don't know much, but maybe I could do some videos on jewelry making."

Morgen tamped down a smile—barely. "That would be nice. I'd love to include that in my program."

She felt a little dirty, as if she'd manipulated Wendy into teaching her how to make the key component for werewolf talismans, but she hadn't been the one to bring it up. Besides, Morgen didn't yet know if magical jewelry making was easy enough for someone like her to learn. Just because she could type over a hundred words a minute didn't mean she had a knack for hand crafts. She distinctly remembered being nine years old and inadvertently braiding her hair—more than once—into an embroidery-thread friendship bracelet she'd been making for her sister.

Morgen wondered if Sian had kept that bracelet or known how much work—and hair—had gone into it. As the younger by two years, Morgen had often wanted to hang out with her older sister but had struggled to make inroads with her. Sian had always seemed to regard her as a pest, though Morgen understood her well enough now to suspect it had simply been that Sian preferred to be alone and grew tired of having to deal with people. Even siblings. Or *especially* siblings. She wouldn't be any happier than Wendy to arrive and find werewolves all over the property.

Maybe Morgen would get lucky, and the Lobos would be done before Sian arrived.

"I just need a table," Wendy said, gazing around thoughtfully, "a cauldron, a few powders for the ritual, and someplace to plug in my soldering gun."

"A soldering gun? Is that a jewelry-making tool that witches have traditionally used?"

"It's a tool that *I* traditionally use. We couldn't fit a forge and anvil into the treehouse."

"A soldering gun does sound more practical. You can set up in the root cellar. All the powders you need are probably down there."

"Oh, I get to see Gwen's workspace? That's so dope."

"Yes, I'm sure that's the word my ninety-year-old grandmother used to describe it. Not kooky or emotionally disturbing," Morgen watched as Amar left the deck and headed toward the barn. He ran his fingers over the stump and gave it a sad look as he entered.

"What do you mean?" Wendy asked. "Why would it be disturbing?"

"Before I came up here, I didn't know about my unique

heritage or that Grandma was a witch. Stumbling across the root cellar with her pentagram and paraphernalia was a little alarming." Especially since she'd expected to find canned tomatoes down there.

"For real? I've never *not* known about my heritage. I always had it drilled into me that I'm supposed to be a good witch who can contribute to the family and keep our ways alive." Wendy rolled her eyes. "You said I could park anywhere?"

"Sure."

Wendy eyed the laboring werewolves again. "Where's your bedroom?"

"Uh, that window up there." Morgen pointed.

Would Wendy feel safer if she were closer?

"And where's your router? I can use your wifi, right?"

A curious chitter came from behind Wendy's seat. The ferret presumably. He was probably asking about lunch rather than internet access.

"There's no wifi. Grandma wasn't into the internet, and I... haven't decided if I'm staying long-term yet." Morgen *had* been having longing thoughts about wifi, even if it would have to be satellite-based internet out here. "The cell reception is all right. I use that to get online when I need to look things up for the database project."

"You don't have *wifi*? I can't game off my cellphone. It's too slow, and I'd blow through my bandwidth and get throttled."

"Sorry. Is that a deal breaker?" Morgen had a hard time believing Wendy's wifi had been amazing in her family's *treehouse*.

Wendy's wide eyes conveyed an emphatic *yes*, but she caught herself before voicing it. "I guess not. The campground had horrible wifi. I might as well have been on my phone. I've just been missing..." Wendy gazed fondly over her shoulder at the computer set up on the tiny table inside the van. It had to be locked down somehow, since she hadn't put it away for driving.

"Playing a favorite game?" Morgen guessed.

"*Castle Crawler*. I'm a rogue elf with an archery specialization. I have an eagle for a pet. He's cool, but if I get to level sixty, I can earn a *gryphon*."

"Not a dragon? That's a little disappointing."

"You can go on a quest at eighty to get a dragon, but it's such a grind to get those last twenty levels. It'll take *forever* if I can't get some high-speed internet. Bellrock sucks."

Said like every other teenager who wanted to ditch the town she'd grown up in. Morgen couldn't blame Wendy but hoped she would pass along that jewelry-making knowledge before leaving.

"Maybe if you learn to work on apps, you can get hired by someone who can actually pay you. Then you can buy a place with broadband."

"A place of my own would be *amazing*. I don't know anything about programming though. Besides, I'd want to make games eventually. Do you think a game based on witches would sell? I know *all* about that. It could be super realistic. And I'd let the players get a gryphon at level twenty. You shouldn't have to wait so long for such a cool pet."

"Realistic, you say."

Wendy grinned. "Well, kinda. I'll park and sketch some drawings for you. I have ideas."

"Sounds good."

Wendy steered the van toward Morgen's bedroom window. Morgen imagined waking up to *Frogger* music wafting up from below.

Since Amar hadn't come out of the barn yet, she headed over to check on him. A clamshell crunched under her foot, and she sighed. She'd thought she'd gotten all of those cleaned up. Hopefully, the seagulls wouldn't bring another round. She'd been doing her best to avoid dwelling on what she would do if the witches truly tried to force her to leave.

Originally, she'd been thinking of making the Lobos talismans purely as a favor to Amar, but if she managed to do it, maybe the pack would help her defend the property. They could be like the A-Team. The Wolf-Team.

But did Morgen *want* to fight a war with the witches here in Wolf Wood? No. She wanted to figure out how to get along with them. She didn't need any more enemies. She couldn't help but feel that if she could do something for them, they would be more open to having an amicable relationship with her. Or they'd at least feel too guilty to contemplate annihilating her and her home.

Whether she'd meant to or not, Wendy had given Morgen the time of the next witches' meeting—tomorrow night. Morgen intended to show up at it and make her case while offering her app to any of the sisters who would take it. She'd won Phoebe over to some extent by getting her store online and helping to make it profitable. Maybe she could woo the others with technology that would improve their lives, or at least make it much easier for them to research spells and potions.

"Just need Amar's help," she muttered. If she had to, she would go to that meeting by herself, but she would much prefer to have him for backup and support. And to protect her if Olivia was there and sicced her fox on her.

Morgen leaned inside the barn as she knocked on the door. "Everything okay, Amar?"

It was late afternoon, and the shadows were deep inside. He'd repaired the electrical, so she thought about turning on the lights, but maybe he preferred the gloom.

A grumble came from a back corner. "I'm behind on my work."

"Do you have clients waiting for furnishings?"

"Yes."

Morgen weaved through his projects to find him sliding recently varnished drawers into a dresser. "Did the rest of the Lobos tell you that you have to help them? Because I never expected you to put everything aside to work on the house. I never expected *them* to either."

"You know what they want."

"Yes. But you already have what you want." She wondered if he felt compelled to help his pack acquire matching talismans. She hoped she'd made it clear that she wasn't trying to finagle free work out of them. As soon as she had everything she needed for the ritual, she would try to make the talismans. Whether the coven wanted her to or not.

Amar gazed at her, his face in shadow, and she thought he might refute her statement. But he only shook his head and slid the last drawer into the dresser.

"I have three clients waiting for art pieces," Amar said, "but the pack is always around now."

"Did they say something about you making your art?"

She'd seen the men tease each other, Amar included. He returned their jabs easily enough and didn't seem fazed by the insults, but maybe that was an act. Maybe the taunts *did* bother him.

"Just that it's not manly work. And they mock the content." Amar twitched a shoulder. "I make what people want. What sells. Whether it's bears holding fish or mermaid mailboxes."

"Mermaid mailboxes?" Morgen raised her eyebrows, trying to envision such a thing carved out of a log by a chainsaw.

"I have a client who wants a mermaid and two dolphins for her yard. Pedro would tease me. A lot."

"Does it matter?" she asked quietly, though she would also be embarrassed by her family teasing her. She always told herself that what people thought didn't matter, but the need to belong was hard-wired into human DNA. For tens of thousands of years, being kicked out of the tribe had been synonymous with death. Maybe it still was.

"It matters."

"Even for a lone wolf?"

"Yes."

Morgen stepped forward and clasped his hand. "I might be able to try making the jewelry we need for the talismans project soon. Where did you get that last block of silver? I'd like to buy some for the receptacles." She doubted Wendy had used the bar Morgen had left in her van as payment for the two necklaces she'd taken, but she didn't want to ask for it back.

"I can get more."

"Do you have a secret silver stash in the woods?" she asked lightly, though his vagueness made her worry that the first bar might have been stolen.

She didn't want to accuse him of that or make assumptions. He always spoke of honor and refused to use trickery—such as witch magic—when dealing with enemies, so he didn't seem like someone who would condone stealing, but... he had ignored a parking ticket and said nothing about *her* taking materials for his talisman.

"Essentially." Amar extricated his hand and grabbed a piece of sandpaper for an electric sander.

"Uh." Maybe that was all she would get from him.

Before turning the tool on, he gazed at her again, his hair hanging in his eyes.

"Does that look mean I don't want to know and shouldn't ask?" Morgen smiled, though she was concerned.

"There was a hunter who took over an old cabin in the woods up on Goat Mountain." Amar waved toward one of the high points in the area. "He heard about the packs here and came to hunt werewolves. He was experienced, and he came prepared. He brought bricks of silver and molded them into bullets, because he believed the tales that silver bullets kill werewolves."

"Do they?"

"*Any* bullet can kill us if it hits a vital target. Admittedly, werewolf magic makes us sturdy and quick to heal, especially when we're shifted into our wolf form, so most bullets don't do a lot of damage. Silver *does* do more." Amar shrugged and touched his hip. "I've only been shot by a silver bullet once. I remember it burned a lot until I could get it removed."

"Only once? That's more times than is recommended to be shot."

"It was the hunter. He got two of the Loups and Carlos before both packs descended on his cabin during a full moon." Amar's eyelids drooped. "He didn't survive the night."

"Oh."

He'd been right. She would have preferred not to know. Prying had been a mistake.

"The cabin has since been looted by locals roaming the woods, but I saw him making the bullets one night when I was sent to scout. He kept the silver bars in a nook under the floorboards. They're still there. Most of them."

"I'm sorry you've had to deal with people hunting you for being a werewolf," Morgen said.

"He was hired by the witches."

She slumped. Of course he was. "Are you going to remind me how awful witches are and that you were a fool to kiss one?"

"No. You already know that." Amar lifted an arm, wrapped it around her shoulders, and pulled her close. His voice lowered to a rumble as he added, "And you're *my* witch."

A part of her felt she should object to the idea that she belonged to him or any man, but with his arm around her and her cheek pressed against his chest, she didn't feel inclined to object to anything.

"I think you should make your mermaid and dolphins," she said, "and if anyone teases you, tell them they're not getting a talisman from me."

Amar snorted softly. "I would not say that."

"What if *I* said it?"

He gazed down at her for a long moment, then bent his mouth toward hers. Relieved she had apparently said the right thing, Morgen leaned into the kiss, but a knock came from the doorway before they'd touched lips for more than a few seconds.

Amar lifted his head and growled, as if he might bite whoever dared interrupt them.

"Uhm, Morgen?" Wendy called, not looking in. "Sorry, but I backed into your dryer vent."

"What happened?"

"A werewolf stuck his head in the window of my van and startled me and also Napoleon. That's my ferret. He feigned death, fell off the dashboard, and hit the gear shift. It put the van in reverse when I wasn't ready for it. Do you want me to... park somewhere else? And try to fix it?"

"I'm sure it's fine, but I'll be right there." Morgen reluctantly leaned back from Amar, intending to step away.

But he didn't release her. "You're going to leave me to attend to a dryer vent?"

"Well, my guest sounds flustered. I thought I'd help her park. Also, kissing you isn't the reason I came in the barn."

"No? What was the reason?" He massaged her back through her shirt, making her wish Wendy hadn't interrupted them.

"I'm planning to woo some witches tomorrow night and was hoping you'd come along to watch my back."

"Woo? As I am wooing you now?" Amar slid his hand down to her butt.

"Sort of." She found herself leaning into him and enjoying his touch. "I'm planning to use technology instead of werewolf machismo."

"That may not be as effective."

"Maybe not, but it's scalable."

"Come into the woods tonight, and I will let you scale me." His eyelids drooped again. "My witch."

With her chest pressed against his again, she could feel her heart hammering against her rib cage. Or maybe that was *his* heart? Beats fast and full of anticipation.

"Okay," she whispered. "Where?"

"The spring. Ten o'clock." He kissed her again, a promise of more to come.

She might have stayed there, enjoying it and him, but a bang sounded outside the barn, followed by Lucky barking. Afraid that unwanted company would barge in, and reminded that Amar didn't want the werewolves to know about them, Morgen made herself break it off. At first, Amar tightened his grip, clearly not wanting her to leave, but another bang sounded, along with someone's suggestion to *Look for it in the barn*, and he released her.

"Tonight," he said, his voice raspy.

"Tonight," she agreed.

7

As the sun set outside, Morgen ran through a list of incantations in one of Grandma's grimoires. In part, it was to sort and load them into her database, but she also hoped to find a few she could memorize that might be useful if her attempt to woo the witches didn't go well. They might not appreciate her sauntering into their meeting, no matter how delightful the software was that she wanted to share with them.

She wasn't even positive where the meeting *was*. Wendy hadn't said, and Morgen was reluctant to ask her, lest Wendy warn the others that Morgen would be coming. If the witches found out and didn't want to talk to her, they might change the venue. Or they might set a pack of snarling dogs to guard the perimeter.

Unfortunately, Morgen was struggling to find any incantations that would be as useful as the werewolf-control spell. One supposedly removed mildew from shower grout—she dog-eared that one to try later—and another extended the life of produce, but she couldn't find much that would help in a battle. Since she'd had magical power used against her, she knew that stronger incantations existed. And since her grandmother had lived up here alone, it seemed that she would have wanted a collection of spells that could be useful for self-defense. And yet... grout cleaning was what the grimoires offered her.

A hint of heat warmed her chest through the fabric of her T-shirt. Her grandmother's amulet.

Morgen pulled it out and wrapped her hand around it, wondering what had caused it to warm. She hadn't mumbled any of the incantations aloud or done anything that should have invoked its power. Was it warning her of an impending threat?

A thump came from somewhere above the root cellar, followed by the whir of a drill. All she could hear were impending home improvements.

With the sun sinking toward the horizon, Morgen was surprised the Lobos were still working. She glanced at the clock on her phone. At eight, she planned to break off her own work, have a bite to eat, take a shower, and shave all of her prickly bits. That would take an hour or so, and then she could sit and be nervous until her date with Amar at ten.

Maybe she would wander out early to meet him. The thought of having sex with him on the forest floor was surprisingly titillating. In all of her staid and proper life, it had never occurred to her to have sex outdoors with anyone. Her ex-husband hadn't even *liked* nature, complaining of bugs and dirt and his grass allergies. But the outdoors was the perfect setting for Amar. She imagined him crouching on a log, the quintessential wild man, as he waited for her. He would watch her coming and undress her with his eyes before springing out to capture her in his arms...

Another thump made her jump. She rubbed her face.

"Okay, Morgen. Enough fantasizing. Incantations, remember?"

She truly did want to find something that could be helpful. Given the enemies she'd inadvertently made in town, this meeting might turn out to be dangerous for her. Olivia might be there. She might be *leading* it.

Aside from wanting to be able to defend herself at the meeting, Morgen had felt useless too many times when she'd run into trouble with Amar. She'd had to leap back and do little more than throw beer bottles or swing her purse as he battled deadly enemies. Even if Wendy and Phoebe had said witchcraft was supposed to be about helping people and not a way to hurt others, she'd seen for herself that there were applications useful in battle.

She glanced toward the wands in a rack on the root-cellar wall, wanting to know what they did and how to use them, but she had come across only general and scant information on them in the grimoires. Further, her attempts to point them at various things and will them to shoot out magical laser beams hadn't resulted in anything except her feeling silly. Maybe the owner was supposed to explain a wand in detail when handing it down from one generation to the next.

At least with the incantations, she'd thus far been able to make them work simply by wearing Grandma's amulet and saying the memorized words.

The buzz of Amar's chainsaw started up. Morgen didn't know if that meant he'd started working on a piece outside of the barn or had lent it to someone who needed to cut wood, but she hoped for the former. She wanted him to be a part of his pack, to be accepted as family, but if it meant he didn't feel he could be himself without being ridiculed... that saddened her.

"Incantation for weaving, incantation to bring on sleep, to bless an object, to banish evil from a room..." She couldn't imagine any of those being useful on enemies in a dark alley, unless that sleep spell caused them to fall unconscious at one's feet. But as she read the description, it talked about curing insomnia and softening one's pillows, not causing bad guys to drop unconscious in their tracks and start snoring. "Here's a possibility. The Illusion of Invisibility."

Morgen imagined herself running through the streets of Bellrock with a werewolf pack on her heels only to turn a corner, chant the spell, and turn invisible.

"It probably doesn't really do that," she said but read the entry with hope. *While holding a suitable amulet of power, chant the words 'Under the moon's magic, avoid cruel and obscene by turning the caster unseen,' and fade into the background to avoid notice from nearby people.* "Huh. Maybe it actually is what I imagined." *Swift movement may cause people to see the witch through the illusion, as will letting go of the amulet. For maximum effectiveness, stand still or move slowly. Also, remain silent and unscented. The illusion works only on the eyes.* "Unscented, huh. And to think, I was going to bathe myself in La Vie Este Bell Intensément before showing up."

She only knew the name of the perfume because one of her sisters-in-law liked to marinate in it before going out. Years ago, Morgen had owned a couple of sedate scents that she'd occasionally worn when she and her ex had been dating, but it had been a long time since she'd used anything like that. Were there any perfumes that werewolves liked? Olor de Carnitas?

"Focus, Morgen." Besides, anyone who wanted to have sex in the woods probably didn't care how elegant she smelled.

She spent a few minutes writing down and memorizing the incantation, as well as the sleep one, since she *did* occasionally have bouts of insomnia, then closed the books.

"Time to test this," she murmured and headed for the doors.

Morgen pushed one open before trying the incantation, figuring she would give herself away if someone was out there and saw the door seemingly open of its own accord. Before venturing out, she gripped the amulet and whispered the incantation.

The chainsaw buzz had paused, but a few thuds and voices floated to her from the back of the house, promising people to practice on for her trial run. Reminded that the werewolves might hear or smell her, she stepped softly out of the cellar and vowed to keep her distance from them.

Lucky ran past, barking at a seagull flying overhead. He didn't seem to see her, but since he was busy, that didn't mean much. Fortunately, there was only one seagull in the twilight sky, and it didn't drop anything dead or disgusting on the yard.

Morgen couldn't see Amar's stump or the front of the barn from her position but didn't want to distract him anyway if he was working. She headed toward a couple of Lobos finishing up attaching wood to the deck for the day.

It looked nearly complete, but someone had started building benches around the edge, as well as what looked like the start of an outdoor kitchen near the laundry-room door. The amount of work the men were doing, free of charge and unasked for, amazed her. Even though they didn't interact with her much, and she was never sure what to say to them, it touched her that they were being so thorough. She might not have as much trouble as she'd feared summoning up feelings of caring and getting the spell for the talismans to work.

As she walked into what should have been their view, they didn't glance at her. She wasn't positive that meant they didn't see her and was debating whether to wave, but the book had mentioned that movement could ruin the illusion.

One of the men was kneeling on the deck with a hammer and glanced in her direction, but he didn't seem to see her. He focused on Lucky, who was running back across the yard, having failed to catch the seagull from twenty feet below. He bounded up on the deck toward the man.

Before catching herself, Morgen almost shouted for him to stay out of their way. But if one didn't want a werewolf to see through one's illusion spell, one shouldn't shout reprimands.

Lucky planted himself in front of the man and wagged his tail vigorously. This earned him pets. He seemed to have known it would. Maybe he'd picked out all of the Lobos who would stop their work to pet him.

The man crooned, calling him a *perro bueno*, and Lucky flopped onto his back with his legs in the air.

Morgen walked around the deck, still not drawing any attention, and began to believe the illusion was working. If so, it could be one of the best things she'd stumbled across. She imagined herself sneaking into Calista's new compound—wherever that was—and spying on her. That could give Morgen the insight and information she needed to defend herself from her unasked-for foe. Maybe she could even drive Calista out of the area by stealthily doing vile things to her personal belongings. How could a witch set a revenge plot into action if all of her socks had been stolen and her bra straps snipped?

Morgen snorted and rolled her eyes at herself. She *was* turning into a criminal. She needed to figure out a way to get those witches to leave her alone so she could return to being an upright citizen who didn't scheme against anyone, bad guys or not.

The werewolf who'd been working on a bench looked in her direction. Morgen froze, thinking the spell had worn off and that he'd seen her. The book hadn't mentioned how long the magic lasted. Then she realized she'd snorted and that he must have heard it.

He sniffed at the air. She wasn't close to him and had no idea how strong his olfactory senses were when he was in human form, but she'd seen Amar sniffing and had to assume their noses were better than average.

Morgen stood frozen, torn between waving and explaining herself and being afraid the men would be mad if they realized she'd essentially been spying on them without their knowledge. She should have explained from the beginning what she was doing and asked for their help in testing the incantation.

Whatever he smelled, it must not have been enough to convince him that an invisible woman was peering at him, for he returned to his work. Lucky was still rolling shamelessly on his back while the other werewolf rubbed his belly.

Morgen continued on around the house. She passed another Lobo, this one taking a smoke break, and he didn't notice her. She bit her lip, pleased with the spell. It was working.

She continued around to the front of the house, planning to return to the root cellar, but she paused as the noisy buzz of the chainsaw started up again. Amar was indeed at his stump, carving chunks out of a piece taller than he was. He was shirtless, fine wood dust coating his chest and arms, save for the spots where rivulets of sweat had run through it.

Her legs headed in his direction of their own volition. She hadn't intended to disturb him while he was working, but maybe she would say *hi*, let him know she was looking forward to meeting him later, and ask if he wanted her to sponge off his chest...

This time, she managed not to snort out loud. She would go over there and tell him about the spell and make sure it worked on him. That was all.

But as Morgen approached, she noticed someone else in the area. Maria leaned against the tailgate of one of the trucks, smiling as she watched Amar work. She looked like she'd been in the process of retrieving someone's toolbox until she'd been distracted. Shirtless Amar *was* a distracting sight.

Morgen hesitated, not sure if she should let go of the amulet and reveal herself or not. She didn't want to speak about the spell in front of Maria. Though she doubted the female Lobo would prove herself an enemy, someone Morgen needed to be invisible around, something told her not to give up any of her secrets to her.

The buzz of the chainsaw halted. Amar lowered it and dragged an arm across his face to wipe away sweat.

Maria called something quietly in Spanish and sashayed toward him. Amar blinked, looking startled to find her there, and turned to face her. Maria glanced toward the house—toward Morgen.

Morgen had already stopped moving, but she stood utterly still now, her hand tight around the amulet. As with the other werewolves, Maria didn't seem to see her. Nor did Amar, though he didn't glance in her direction.

As Maria walked closer to him, she paused and glanced around.

Morgen frowned. Had Maria been checking to see if anyone was watching them? Why did *that* matter? Because she wanted to speak privately to Amar? About what?

Her jaw clenched.

Maria asked him something softly and stepped up to put a hand on his chest. Horror and anger mingled inside Morgen. And indecision. She wanted to spring over and knock the other woman away. She wanted to flee so she wouldn't see what happened. She wanted to shout and ask Amar what he was doing, standing there and letting Maria *touch* him.

But her feet were rooted in indecision, and she didn't do any of those things.

Amar asked her something. They were speaking in Spanish and too softly for Morgen to make out more than a few words, but he asked about Pedro.

Yeah, Maria's *mate*. Maybe Maria should be thinking about him instead of ogling and touching Amar.

Maria wrapped her arms around Amar's shoulders, rose on tiptoes, and kissed him. Morgen gawked.

Push her away, push her away, she chanted in her mind.

But he didn't. He stood there and *let* her kiss him. And why wouldn't he? She was his former love, the love he'd never stopped pining for, the love he'd drawn and still had a picture of in his truck. And who was Morgen? The woman who'd puked in the driveway at his feet the day before.

Morgen wrenched her gaze away and whirled to run into the house. She almost tripped over Lucky, who was bounding past on his way to the garden. She flailed, barely keeping from pitching face-first into the grass, and raced to the porch. Not caring if they heard her or not, she flung the door open and ran aside.

Whatever happened after the kiss, she didn't want to see it.

8

It was dark in her bedroom when Morgen woke, her grandmother's amulet warm against her skin. She'd been sleeping on her side, the green star-shaped pendant dangling onto her bare arm. It didn't glow or do anything else obviously magical except emanate warmth.

With her thoughts muzzy from sleep, she fingered it in confusion. This wasn't the first time it had warmed up, but it was the first time it had done it in the middle of the night when nothing was happening. At least... she didn't *think* anything was happening.

Frowning, Morgen sat up and looked warily around with her ears straining. The curtain was pulled, so little illumination seeped in from the handful of landscaping lights that stayed on all night. Her faithful watchdog was snoozing, his legs sticking straight out as he occupied more than half the bed.

"If I ever get a boyfriend again, we're going to have to discuss the sleeping arrangements," she told him, then winced as the memory of Amar's kiss with Maria flashed in her mind. "I guess you don't have anything to worry about," she added in a dark mutter. After witnessing that kiss, she'd cast aside all thoughts of meeting Amar in Wolf Wood. He was probably out in the trees with *her*.

An orange glow started up in the corner of the room.

"Uh."

Morgen gaped as it grew brighter. Fear ran through her veins, and she tried to think of something nearby she could use as a weapon. The antler staff. Where was it? Leaning against the wall next to the coat rack in the living room.

She slid her feet to the floor, thinking of darting downstairs to grab it, but how was she supposed to attack a glow?

As the light brightened, she could see that nobody was in the bedroom with her, not unless they were hiding in the closet. She eyed a gap by the sliding door, wishing she'd shut it fully.

The orange glow wavered and shifted, and colors appeared inside it. A blue sky, green grass, brown and green trees, and the perky red of the barn. It was the barn before it had been burned— Amar had replaced all of the scorched wood, but he hadn't yet repainted it. The garden was also visible, an early-spring version of it. Rows of kale and lettuce had barely started, and most of the beds were more dirt than green growth, save for some strawberry plants that had survived the winter. Those weren't there now. How many years ago was this?

"Are you seeing this, Lucky?" Morgen whispered, still debating on running downstairs for the staff.

But the magic didn't feel threatening, even though the amulet remained warm against her skin. Was it the *source* of this vision? If so, it would be the first time it had shared something like this with her.

Lucky hadn't stirred, and Morgen rested a hand on his side. It rose and fell with steady breaths, his skin warm through his fur.

In the vision, a person stepped into view. Amar.

He had on his usual jeans, but instead of the typical leather vest, he wore a plaid flannel shirt with the sleeves ripped off.

"Who would have thought the leather was an *upgrade* to his wardrobe?" Morgen whispered.

The Amar in the vision carried a huge slab of driftwood in both arms. He strode up to the porch and knocked on the door with the toe of his boot.

To Morgen's surprise, she *heard* the knocks. Thus far, she hadn't heard sound in any of the visions Lucky or Zorro had shared with her. But she didn't think this one was coming from an animal.

The door opened, and Grandma stood there, her white hair in a braid that hung over her shoulder, her skin weathered with age, her body leaner and frailer than it had been the last time Morgen had seen her alive. Pangs of sorrow and nostalgia and regret tangled in her gut.

"Did you knock on my door with your foot, wolf?" Grandma squinted and looked him up and down, her gaze lingering on the boots.

"My hands are full."

"So you've decided to be impertinent?"

"My foot was impertinent. The rest of me is too busy holding this slab for that."

"Uh huh. You're lucky you didn't surprise me a minute earlier. I was handling..." Grandma glanced back into the house. "Affairs."

"Cryptic," Amar grunted. "I found this piece down on the beach. It feels magical. The driftwood usually isn't. I'd like your opinion on it."

"You want to know if it's cursed and will wilt your cranny hunter?"

"My what?"

Grandma shook her head. "There's little point in being ribald with youth who don't know good slang when they hear it, is there?"

"No, ma'am. The magic?"

Grandma slid a hand over the slab of driftwood. "She's a beaut. Mesquite. You don't see that float all the way up here generally. A hint of magic, yes. Not from a spell or incantation. Natural. The tree grew that way, like ours do in Wolf Wood."

"So it's safe to work." Amar nodded toward the barn. The vision might have been from some past year, but the chainsaw leaning against the stump out front was familiar. "For my... cranny hunter."

"And other body parts, too, likely."

"That's good. You don't object to me using it?"

"Not at all. My objections start and end with your muddy boots being used to pummel my door."

"Next time, when my hands are full, I'll knock with my head."

"Excellent." She smirked at him. "You ought to find some use for that thing."

"You're a loathsome witch."

"And you're an odious wolf." She shut the door on him.

The vision showed Amar's faint smile as he ambled off the porch with his load. Then it shifted to the inside of the house, following Grandma to the kitchen where an ancient leather-bound grimoire half the size of the table lay atop it. The front cover was ornate with gold designs at the corners and a matching emblem on the front. It reminded Morgen of the book in *The NeverEnding Story*, a movie her sister had adored in her youth and made the family watch dozens of times.

Not only did the size and embellishments make the book remarkable, but even more interesting was that Morgen hadn't seen it before. She'd been through every book, tome, grimoire, treatise, and compendium in the root cellar, and had read the contents of many of them while creating her database. She was positive that one wasn't down there, nor had she seen anything like it in the upstairs library of more mundane books. It wouldn't have fit on any of the shelves.

Grandma didn't open the ornate tome, instead sitting down to continue what she'd been doing. Writing a letter, it looked like, but the vision wasn't sharp enough or close enough for Morgen to make out the words on the page. As Grandma picked up a pen and resumed writing, the glow faded.

"Wait, no." Morgen lifted a hand in protest. "I want to see what she's writing."

And she wanted more of Grandma, to see her alive again, even if only in a vision, and to see her bantering with Amar.

But the glow faded completely, leaving Morgen wondering what was in that huge book and who Grandma had been writing to. Soon, full darkness shrouded the bedroom once more.

"Was that real?" Morgen rubbed her face. "Or did I dream it all? Am I dreaming *now*?"

Lucky shifted positions, managing to jab a paw into her side.

"Normal people don't dream of being pronged in bed by dog claws. I'm sure of it."

She flopped back down onto her pillow. The warmth from the amulet was gone.

∾

Morgen sat at the kitchen table with her laptop open, doing her best to focus on writing the code that would allow her to add video clips to the database. That was something useful to do with her time. Dwelling on Amar was not.

Amar, whom she hadn't seen since the evening before. Other than opening the door to let Lucky out to do his business, she hadn't gone outside. After witnessing the kiss between him and Maria, she hadn't known what she would say if they came face to face. A part of her had hoped that he would knock on the door that morning and confess to the kiss—and say that it hadn't meant anything.

But he hadn't. Maybe he'd spent the night with Maria. Maybe, as far as Maria was concerned, Pedro was out and the hunky wild man Amar was back in, and that was fine with him.

The laptop bleeped an error at her, and Morgen scowled at it. She'd been staring blankly at the screen, her mind elsewhere, so she didn't know how she'd managed to elicit an error.

"Error with my life, maybe," she muttered.

Her phone buzzed, and she picked it up, needing a distraction. Besides, she was expecting word from Sian. The night before, she'd texted to let Morgen know she was returning to the United States and flying into the Bellingham airport that afternoon.

Morgen doubted this was the best time, since she had a witch-meeting infiltration to finish planning, but she wouldn't mind company. Company that couldn't turn furry at night. Company she could talk to about her tangled emotions.

A part of her was sad that her mom wasn't the one coming to visit, that her mom could never again come to visit. Morgen could have used a maternal hug and someone to talk to who wouldn't accuse her of being irrational. Their mother hadn't been the most touchy-feely person, something that definitely did not run in the family, but she hadn't been as puzzled by the emotional needs of others as Sian.

Morgen sighed and wiped moisture out of her eyes. She'd thought she'd gotten past her mother's death, but this summer—this whole past year—had her longing for maternal companionship again.

I'm on my way, Sian's text said. *The address is 137 Alder Lane, correct?*

Yes. Morgen was surprised her sister remembered it, since she didn't think Sian had ever driven up here, but Sian didn't forget much. *If one of the tires on your rental car falls off in a pothole, you turned up the right driveway.*

It's an Uber.

Then I guess the tires are someone else's problem.

Yes. And I am accustomed to potholes. None of the roads around our camp were paved. Some of the potholes were so substantial that when they filled up with water, Siamese crocodiles would move in.

Are those like Siamese cats?

They are not. I am approximately fifteen minutes away.

I'll meet you outside.

That is unnecessary. So long as the door is open, I can find my old room.

I'll meet you outside anyway. There are a few... updates to the house that I should tell you about. Like the werewolf pack engaged in weeks-long construction projects.

Very well.

Morgen waited until Lucky barked at the window to go outside. The chainsaw had started up, meaning Morgen wouldn't be able to avoid seeing Amar. That made her wish she hadn't promised to meet her sister outside, but she probably *did* have to explain the construction crew. Otherwise, Sian might take one look at the hordes of people, leap back into the car, and tell her driver to take her to a hotel.

As a blue sedan with the sides freshly spattered with mud drove up, Morgen stepped out onto the porch. The chainsaw stopped, and Amar looked over, not at the vehicle but at her. She saw him out of the corner of her eye but didn't glance in his direction. Maybe it was immature, but she didn't want to meet his eyes. Not because she was mad or feeling petty but because she was hurt, and she was afraid she might get weepy again if she let herself look at him.

Bangs came from the deck project in the back, and loud whirs emanated from the second floor of the house, where a team was sanding and refinishing the hardwood floors. The furniture in most of the bedrooms had either been removed and stored on the small third floor or was shoved up against the walls. She hoped one of the guest rooms was still intact. Otherwise, she would have the joy of telling her reclusive sister that they would be sharing a room for a couple of days.

The trunk opened, popped by the driver, but none of the car doors followed. A back-seat window rolled down, revealing Sian's stunned face as she looked at Amar, the men walking about, and the construction trucks filled with piles of drywall and lumber. A noisy drill started up, and Sian winced. Even Wendy's camper van was making noise, the refrains of a pop song booming out an open window.

Had the driver not asked her a question, Sian might have stayed where she was. Morgen waved and headed toward the car, but that didn't encourage Sian to get out.

"The remodeling is almost finished," Morgen said as she walked up.

"You didn't warn me." Sian looked bleakly around and shuddered. Or maybe that was a shiver. She wore two thin hoodies zipped up to her chin, as well as a rain jacket, as if it were November instead of August. Maybe after the tropics, the drizzly gray Bellrock day felt frigid.

"I know," Morgen said, "but it'll be an improvement when it's done."

"Grandma's serene and peaceful woodland retreat is noisy and full of people."

"We're getting a deck and an outdoor kitchen."

"I had an *outdoor kitchen* in Borneo."

"Was it in lieu of an indoor kitchen? And next to an outdoor toilet?" Morgen had seen pictures of her sister's camp. Posh, it had not been. The orangutan nests had appeared more comfortable.

Sian gave her a scathing look, grumbled a grudging *thanks* to the driver, and climbed out. She'd lost weight, though she was still on the heavier side. Thankfully, she didn't appear as wan and sickly as Morgen had feared she would. It had been a couple of weeks since Sian had been in the hospital, and she appeared to have mostly recovered.

After her sister retrieved her luggage and set it down, Morgen leaned in to give her a friendly pat—the amount of touching Sian tolerated without commenting on how deplorable it was—but it turned into a hug before she could stop herself. She still felt wrecked and wanted sympathy and support. Too bad Sian wouldn't understand man troubles. She was like an android, indifferent to relationships, indifferent to feelings. No, that wasn't true. She had feelings; she just wasn't ruled by them and didn't seem to be attracted to people at all, neither men nor women.

Just as she had when they were kids, Sian stiffened and grimaced at the hug. Morgen sighed, wishing she'd invited her cousin Zoe up. But she hadn't planned to need emotional support today.

"Is that necessary?" Sian gave her a quick, awkward pat on the back, her grimace not fading until Morgen released her and stepped back. "You know how I feel about being squeezed."

"Yes, but we've both almost died since last we saw each other. I thought squeezing might be appropriate." Morgen wouldn't bring up Amar's kiss, as she knew her sister would be unsympathetic about that and probably confused as to why the recently divorced Morgen would even be dating anyone.

"You almost died?"

"A witch tried to magically compel me to get in a gyrocopter and crash it into a ravine."

Sian gazed at her with a flat unreadable expression, but Morgen knew her well enough to interpret it as wild disbelief.

"I'm going to sneak into a meeting of witches tonight if you want to come with me and see them performing rituals." Or whatever they did at their meetings. It was possible they noshed cookies, gossiped, and complained about their gardeners.

"I do not," Sian said.

"Do you want to see Grandma's stash of grimoires and spell ingredients? There are organs in jars too. I know scientists are into those."

"It may be interesting to examine someone's cabinet of curiosities."

"It's an entire root cellar of curiosities. Now organized, de-cluttered, and labeled."

"As I'd expect from you."

"Don't judge me. You like things tidy too."

"It wasn't a judgment." Sian frowned as two shirtless Lobos strolled past, sweat glistening on their arms and chests. They grabbed lumber out of the back of their truck and headed back toward the deck.

Zoe would have ogled them openly while fantasizing about bedroom activities. Sian looked like she'd bitten into a bad clam.

Another shirtless Lobo walked past, smirking over at them and flexing his muscles as he passed. Morgen didn't know if that was better or worse than being ignored by the men. Worse, judging by Sian's nose wrinkle.

"He smells," she said as he headed for one of the trucks.

"Of woods and musk and werewolf pheromones, I know. They're all like that." Morgen *liked* it on Amar.

"Disgusting." Sian pointed to a wet spot on the gravel driveway. "He dripped sweat."

"Do you want me to disinfect that spot?"

"I'd say yes, but I sense you're teasing me."

"You've gotten better at detecting that."

"I'm working on blending in better with neurotypical humans."

Morgen doubted she qualified as one of those, but all she said was, "A tall order."

"Tell me about it." Sian kept eyeing the damp spot on the gravel, as if she could will it away with her mind.

"You're fantasizing about buckets of disinfectant right now, aren't you?" Morgen asked.

"Pools." Sian must have been a blast in that rugged, remote camp.

Morgen's phone buzzed with a text from Dr. Valderas.

Zorro is ready to return to the woods if you want to come pick him up.

"If you're interested in werewolves, our town vet might be more your speed." Morgen texted back: *I will. Thank you.*

"I am not interested in werewolves. You are the one with this dubious new obsession." Sian eyed her up and down. "Or hallucination."

"Once it gets dark, I'll talk one of the Lobos into shifting into a wolf so you can see for yourself whether it's a hallucination." Morgen wasn't sure which one she would ask. She didn't want to speak with Amar, even though he kept glancing in her direction. Sooner or later, she would have to talk to him, but she wasn't ready. It would be too hard with the lump in her throat threatening to swell every time she thought of him kissing someone else.

Bleakly, she realized she would have to talk with him at some point during the day, if she still meant to take him to the witches' meeting. Did she? She would be a fool to go without backup.

"I need to pick up a patient," Morgen said. "Do you want to ride along to the vet?"

"You got another pet?" Sian glanced toward the garden beds, where Lucky was sniffing between the stalks of corn.

"An owl familiar." Morgen decided not to mention that Lucky had also been promoted from companion to familiar. "I'm a witch now, you know."

A drill buzzed somewhere, and Sian shook her head. "This is too much to deal with. I should stay at a hotel."

"At the Wild Trout Inn? I hear it's drenched in werewolf sweat."

"I would think from the name it would be fish guts."

"Probably so, but they don't mention that in the brochure."

"Just the werewolf sweat?"

"Marketing departments always highlight the key selling points."

Sian shook her head.

"I'll get my keys, and we can head to town." Morgen pointed to the house.

Sian didn't pick up her suitcases to carry them inside, suggesting she did indeed want to be taken to a hotel. Morgen couldn't blame her, but she'd been hoping for a little sister-sister time together, talking about the last couple of years' events over a glass of wine. Though maybe it would be better for Morgen to deal with the witches before settling down for family get-togethers. She hoped it hadn't been a mistake to invite Sian up here.

9

As Morgen drove Sian into town, what had been light cloud cover turned into an ominous gray sky, and it started raining. The windshield wipers came on automatically.

"That ought to take care of the sweat in the driveway," Morgen said.

"It'll be sufficient," Sian said from the passenger seat.

Morgen wondered if the coven would move their evening meeting indoors. She didn't know for sure that it usually took place outdoors, but the graveyard behind the church, a favorite witch spot that Amar had once mentioned, was at the top of Morgen's list of possible places to check. If the witches weren't there, she planned to send Zorro scouting around town to look for sign of lots of women congregating. Assuming the owl didn't mind working his first day back on the job.

"You might like the vet," Morgen said as she parallel parked a half a block from the Victorian house that held his office. "He's kind of quirky."

"Thus, I should find him appealing?"

"Well, you're quirky. Quirky people like to hang out with their own kind, don't they?"

That earned her another flat look.

"It probably won't come up, but just in case, I'll warn you that he's a werewolf." Morgen wondered if she could convince Valderas to shift forms and show his furry side to Sian. With that cloud cover, it might be dark enough for it.

Amar, however, had once admitted that shifting was a little painful. Asking someone to do it for show-and-tell didn't seem right. Still, Morgen would hate for Sian's whole visit to pass without anyone turning into a werewolf or casting a spell in front of her. Without evidence to the contrary, she might go on thinking Morgen had gone nutso.

"Is *everyone* in town a werewolf?" Sian asked with a sigh.

"No. Just the two packs, the Loups Laflamme and the Lobos Sanguientos. And Dr. Valderas. He said he was forcefully turned by a Loup, and they wanted him as one of their own, but he's a lone wolf now. Amar kind of is too, though he's getting along better with his pack these days. I've heard that the mayor and some other high-profile citizens—inasmuch as Bellrock *has* high-profile citizens—have also been turned and are associated with the Loups. I guess that *is* a lot of people."

Sian eyed the weathered siding of the Roaming Elk Inn and the soggy putt-putt course down the block. "Indeed."

"Dr. Valderas was the one who mentioned that the Loups forced some people to become werewolves to try to bring them under their sway and control the town. I haven't met the mayor or any of the other big guns though, so I'm not sure how much is the truth. Valderas might be a big gossip who spreads rumors." Morgen doubted that. He'd seemed more like a bitter man who'd wanted to rant. Given that he'd been turned into a werewolf against his wishes, she couldn't blame him for his bitterness.

"And he's the one you think I'll *like*?" Sian made air quotes around the word.

"Yeah. Because he's quirky, not because he's a gossip. And because you two have both studied animals."

Sian shook her head. "I'll wait in the car."

She looked toward the hotel again, as if she was contemplating trotting over and checking in, but the rain may have squelched such notions, for she merely leaned back in her seat.

"Don't be a doorknob," Morgen said, trotting out the heinous insult they'd thrown at each other as pre-teens. "Come in with me. See the town. Experience Bellrock. Don't you want to meet Zorro?"

"Who?"

"My owl familiar. You helped me identify him, remember? The —at the time—green-glowing spotted owl. He's lost the magical glow since then."

Sian stared at her. "See if the vet can write you a prescription while you're in there. Thorazine, perhaps."

"If you come in with me, I'll buy you a vanilla latte and a scone."

"Fine." Sian put up her hood, climbed out, and strode quickly toward the covered porch of the Victorian house.

"I should have started with that." Morgen had forgotten that Sian had even more of a sweet tooth than she did.

She caught up to Sian at the door and pointed at her shoes. "You'll want to take those off. Dr. Valderas doesn't like muddy feet in his office." She rang the doorbell.

"What about muddy dog paws?"

"I made sure Lucky's were clean when I brought him in."

Lucky was back at the house, overseeing the deck construction. He'd been more agreeable about staying home lately, now that there were so many people there to attend to his petting needs.

Dr. Valderas opened the door, glanced at them, then peered past them and into the rain before waving them into the foyer.

"Are you expecting another client?" Morgen tucked her damp shoes into one of the cubbies under the bench.

Sian hesitated, then removed her own shoes, revealing pink socks with chubby green dragons flying all over them. Practical whimsy.

"Nobody else has an appointment." His tone and wary eyeing of the street suggested he might be expecting someone anyway. Had Olivia and her odious fox promised to return? Or threatened him because he dared wear that talisman?

As Valderas closed the door, he glanced at their feet, then glanced a second time at Sian's socks.

"Dr. Valderas," Morgen said, "this is my sister, Sian. She just got back from Borneo where she studies orangutans."

"Oh?" Valderas arched his eyebrows.

"I studied them for two years there, yes." Sian didn't go into details. She wasn't one to expound on her personal life or her work. If he asked questions or showed even remote curiosity, she would likely refer him to some of the more recent papers she'd written.

After a moment, Morgen realized her sister had spoken in past tense. Did that mean she wasn't going back to Borneo? Or field work at all?

"Your background is in primatology?" Valderas headed into his office.

"Yes."

"She has a PhD and has published all sorts of papers," Morgen said, feeling she should talk up her sister to strangers. "Some in magazines and journals that people actually read."

Sian shot her a dirty look but didn't argue the fact that most of the dry scientific journals where she published appealed only to other scientists, and then only because those scientists were looking for papers to reference in their own papers.

"She hasn't had a lot of experience with werewolves though," Morgen added, "and doesn't believe they exist."

"That is a common opinion." Valderas gestured to Zorro, who had regained the perch overlooking the office.

His eyes were closed with his head tucked under his wing.

"I see he's missed me terribly and is relieved I've come." Morgen wondered if the owl wanted to leave with her. He was a wild creature and could simply fly off if Valderas left the door open. It wasn't as if Morgen needed to tuck him into a cage and take him home in the car.

"He had an eventful day yesterday." Valderas touched a hand to his chest, the silver chain of the talisman visible around his neck, even though the admittedly ugly medallion was hidden under his sweater vest.

Morgen couldn't blame him for keeping it out of sight. It touched her more than a little to know he wore the talisman and seemed to value it. If Olivia regularly came looking for him for sexual favors and who knew what else, that was understandable.

"As did I," he admitted. "I must thank you again for your gift." He bowed to her.

"Is this the *werewolf* you've been spending time with?" Sian asked.

"No, no," Morgen hurried to say. "That's Amar. It *was* Amar. And we're just... roommates."

Valderas's eyebrows rose again, and Morgen blushed.

"We're not even that," she said. "He lives in the barn. Grandma let him. They were friends. We're just... adjacently domiciled."

Her cheeks grew even warmer. Why was she babbling about this in front of Dr. Valderas?

"He said he cares about you," Valderas surprised her by saying, then smiled faintly. "Even though you're a witch."

"He cares for Maria even more," Morgen grumbled, then shut her mouth, wishing she hadn't said that or anything at all.

"Ah," was all Valderas said, though his brow creased, as if he were confused. "Relationships are often fraught. I prefer the company of animals."

"Unlike humans, they do not lie, scheme, or gossip," Sian said.

"Indeed."

"They just poop on your shoulder." Morgen noticed that Zorro had stirred and was flexing his wings.

Sian and Valderas regarded her with the same long-suffering look. Maybe Zorro had been respectful of the vet and his belongings while he'd been here.

"We're heading back to Wolf Wood, Zorro. Are you ready? Do you want to ride in the car or fly on your own?" Morgen didn't know if the owl was up to flying miles or if it would take him a while to work up to that.

Neither Sian nor Valderas gave her a strange look for speaking to a bird. Maybe they considered that perfectly normal.

"Wait." Valderas held up a hand and walked to a window. He opened it a crack and inhaled deeply. "I was afraid of that."

The rain was coming down hard, droplets bouncing off the pavement in the street. Morgen couldn't imagine what he could smell through it. But when he turned to face her, his eyes grave, her gut told her it was trouble and that it would affect her.

"Ms. Braybrooke didn't appreciate being booted out yesterday," Valderas said. "She's returning, and she's not alone this time."

"Werewolves?" Morgen guessed.

"One of the Loups, yes, and I believe another witch as well."

"Calista?" Morgen glanced at her sister, already regretting inviting her to visit. It wasn't that she hadn't taken Calista's or the coven's threat seriously… She'd just believed she could figure out a way to change their minds—at least the coven's minds—before they did anything too drastic. Maybe that had been naive.

"I don't know her that well, but I don't believe so. You should go out the back. Leave the door open, so the owl follows you. Ms. Braybrooke may have her fox with her." Valderas glanced out the window again. "I see her now."

"Let's go, Zorro." Morgen pointed toward the back of the house, willing him to come along obediently and thinking of Olivia's fox.

He squawked, ruffled his wings, and launched himself from the perch. The ceilings in the old Victorian weren't that high, and Morgen and Sian had to duck as he flew over their heads. Wings still brushed Morgen's hair.

"Perhaps you should have opened the door before giving that order," Sian said.

"Perhaps so."

Morgen jogged after him, through a dining room that held another exam area instead of a table and into a kitchen. Its bones hadn't been changed much when the first floor had been converted for veterinary purposes, but several cages and terrariums occupied the tile countertops.

Zorro landed on an upper cabinet and hooted with concern.

Morgen strode around the kitchen island to a back door with a window, curtains covering the glass. A hiss came from a large terrarium full of sand and rocks on the counter next to the door, and she jumped back, almost bumping into her sister. A long snake with black, yellow, and brown bands was twined among the rocks inside. A sticky note on the glass read *Ralph*.

"This is quite the kitchen," Morgen muttered. "Think Ralph is venomous?"

"Ralph is a California kingsnake," Sian said from behind her, "so no. They are escape artists, however, so don't bump his terrarium."

"I wasn't planning on bumping anything of his." Morgen reached for the knob again, but some instinct warned her to pause. She nudged the curtain aside and peered out onto a covered deck, a garden, and small grassy lawn beyond it. A wolf stood on the walkway in the rain, looking at the door. It was still afternoon, but the storm clouds must have made it dark enough for someone to shift. "Ugh."

Morgen stepped aside so Sian could look.

"The good news," Morgen said, "is that his eyes aren't glowing. The bad news is that he's there and probably under Olivia's control."

Sian moved the curtain aside to look out. "That's the largest gray wolf I've seen."

"That's because it's a werewolf."

10

"A werewolf?" Sian asked skeptically.

"Yes. You can tell by the size." Morgen closed the curtain on the door window. They weren't escaping the house that way. "According to Amar, they keep the same body mass as when they're human. They—"

"Ms. Braybrooke." Dr. Valderas's voice floated back to the kitchen. "I'm quite positive I locked the front door."

"Are these not your office hours?" Olivia asked, then lowered her voice. "That's the talisman. It's under his shirt." She had to be talking to someone else. The other witch? "If you get it off him, it's yours."

No, not the witch. The werewolf. There had to be another one inside with them. Who else would want a talisman that kept witches from controlling their kind?

"Really, Ms. Braybrooke," Valderas said. "Theft?"

"Check the rest of the house," Olivia said. "I'm sure that was Keller's car we passed."

Morgen swore under her breath. She wouldn't have guessed Olivia was keeping such close tabs on her—and her car.

Sian, who was doubtless confused about what was going on and didn't know what to expect, arched her eyebrows. Morgen glanced through the gap in the curtains again, hoping the wolf had gotten tired of standing in the rain, but he remained, his fur wet and his eyes displeased.

"We'll try the invisibility incantation," Morgen murmured, though she doubted it would fool the wolf, not if he saw the door open right before his eyes.

"The what?" Sian whispered.

A floorboard creaked in the adjacent dining room. Morgen gripped her amulet with one hand, Sian's forearm with the other, and quietly spoke the incantation. She had no idea if the illusion would extend to someone she was touching, but she hoped so. If not... at least Olivia's people shouldn't recognize Sian and think much of her. Maybe they would believe she was Ralph's owner.

A big man leaned through the kitchen doorway. Morgen recognized one of the Loups that she and Amar had fought a few weeks earlier. She'd ensorcelled him briefly and severed his belt and bootlaces before the incantation wore off. He wouldn't have fond memories of her.

She held her breath as he looked around the kitchen, but his gaze skimmed over them without any indication that he saw them. Next to her, Sian stood utterly still. She might not know what was going on, but she understood that they were in trouble.

Maybe Morgen could whisper the werewolf-control incantation and take the Loup out of Olivia's control. But he would hear her if she spoke and was close enough that he might be able to attack before she finished. Besides, focusing on another spell might cause the invisibility illusion to fail immediately.

The werewolf's nostrils twitched. Damn it, he smelled them.

He took a step inside, but a crash came from the front of the house.

"You're not taking my talisman," Valderas barked. "It won't even *work* on another werewolf."

"Of course it will," Olivia said. "If it doesn't, I'll alter it. I believe in treating my helpers well."

Yeah, right.

"Your *servants*, you mean," Valderas snarled.

Another crash sounded, followed by a fierce lupine growl. Had Valderas shifted forms?

The Loup in the kitchen ran toward the front of the house. Furniture skidded across the floor, and a woman—not Olivia—yelled, "Look out!"

"Is there another door?" Sian whispered.

"I don't know." Morgen dug her phone out of her pocket. But who could she call? She still didn't have a number for Amar and didn't know if he even *had* a phone. Would he pick up if she called the land line at the house? She had no idea and dialed Pedro instead, finding it ridiculous that she knew how to get in touch with him and not Amar. Why hadn't she told Amar where she was going? He and a couple of the Lobos might have come along to protect her, the same as they had at the coffee shop. "Because you were acting like a drama-wrought teenage girl and not talking to him," she whispered angrily to herself.

As the sounds of fighting continued out front, Sian peeked through the curtains again. "The wolf is still there. He looks wet and pissed."

"I know."

Pedro answered.

"Pedro," Morgen whispered, speaking first. "We need your help. It's me, Morgen. I'm with Valderas. The Loups are here at his office, and so are two witches. They're attacking him. Send Amar to help if you're busy. Tell him, please."

"Amar can suck it." Pedro hung up.

Morgen gaped in disbelief at the phone. Pedro must have found out that Maria had kissed Amar. That was the only reason she could think of for the turnaround.

But why wouldn't Pedro come to help *her*? She had nothing to do with that betrayal. And neither did Dr. Valderas.

What sounded like heavy books thumped to the floor. A lupine yelp of pain followed. Valderas? Morgen couldn't tell, but he was outnumbered, and she couldn't imagine him fighting off a werewolf *and* two witches.

"We have to help him," Morgen whispered.

"*We?*" Sian pointed to herself.

"Me. Stay here." Morgen released Sian—it wasn't as if she knew any magic and could help against witches—and pointed to the floor in front of the door. "And lock that," she added as it occurred to her that the wolf could revert to a man and turn the knob.

Morgen crept to the other doorway and peered through it. Most of the fight was taking place in Valderas's office, and she couldn't see him, Olivia, or his werewolf foe, but a white-haired woman in a dress stood in the foyer. She gripped an amulet similar to Morgen's and was pointing a wand into the office.

Morgen clenched her jaw, tempted to sprint across the exam room to bowl her over, but with shards from a shattered vase littering the floor and upturned chairs half-blocking the way, the woman—the witch—was sure to hear her approach. With her luck, Morgen would trip and fall flat on her face.

Instead, she whispered another incantation, the one that showed enemy weaknesses. She barely got the last word off before a silver wolf skidded out of the office and into view. Valderas. Blood matted his left flank, but he sprang to his feet and charged back into the fray.

The air blurred around the unfamiliar witch, and Morgen saw

two of her, one pointing the wand and acting as Olivia's backup and one shrieking and backing away from a floor covered in spiders and snakes. Those were her fears? If so, Morgen had a perfect tool to use against her.

As she backed into the kitchen, Morgen whispered the invisibility illusion again, not certain if it had dissipated when she'd uttered the other one.

"I need Ralph," she whispered, stepping toward Sian and the door again.

Her sister jumped. "Morgen?"

Sian was looking right at Morgen but didn't see her.

"Here," Morgen said, encouraged by this proof that the invisibility illusion was working. Maybe, when she'd been touching Sian, Sian had been included in it and hadn't seen her disappear. Morgen touched her shoulder. "I'm invisible."

"How?"

"Magic." Morgen found the access panel on the top of the terrarium. "Will he bite me?"

"Not unless you're another California kingsnake."

"Uh?" Morgen had already been reaching inside but paused. What if the snake was confused when an invisible person grabbed it and *did* bite her?

"They're known to eat each other."

"Cannibalistic reptiles, the perfect choice for a pet." Grimacing, Morgen picked up the snake with both hands. She wasn't much more enamored with snakes and spiders than the witch out there, but she trusted Sian would know if it was venomous or otherwise dangerous. Her hope was that the *witch* wouldn't know that.

Growls, snarls, and a thud preceded a thunderous crash in the office. It sounded like a bookcase had fallen over, with all of the tomes tumbling out.

Another yelp of pain followed. Dr. Valderas might not have much time. If he was knocked out of the fight—or *killed*—Olivia and her assistant would be free to stroll through the house until they found Morgen and Sian.

As quickly as she dared, Morgen carried the snake across the kitchen. It stirred but didn't do anything threatening. Hoping her illusion spell would hide her *and* the snake until the last moment, she crept through the dining room toward the witch.

Pained pants came from the office, and Morgen wanted to move more quickly, but she had to step carefully around the broken ceramic and overturned furniture. The witch grimaced and glanced away, her gaze skimming the dining room as she avoided looking at whatever was playing out in the office. Hopefully not a death blow.

Morgen froze as the woman looked at her, but as with Sian, the witch didn't see her. She must not have seen the snake either, because she didn't react. The witch took a bracing breath and looked back toward the office, raising her wand again.

Morgen suspected the woman didn't want to be there. Well, she was about to want to be there even less. A few more steps...

Saying a silent apology to Ralph and hoping he wouldn't be hurt, Morgen gently tossed the snake onto the witch.

For a stunned second, the woman didn't react other than to step closer to the door and try to brush off what was touching her. Instead of letting himself fall to the ground, Ralph caught her shoulder and coiled part of his body around her, as if she were a handy tree. As soon as the witch realized she was dealing with a snake, she shrieked loudly enough to be heard in Canada. *Northern* Canada.

Morgen spun toward the office where a huge gray wolf wrestled on the floor with the silver Dr. Valderas and started her incantation. But Olivia spotted her right away, somehow seeing through the invisibility illusion, and threw something at her.

Between the attack and the other witch shrieking in her ear, Morgen didn't finish her incantation. She was too busy leaping to the side to avoid the projectile. It was a clear vial with green liquid inside and hit the floor where she'd been standing. The glass shattered, and greenish vapors wafted upward.

Holding her breath, Morgen skittered backward. That didn't keep the sharp rotten-eggs odor from reaching her nose and making her eyes water.

Morgen groped for a way to defend herself, to keep Olivia back. She'd used the weaknesses incantation on Olivia before and knew her fears weren't anything that she could exploit. All she could do was try to get the werewolf-control incantation off in time to turn Olivia's Loup against her.

"Under the moon's magic—" Morgen blurted, but Olivia was too fast.

She charged out of the office with a wand raised, and an invisible buzz of electricity—or pure, raw magic—wrapped around Morgen. It made her heart flutter and her jaws clatter, cutting off the rest of her words. Her amulet grew hot against her chest as its magic tried to protect her, but all it did was distract her.

As the other witch flung open the front door and ran out into the rain, leaving Ralph on the floor and slithering behind the bench, Olivia strode straight at Morgen.

With the buzzes coursing down her veins like electrical currents, Morgen couldn't run away. She barely managed to stay on her feet as her spasming lungs struggled to draw in air. Air tainted with those awful vapors.

Olivia had murder in her eyes as she switched her wand to her left hand and drew a curved dagger with her right. "You killed my sister, you bitch."

"She tr-tr-tried to burn my—" Morgen broke off with coughs. She'd thought she'd evaded most of those green vapors, but the pungent stuff clawed at her throat as if she'd swallowed blackberry brambles.

Unfortunately, it didn't affect Olivia at all. She lunged forward, the dagger tip aiming for Morgen's stomach.

Someone sprang in from the side and kicked Olivia's arm. The dagger flew out of her grip and lodged in the ceiling. Sian attacked again, a roundhouse kick that slammed into Olivia's stomach. The woman pitched over, and Sian kicked her one more time, the ball of her pink-socked foot clipping Olivia in the chin and sending her reeling backward and to the floor. Her wand skidded across the floorboards to join Ralph behind the bench.

The magical attack stopped, and Morgen gasped in air as she stumbled to a wall, planting her hand against it for support.

Wolves charged in the front door, and Sian yelled and sprang out of the way. She bumped Morgen's shoulder as she joined her against the wall.

As the wolves ran over Olivia and into the office and the rest of the house, Morgen's first thought was that they were more Loups, here to protect their allies, and she glanced toward the closest window. If she flung it open so they could climb out, maybe they could evade the wolf in the backyard and escape.

Then a familiar gray-and-black-furred wolf ran into the house. Amar. Instead of following the others into the office or elsewhere, he looked around until he spotted Morgen. He ran toward her, prompting another alarmed yell from Sian. Sian started to lunge away, but Morgen grabbed her arm.

"It's okay," she blurted. "He's on our side."

Amar turned to put his back to them, his stance making it clear that he would defend them. Morgen appreciated that, but she also didn't want Olivia to get away.

A crash came from the rear of the house—the back door being forced open? Yes. The big wolf that had been in the backyard ran out of the kitchen and charged the Lobos in the front of the house. For a moment, there were so many wolves in the exam and waiting area that Morgen could barely see Olivia. She was rolling away from them and toward the front door.

"Stop her," Morgen yelled. "She's the ringleader."

But the wolves seemed to find the *other* wolves more dangerous than a woman down on the floor. They sprang into battle with each other, jaws snapping and growls filling the house.

Though Morgen's legs shook, she skirted around Amar and the fight to try to reach Olivia. But more glass shattered as the woman threw another vial. A thick black cloud quickly formed in the air.

With her eyes already watering, Morgen dared not charge into whatever it was. Two fighting wolves rolled close, jaws snapping alarmingly near her thigh.

Something grabbed her shirt from behind and tugged her back from the fight. She thought it was Sian, but Amar had his lupine teeth in her shirt.

"I know, I know," Morgen said, letting him pull her back to the wall, "—but Olivia—"

The front door banged open, and Morgen slumped, having a feeling Olivia had already escaped. Sian grabbed her arm and pulled her close as Amar repositioned himself so that he was protecting them from the fight. He looked over his shoulder, blue eyes hard as he growled at Morgen, the wolf version of *stay there*.

"Are you *sure* he's on your side?" Sian asked.

"Yes." Morgen leaned the back of her head against the wall, confident the Lobos would handle the rest. No fewer than six of them had charged in, and Valderas, though wounded, was still fighting too.

The two Loups realized they were outnumbered—or maybe Olivia's control over them wore off—and soon limped or ran out the front door.

Once the Lobos determined that they'd chased off their enemies, some of them went out to the front and back porches to watch for further threats. Amar, Pedro, and Valderas remained inside and shifted forms, arms and legs thickening, fur disappearing, and bones altering until they stood in the house as men. Naked men.

Sian managed an "Uh," but nothing further. Her mouth dangled open as she stared at them.

It had almost been worth being caught in the fight to see Sian speechless. She couldn't have delivered a lecture right then even if someone had paid her a million dollars.

Wings flapped and Zorro, who'd wisely spent the battle on his high perch in the kitchen, flew past. He arrowed out the front door and into the rain.

"I guess he'll meet us back home," Morgen said. Or maybe he was going to flee to another state, one that wasn't infested with witches and werewolves.

"Uh," Sian uttered again, shaking her head slowly.

Pedro went to help Valderas, who was retrieving some of the medical supplies he used on animals to bandage himself, and Amar faced Morgen. His eyes had the same stern mien as before.

"Are you going to growl at me again?" Morgen asked.

"I might. The witches are after you, and you know that. You shouldn't have left without telling me where you were going."

Even though she'd been thinking the same thing earlier, Morgen didn't appreciate the chastisement. She blurted the first response that came to mind, "Well, you shouldn't have kissed Maria!"

Surprise flickered in his eyes but only briefly before it turned into a frown. "I did not kiss her. She kissed me."

"And you let her. I *saw*. You let her because you *liked* it."

He scowled, but he didn't refute her. Disappointment punched her in the stomach. She'd wanted him to say he hadn't, that he'd pushed her away as soon as he recovered his wits. But maybe they'd ended the day entwined in each other's arms.

Pedro and Valderas had stopped their discussion about bandages and were staring at them.

Embarrassed and discombobulated, Morgen grabbed Sian's hand. "Come on. We're going back to the house. Pedro," she said as she maneuvered past Amar, who didn't try to stop her this time, "thank you for your help. Dr. Valderas, I'm very sorry this happened and that you were hurt."

Not waiting for anyone's responses, Morgen hurried out onto the porch. She'd forgotten that several of the Lobos were out there, still in wolf form, and ran into someone's backside.

"Sorry," she muttered, hurrying past. She almost missed a step on the way down from the porch and might have landed face-first on the walkway, but Sian caught her.

"You're acting like you're fleeing a crime scene," Sian said, having found her voice.

"Because I'm *embarrassed*," Morgen said over her shoulder, relieved when she spotted her car still parked at the curb. With the way things were going, she'd half-expected Olivia to have called someone to tow it away.

"Because of your outburst?" Sian asked, as if it hadn't been obvious. Maybe to her, it hadn't been.

"*Yes.*" Morgen reached the car and halted. Something was wrong with it.

The little electric vehicle wasn't large to start with, but it was too low and slumped oddly toward the curb. Morgen bent to examine a tire and groaned. It was flat with a huge puncture hole in the side. It looked like someone had stabbed it with a knife. The knife Olivia had been holding.

She moved around the car and groaned again. *All* of the tires were flat.

"And you were worried about what the potholes would do to a car?" Sian asked.

Exhausted and angry, Morgen sank to the curb, hardly caring about the rain striking her shoulders. She dropped her face in her hands, annoyed with Olivia and all the witches in Bellrock and even more annoyed that she was going to have to ask the werewolves for another favor, a ride home.

11

"Your... werewolves are coming," Sian said.

Morgen didn't lift her face from her hands, but she took a few deep breaths, trying to get herself together. So what if Amar had kissed Maria and half the Lobos had heard her shout about it like a jilted lover? They had far bigger problems to deal with. She could handle this.

"They've put clothes back on," Sian added.

"I'm sure you're relieved," Morgen said.

"I am indifferent to nudity."

"Then *I'm* relieved."

A hand came to rest on her shoulder. Morgen knew right away that it wasn't Sian, since offering comfort with touch wasn't in her playbook.

After another deep breath, Morgen pushed herself to her feet and faced Amar. Despite the rain, he wore his usual leather vest and appeared indifferent to the damp or chill.

"I'll give you a ride home," he said. "We can come replace the flats tomorrow."

"Thank you," Morgen said.

"If you're so motivated," Sian said, tugging her luggage out of the car, "you can give *me* a ride to the better of the two hotels in town." She shot Morgen a dirty look, as if this failure to warn her about all the chaos in Bellrock was Morgen's fault.

Technically... it was.

"I'm not sure which hotel that would be," Amar said.

Neither was Morgen. The Wild Trout had been underwhelming, and the Roaming Elk appeared far from luxurious. Maybe there was a reason so many tourists brought tents and RVs and stayed at the campground.

"My first night in town, I stayed at the Wild Trout," Morgen said. "It was old and a little mildewy smelling but otherwise fine. No noticeable werewolf sweat odors."

Amar frowned slightly at the comment, but all he said was, "I'll get the truck and pick you up."

"Thank you," Morgen said, then added to Sian, "The Wild Trout also allows dogs."

Given Sian's quest for quiet and her lack of a pet, Morgen thought that might make her choose the other hotel.

"The owners must be amenable to animals then," Sian said.

"I think they're amenable to the twenty-five-dollar pet fee they charged me."

"I will support them with my patronage." Sian rolled her luggage over to stand under a tree while they waited for Amar to return. It didn't offer much protection from the rain.

"Are you sure you don't want to come back with us? The contractors will probably go home instead of sleeping outside tonight, and they're decent guys anyway." Morgen pointed her thumb toward Valderas's house. "Those werewolves were some of them, in case you didn't recognize them in their furry forms."

"I will stay in the hotel tonight while relaxing and contemplating the day's events. Besides, it sounds like you need to speak with our driver."

"Amar." Morgen realized she hadn't introduced her sister to him or to any of them. She'd been too eager to escape the area and avoid speaking with Amar. Childish. She would talk to him on the way back and straighten this out. "And you're right."

"That is usually true."

"You were wrong about witches and werewolves existing. Nice kicking, by the way. I'd forgotten that you took Tae Kwon Do as a kid."

Their mother had forced both of them to sign up for a sport when they'd been in middle school, noting that they'd "gotten chunky" and that "reading books doesn't burn a lot of calories." Morgen had begged to take horseback riding lessons, as all animal-loving children did, but had ended up suffering through two years of volleyball. Since Sian had been devouring fantasy novels at the time, she'd begged to sign up for archery, but Mom had called that too sedate and unlikely to result in weight loss. Sian had agreed to martial arts so she could learn to fight like Legolas. Morgen had said she was built more like Gimli, which had earned her a kick from Sian early in the Tae Kwon Do training.

"I would have knocked her across the room if I'd been wearing my shoes," Sian said.

"Knocking the knife across the room—or into the ceiling—was sufficient. I'm impressed that you've kept up with your martial arts practice."

"I haven't. If you'll recall, I dropped it as soon as I entered high school and switched to chess club."

"Then I'm impressed you can take down enemies."

"It's not like she was a professional MMA fighter. Toppling a distracted woman in heels is within my sphere of competence."

Amar pulled up, helped Sian with her luggage, and they drove the four blocks to the Wild Trout. Morgen sat in the middle on the single bench seat, aware of the warmth of

Amar's side through her damp clothing. She resisted the urge to scoot closer to him and soak up his body heat. Instead, she shivered and longed for a shower and a change of clothing.

"It may not be safe for your sister to stay here alone," Amar said as he pulled up to the hotel's front door. "The witches know about her now."

Sian had been reaching for the handle to get out but paused. Morgen wanted to say that the witches wouldn't care about her and that it would be fine, but would it? Sian had kicked Olivia, and Olivia had demonstrated that she was the kind of person to hold a grudge.

"How did Olivia know you were at Dr. Valderas's house?" Amar asked. "She must have had time to gather her forces."

"Actually, I don't think she came there for me." Morgen touched her chest. "She had an altercation yesterday with Valderas, and it sounded like she came back to try to get his talisman from him."

"An altercation? With the vet?"

"Well, he wouldn't sleep with her. She didn't like that."

Amar frowned at her.

"Women like being slept with," Morgen explained, smiling slightly, though he probably wasn't in the mood for humor. She wasn't sure she was either.

"Then *women* should show up to meet their dates in the woods."

"Women would do so if they hadn't seen their *dates* lip wrangling with other women."

The door opened, and Sian slid out. "I'll risk the ire of the local witches to avoid listening to this. Goodnight."

"See you later, Sian." Morgen scooted over to take her vacated seat and put some distance between her shoulder and Amar's shoulder. "Call me if you need anything."

"That apartment in Shoreline is sounding appealing," Sian grumbled.

Morgen hesitated. "I can get you a key if you want to go down there today." She glanced at the dark sky, the sun only a couple of hours from setting somewhere behind the clouds. "Tonight."

"I'm wet and tired. The hotel is fine." Sian headed in without a goodbye or looking back.

Morgen felt like a bad sister. Sian was recovering from a life-threatening illness, and Morgen had invited her into a war zone. What had she been thinking? Besides that she'd wanted to see her sister and maybe have an ally up here in all of this. But she already *had* an ally. One far better suited to battling werewolves than Sian.

Amar put the truck in drive and headed out onto Main Street.

"I'm sorry for sniping at you in front of the others," Morgen said quietly, looking at the dashboard instead of over at him. "I should have talked to you this morning. I just didn't know what to say." Maybe she shouldn't have said anything and also shouldn't have acted as if she'd been vastly betrayed. It was sad to admit it at forty, but she wasn't that experienced with dating and didn't know all the rules. Like if they were, after three kisses, supposed to be exclusive to each other and not spend time with others. Not *kiss* others. They hadn't made any promises to each other about that. They hadn't even defined the parameters of their relationship or admitted that they were boyfriend/girlfriend, or whatever the hell people called it these days. "I'm not very good at... men," she added lamely. "And werewolf men seem *extra* complicated."

Yeah, that was the way to go. Put the onus on him. Call *him* the weird one. As if she hadn't been fighting with witches and casting incantations twenty minutes earlier.

Amar focused on the road as he took the turn toward Wolf Wood and didn't answer right away. A soggy leaf fell onto the windshield, and the wiper struggled to dislodge it.

"Werewolf men *are* complicated," Amar finally said.

"I thought so."

"Witches are also complicated."

"I'm not complicated. I'm just not the best at saying what's on my mind. I get shy and nervous around strangers." She lowered her voice. "And you."

He glanced over.

"Are you..." She nibbled on her lip and debated what she wanted to ask. He wasn't the best at saying what was on his mind either. He'd seemed insulted that she hadn't shown up for their tryst in the woods, but was that because he hadn't thought Maria's kiss meant anything or because he hadn't known she'd seen it? "I shouldn't have been spying on you and didn't really mean to, but I did, and so I know Maria is still into you. Or wasn't but is now. I don't know. Are you still into her? You let her..." She didn't finish the thought. She'd already pointed it out, that he hadn't pulled away from that kiss.

"I know," he said quietly. "I didn't ask her to kiss me, and she took me by surprise."

"In a good way? I... get that you still have feelings for her." Morgen kept herself from pointing out that he *shouldn't* have feelings for someone who could bounce back and forth between him and Pedro. Besides, she didn't know what had happened. Maria might have broken up with Pedro before planting her lips on Amar.

"We were together for two years. I still..." Amar spread a hand upward.

"Care for her?" *Want* her?

"Yes. When she kissed me, it was... I don't know. Nostalgic. For when we were together and when I was a part of the pack and things were better between me and Pedro. My blood family has been gone for a long time. The pack is—was—all I had. Have."

A part of her wanted to say that he had *her*, but that would be silly. They'd only known each other for a month. A lot had happened in that time, but it didn't mean he thought of her as family. After three years of living in Grandma's barn, he'd probably thought of *her* as family. But she was someone else he'd lost.

"I get that," Morgen said.

"I didn't know you were there, or I would have stepped away sooner." He glanced at her again. Funny how neither of them was holding the other's gaze for more than an instant. "I wouldn't want to hurt you."

She wanted to say that she wasn't hurt and he didn't have that power over her, but it would have been a lie. How had she come to care for him in such a short time? He was surly and grumpy and... kept watching her back and saving her ass.

Morgen swallowed and looked out the window at the passing trees. "Did she dump Pedro? Are you going to get back together with her?"

"She told him she's been having second thoughts." Amar turned the truck up the driveway. "I guess he read between the lines that her second thoughts involved me. He's not happy with me. Again."

It took Morgen a moment to realize that he wasn't going to answer the second half of her question. Did that mean that he and Maria *were* getting back together? She would have let her head lean against the window, but they were driving through the potholes now and that would have hurt.

"I like you, Morgen. I appreciate that you made me the talisman and that you stood up for me when those witches disparaged me."

"But in the end, I have witch blood, and werewolves are drawn to other werewolves, and that's just how it is?" Morgen probably looked like a hurt puppy dog when she glanced over at him, but she couldn't help it. Sian would have scoffed at her for letting her emotions influence her so much.

"Werewolves are drawn to other werewolves, yes, but I am also drawn to you." For the first time on the ride, he met her gaze, the intentness in his eyes sending a spark of electricity through her. What was he saying? That he preferred her to the beautiful Maria? If that was true, it would be a shock. She held her breath. "That *shouldn't* be how it is," he added.

"Because of my blood?"

"Because of what you are, yes."

"Why does it matter? I didn't know there was anything special about my blood before this summer, and it's not like I was raised to be a witch or hang out with the coven. I've never—aside from that one time, I've never tried to control you with that incantation. And you know why I had to do it then."

"I do. What bothers me is that I didn't mind it. I *wanted* to do what you wished. You have power over me, Morgen, and that disturbs me. It makes me think that I might lose myself, my free will and who I am, if I was with you. I might... want to serve you. Maria pointed all that out."

Morgen clenched her jaw to keep from blurting, *Oh, I bet she did.*

They'd reached the house, and Amar parked the truck, but neither of them reached for the doors. The other Lobos had also returned to the house, and their trucks were parked in the driveway. Between the rain and the afternoon's events, she was surprised they hadn't taken the rest of the day off.

"Don't take this the wrong way, but I think you may be imagining things," Morgen said, struggling to sound calm and reasonable. "Even if I could somehow ooze my witchiness over you, that talisman would protect you. I *couldn't* influence you in any way. We tested it, right? And it works. It worked when you fought other witches, and it would certainly work with someone as untrained as me. Even if I *wanted* to try magicking you into doing something, I couldn't."

"If you asked me to do something, I would do it."

"Because we're friends now, not because of magic. If you asked me to do something, I would do it too."

"I told you to meet me at the spring last night, and you didn't."

"Because you were kissing another woman. We already went over this."

"I don't want her," he growled, leaning toward her. "I want *you*."

His eyes burned her with their intensity.

She opened her mouth but didn't know what to say.

"I don't know," Amar said, holding her gaze, "if it's simply because you've been a friend to me and I'm attracted to you, or if it's your power calling to me. But I feel an intense urge to do your bidding, to be your loyal hound." His voice was almost harsh, as if he hated admitting that.

Morgen shook her head. "I don't want you to be like that. You're your own man. I just want... can't we, I don't know, date? See if we're compatible?" She tried to smile, but his expression was so fierce that she couldn't. Fierce, intense, and... anguished.

"I watched you from the woods when you did your ritual. I'd gone out to hunt, but your magic called me back, overriding the call of the moon. It was as if you'd summoned me with your power, the same as you did the owl. I watched you dance naked around the fire. I wanted you then, and I want you now."

He radiated frustrated and dangerous energy, and some instinct warned her to run into the house and close the door, but she couldn't turn away from him. That night, she'd seen those eyes and wondered who was watching her. It had alarmed her then, but now... the thought that he might have been out there, aroused by her nudity, excited her.

She scooted closer to him and lifted a hand to his cheek. "I want you too," she whispered and kissed him.

He groaned against her mouth and returned the kiss, his lips hard and hungry, his hand coming up to the back of her head, holding her there, capturing her in his grip. "To be your loyal hound," he growled against her mouth.

Desire flushed her body, along with the urge to groan *Yes!* back to him, but she sensed that wasn't what he wanted, that he didn't want to feel a prisoner of her power. Whatever the hell power she supposedly had. She didn't want to say that it was all in his mind, not when she still understood so little of the magic that flowed through the veins of witches and werewolves, but the idea of someone being drawn to her power seemed crazy.

"To be Amar," she whispered, breathless, hoping it was the right thing to say.

A distant howl sounded. It didn't come from the house but from the woods. Were the Lobos out hunting in the rain? It wasn't even dark yet.

The howl sounded again. Amar broke their kiss. He squinted at her, as if she were some mystery he was trying to figure out, but his ears were cocked as he listened to that call. It sounded like one wolf, not the whole pack.

"Amar?" Morgen whispered.

Another howl came from the woods. It sounded cranky and insistent.

Cold dread replaced the hot desire coursing through Morgen's veins as she knew with certainty which Lobo was out there calling to him. Maria.

"I have to go," Amar said and pulled away.

He opened the door and removed his vest and jeans as he sprang away from the truck. He tossed the clothing onto the hood, changed into a wolf, and ran off in the direction of the howl.

Stung and disappointed, Morgen slumped back in the seat. "Werewolf men *are* complicated."

12

Between Sian's arrival, the chaos at Valderas's office, and the conversation and kiss with Amar, Morgen almost forgot about her plan to show up at the witches' meeting. She *had* forgotten to make dinner.

The digital clock on the microwave ticked over to 8:00 as she sat with her laptop, uploading the latest version of her app to her phone. She gathered her belongings, stuck a bag of pistachios in her pocket, and was about to go out and ask Wendy if she knew where the witches were when something flew past the window.

A *hoo hoo* reached her ears. Zorro?

She put her laptop in her backpack and jogged out to the porch. Lucky, who'd been stuck inside all afternoon and evening because of the rain, galloped after her.

"We're not going for a walk now," she said but let him outside. It had stopped raining, and he needed to run around.

The owl was perched on the railing and watched indifferently as the dog sprang off the porch and raced into the wet grass.

"Hey, buddy." Morgen grinned at Zorro. Between being chased around the office by a fox and watching a werewolf battle play out the next day, it was a wonder that he'd come back. "Good to see you."

Zorro worked his beak back and forth for a few seconds before hawking an owl pellet onto the porch.

"I see that you've eaten," she said. "Hey, do me a favor, will you? Go molt or poop on Amar's stuff in the barn, okay?"

Zorro looked toward the barn, as if he understood, but he didn't fly over. That was probably for the best. Morgen didn't truly wish Amar's belongings ill will, even if he had left her all hot and horny in the truck to run obediently off to Maria's wolfish call.

"I suppose I don't have any way to know it was Maria. It could have been some *other* beautiful young werewolf." Morgen rubbed her face. "Focus, girl."

The owl hooted.

Morgen lowered her hand and studied him. "You've gone out to look for things for me before. Would you mind checking out the graveyard behind the church and seeing if there are any witches meeting there? And if they're not there, could you try to find them and show me where they *are* meeting?"

It was possible their gathering was already over, but Morgen had a hunch witches waited until after dark to convene. It seemed the proper witchy time for such things.

Zorro spread his wings and launched into the air. He flew over the trees in the direction of town.

"Maybe he really understands me," Morgen mused.

Wendy walked around the corner of the house and into view and peered up at her. Her ferret was draped across her shoulders like a mink fur. "Uhm, Morgen? Can we talk?"

"Sure."

Wendy climbed the steps to join her on the porch. The ferret sat up on her shoulder and sniffed its little nose.

"Zorro is gone," Morgen told him. "And Lucky is doing laps

around the property. There shouldn't be anyone nearby who likes to eat long slinky rodents."

The ferret chattered at her and sniffed again. He looked her up and down.

"Ferrets aren't rodents," Wendy said. "They're in the mustelid family and related to weasels, badgers, and wolverines. They're carnivores, so they'll happily *eat* rodents."

"And avocado crisps. He demolished a bag of them in my kitchen."

"Ferrets aren't supposed to eat non-meat products. He probably destroyed the bag because it was fun."

"As wanton destruction so often is."

"Ferrets like to play." Even though Wendy had said she wanted to talk, she shuffled her feet and looked out toward the garden. Lucky had his nose in the bushy tomato vines. "His name is Napoleon," she offered.

"Because he's a brilliant tactician and leads armies? Did you know he passes out if a werewolf walks by?"

"Yeah, but I do too." Wendy lowered her voice and glanced around, as if worried some of the Lobos would prowl past and she would have to demonstrate, but they'd finally left for the day. "They're scary."

The ferret ran down her back to the porch and sniffed around Morgen's feet. She was tempted to pick him up but didn't know if the mighty Napoleon would appreciate a stranger manhandling him.

"That's what I wanted to talk about," Wendy admitted. "The werewolves."

"They didn't bother you today, did they?"

"No. I stayed in my van with the doors locked. But I heard them talking."

Morgen lifted her eyebrows.

"About how you're going to make them talismans to keep our

people—" Wendy pointed at herself, "—from being able to defend against them."

"From being able to *control* them."

"So you *are* doing it?" Wendy whispered, horror in her eyes. "For *all* of them? I'd wondered why they were here working for you. I figured you were paying them, but even so, they hate us. Hate witches."

"It's what they want, but I don't know yet if I can make them all talismans."

"You *can't*. If we don't have a way to defend against them, they could hurt us. Not only us but the people of Bellrock. When they first came, they turned some of the locals into werewolves against their wishes."

"I've heard that, but it was the Loups that did that, right? Not the Lobos."

"They're all the same. And if the Loups hear you can make talismans, they'll want some too."

"Look, the spell or ritual or whatever doesn't work that way. I have to care about the recipient to make the magic work. And trust me, I do *not* care about the Loups. I'm not even sure how I feel about the Lobos, aside from Amar. Though the new deck they're building me is making me more of a fan."

Wendy shook her head. "They're only doing it to get what they want from you."

"There have to be other ways that witches can defend themselves against werewolves. It's not right for you to turn them into automatons and control them against their will. That's slavery."

"Not as bad as what they've done to our kind. And you're one of us, whether you want to be or not. You have Gwen's blood."

"I know."

The ferret tugged at Morgen's pant leg. Not sure what he wanted, she picked him up. He squirmed around in her arms and climbed up to her shoulder.

"When I saw that you'd used my amulets to make talismans for your Lobo and the vet, I wasn't sure what to think. I'd made those for other witches who wanted to create imperviousness talismans for themselves. Those two werewolves don't seem that bad... but I can't make receptacles for the others. I may want to leave Bellrock, but I don't want to be cast out of the coven or have everyone hate me. And I don't want to be responsible for the werewolves being strong enough to overcome the witches. I realized... I can't make a tutorial on how to craft receptacles. It would be too dangerous. I can do videos for some other things, but not that."

"Ah." There went Morgen's plan to watch the tutorial and learn how to do it herself. "What if I could convince the witches in the coven that it's okay for some of the werewolves—the Lobos—to have talismans? That in exchange, they would help protect the town and defend the witches?" Morgen had no idea how she would talk the Lobos into doing that, but if they were willing to remodel her house for some protective jewelry, maybe they could be convinced to help in other ways. "Would you teach me how to make receptacles if the others said it was okay?"

"They're not going to say that. They all hate the werewolves."

"But if they did, would you?" Morgen grimaced as the ferret—Napoleon—navigated down her hoodie, little claws digging in, to stick his head in her pocket.

"I don't know. I guess. But they won't agree to doing what you want. They, uhm, don't like you much either."

"I'm going to change that. Do you know where their meeting is tonight? I want to stop in, show them my app, and make my case."

"The meeting times and places are a secret. You have to be in the coven and be invited to go."

"I have a form the treasurer left for me. I could drop it off in person and offer to pay my dues."

"Judith does like dues."

"So I've heard. Will you tell me?"

Wendy shook her head. "I can't. I shouldn't even be here on your property. If they hear about it, they'll think... I don't know what they'll think. Morgen?" She took a deep breath and then looked squarely at... Morgen's nose. "What really happened with Nora's death? Olivia gave me a version, but she wasn't there, and since Olivia kidnapped Phoebe and me and hypnotized us with a witch gem, I'm not sure what to think anymore."

"Nora flew here in Calista's gyrocopter, forced the Loups to attack Amar and me, and tried to light the house on fire. It was stormy, and she crashed the thing into the barn. She died in the wreck." Morgen wrestled with her desire to tell the full truth and her fear of alienating Wendy if she admitted that she'd played a role in Nora's death. "I did throw a staff at the gyrocopter blades, and that contributed to the crash. I was trying to stop her, not hurt her. She kept throwing Molotov cocktails at the house, and it was burning in several spaces, and there were way more Loups than we could handle. It was chaotic. I didn't mean for her to die."

"Oh." Wendy looked out toward the yard again.

Morgen pulled the ferret's head out of her pocket. He'd found her bag of pistachios. For an animal that supposedly only ate meat, Napoleon was sure into her vegetarian snacks. It was hard to believe he'd climbed all over her just to play with the *bag*.

"I get why Calista is angry with you," Wendy said, "but I'm not sure why Olivia and Nora are—*were*—so mad. They were worried about Wolf Wood and you selling it before we knew anything about you."

"I noticed."

"And even after you didn't sell it to Calista and said you wouldn't sell it..." Wendy shook her head. "They still want you gone. They said it was for the safety of Bellrock and the coven, but you don't seem that dangerous to me. You barely know how to do... Sorry, but you don't seem to know much about your heritage and how to do things."

"Someone finally noticed."

"I'm surprised you were able to make a talisman of imperviousness."

"Me too."

"If you hadn't done that, maybe the coven would have been okay with you. I gathered from what I heard that they aren't that sure why Olivia and Nora had it out for you either."

"Something I'll be sure to bring up when I visit them at their meeting tonight." Morgen tugged out her phone to check the time. "Where and when did you say it is?"

"I didn't."

Napoleon nosed the phone screen and licked it. Morgen shifted it away from him.

Barking came from the garden. Lucky had found something interesting among the tomato vines and was focused on them, but the fearsome military leader Napoleon fainted in Morgen's arms.

"I'd better go." Wendy extricated him. "This was a bad idea. I don't think I can help you with the app."

"Wait. What if the other witches say everything is okay? Will you do it then?" Morgen hated to lose her assistant—and best resource on the coven—before they'd even started their work together.

"I... probably would, but they won't."

"I'll figure out a way to convince them. My program will be useful for everyone in the coven." And Morgen would also convince them that having a few werewolf allies with talismans would be a good idea too. Somehow.

"Good luck." Wendy waved and headed back to her van. She sounded sincere if skeptical. She hadn't, however, told Morgen where the meeting was or how to find the coven.

"I'll just have to—" Morgen sucked in a breath as a vision came to her—an *owl* vision. She gripped the railing for support.

Through the vision, she saw Bellrock from above. Zorro flew

over Main Street, giving her a bird's-eye view of people coming out of restaurants and heading to their cars and RVs. He soared over the church toward the parking lot and graveyard in the back.

Morgen held her breath, hoping to see witches roaming among the tombstones. Amar had once said that a couple of the mausoleums held some significance to them. But the graveyard was empty. Mostly. With his sharp vision, Zorro spotted a mouse. He dove down quickly, giving Morgen vertigo—and nausea. Her stomach protested even further when he caught the mouse and alighted on a tombstone to eat it.

"Zorro," she groaned, closing her eyes. That didn't make the vision go away. "Please find the witches' meeting, not anything else to eat."

From what she'd determined, she didn't have a way to communicate with her familiars from afar. At least Zorro was a fast eater. And why not? He waited until later to digest his meal and spit out the bones at Morgen's feet.

He sprang into the air again and soared around town, as if he were trying to obey her and find a gathering. But a gathering was not to be found. As he neared the far end of town and headed into a residential area, she decided this was unlikely to work. Either the meeting was over, or it was at someone's house.

But when Zorro flew over the dark playground of an elementary school, Morgen spotted cars in the parking lot. She'd seen one of them in a vision before: a green Subaru. That was the color and make of the automobile that Judith had driven when she'd put a note on Morgen's door. Could this be the same car? Would the coven meet at a school? Most of the women were too old to have school-age children.

Zorro flapped toward the gymnasium. A door was propped open. Given the hour, that was unusual.

He alighted on the rooftop and peered down, having a view of the open door and also the parking lot. Another car was driving in, the headlights skimming across several other SUVs and sedans. When it parked, two white-haired women got out and headed for the door.

"That might be the place," Morgen whispered.

She wished Zorro could swoop through the doorway and spy on the meeting for her, but since sound didn't accompany the visions, that wouldn't be that helpful. She ought to be glad about that lack, since it meant she hadn't had to listen to the mouse die and the crunching of bones as it was eaten, but it would have been handy if Zorro could share nearby conversations with her.

He rotated his head so quickly that it made her dizzy. Another bird had alighted on the roof. A black raven. Was that Phoebe's Zeke?

It cawed and flapped its wings. A second raven descended and landed behind the first. Another familiar? A white owl came down, joining the growing flock. All three birds glared at Zorro.

"You may need to get out of there, buddy," Morgen urged.

She didn't know if the feathered familiars would attack an intruder, but the last thing she wanted was for Zorro to be hurt again because he was working on her behalf.

Maybe he felt similarly, for he sprang into the air and flew away from the area. The vision dissolved.

If Morgen wanted to know what happened at that meeting, she would have to go down there herself.

"It's what I'd planned to do," she muttered, grabbing the bag with her laptop.

So why was she so nervous?

13

Morgen stared at the empty gravel where she usually parked her car, belatedly remembering that it was still near the vet's office, the tires flat until she could get it towed and fixed. She felt silly. She'd coaxed Lucky back into the house so that she could... stare blankly at the vacant driveway.

How was she supposed to get to the gymnasium in time to talk to the witches? Amar was gone, and Wendy wouldn't take her.

Morgen eyed the lights shining through the curtains of the camper van and thought about asking Wendy for a ride into town. If she was vague about her ultimate destination, would Wendy see through that? Probably. The only thing open late in Bellrock was the pub.

Amar's clothes lay across the hood of his truck where he'd left them. His keys ought to be in the pocket of his jeans. Would he be angry if she borrowed his truck? Earlier, he had said he would go to the meeting with her. It wasn't Morgen's fault that he'd left her breathless to run off and meet a wolf in the woods.

"Let's see if they're there before worrying about it," she muttered.

As she walked toward the truck, barking came from inside the house. Not from the living room—Lucky's usual spot, when he was alerting her to people in the driveway—but from the second floor. He was up in her bedroom, his paws on the windowsill as he woofed at something through the glass.

Wendy's van was below that window, but Morgen couldn't imagine a stationary vehicle being that interesting to a dog. Ah, but the door was ajar. Maybe Wendy had stepped out and was doing something to attract Lucky's notice. No, a shadow moved in front of the curtains. Wendy was still in her van.

Morgen almost went over to check out the situation—she only trusted her new roommate to a certain extent—but then she spotted the ferret running around outside the van. He was sniffing bushes and clumps of grass. Napoleon was on the hunt—and had Lucky's attention.

"Country living was supposed to be peaceful," Morgen said.

She hesitated before poking into the pockets of Amar's jeans, feeling like a felon. He wasn't here, so she couldn't ask for permission to borrow his truck, but...

"If the man carried a phone, I wouldn't *have* to do this without permission." She slid her hand into his pocket and fished among his change for a keychain.

"He used to carry one, but he broke three over the course of a year when he shifted form too quickly," came Amar's voice from behind her.

Morgen jumped and lifted her hands into the air, as if he were a sheriff with a gun pointed at her. No, he was a naked man with his eyebrows raised. Nothing else was raised, she noticed before jerking her gaze upward.

"I need a ride to the elementary school in town." Morgen looked past the top of his head toward the barn to avoid staring at his naked chest. "The witches are meeting there."

"Are you sure?" Amar turned to look at the barn, as if

wondering what held her attention over there. "There's a quilt show at the school this weekend. It's a big deal. The locals and tourists come to it every year. For whatever reason, it's more attended than the woodworking show, which is *vastly* more interesting."

Morgen rocked back as she wondered if the women Zorro had seen had been quilters, not witches. They hadn't been carrying stacks of blankets, but what if they'd been attending a meeting to learn where to set up their booths?

"No." She shook her head. "There were familiars there. They drove off Zorro."

"You should have summoned a fiercer familiar that could take care of itself."

Under the bedroom window, Napoleon was on his hind legs, chittering up at Lucky. Taunting him because he was stuck inside?

"Like that one?" Morgen pointed.

"Not that one, no. He wets himself whenever a predator looks crossly at him."

"Owls are plenty fierce. They just can't be expected to fight off three other big birds at once."

"Let's go check." Amar stepped past her and grabbed his underwear and jeans, the latter jangling as he tugged them on.

"Would I have found anything interesting in there if I'd finished investigating your pockets?" she asked.

"You can investigate them now if you like." Amar turned his hips toward her and lowered his eyelids halfway, the suggestion clear, as if he hadn't run off earlier without an explanation. "But I thought you were in a hurry."

"I am, and I wouldn't want to upset whatever werewolf summoned you for a chat. Or a howling match."

"She's already upset."

She. Confirmation. It *had* been Maria. What had she wanted?

To interrupt Morgen and Amar enjoying each other's company in the cab of the truck?

"Because you've moved on, and she can't have you back?" Morgen asked.

Amar shook his head and got in the truck without answering.

Morgen sighed, not sure if he would ever tell her the words she wanted to hear, and climbed in on the other side.

They drove in silence to town, though Amar looked over at her a couple of times, as if he wanted to say something. But each time, he shook his head, and returned his focus to the road.

Morgen couldn't help but feel disappointed, but she would figure things out with him later. For now, she patted her laptop bag and mentally rehearsed what she would say when she strolled into the meeting. As it always did, the idea of talking to a bunch of strangers kicked up butterflies in her stomach. The only time such things didn't terrify her was when she'd been drinking alcohol. Too bad swinging by the Back Alley Pub for a White Russian would be a bad idea.

Amar drove past the school, confirming that the cars were still in the lot in front of the gymnasium, then parked a block away. He probably didn't want a witch to recognize his truck and slash his tires. Understandable.

"Should I wait in the parking lot?" he asked after they got out. "I assume you'll use that invisibility spell to spy on them."

"Actually, I'm planning to go in and address them as a group, but yes, they might be less disturbed if you don't walk in at my side. Witches find you scary."

At least, Wendy did. It was possible the older ladies were more experienced and less concerned by furry men with fangs.

"I'm glad they do," Amar said balefully. "You brought weapons?" He pointed at her backpack.

"My laptop, a demo of the alpha version of my app, protein bars, and banana-oat cookies."

"None of those sound suitable for self-defense."

"I brought the snacks because I haven't had dinner yet. But if a bear leaps out of the woods, I can throw the cookies at it to distract it via its sweet tooth." Admittedly, that was her plan with the witches too. *Ladies, please enjoy these cookies while I show you an app that will improve your lives and make it a breeze to look up spells and potion recipes.*

"There will not be *bears* in the gymnasium."

"That's good news for the small school children who use the facility. Look, my plan is to give the witches things they might need and try to make friends, not get in a fight." Morgen shouldered her pack and headed toward the school.

"You should use the invisibility spell," Amar said. "You have enemies within the coven. You should make sure they aren't there before you stroll in and try to *make friends*." His tone made it clear he didn't believe her plan would work.

Morgen crossed her fingers and hoped he was wrong. Phoebe had been willing to befriend her, up until the rest of the coven had told her to stay away, and the form that Judith left had implied Morgen could apply to join... Most of the witches shouldn't have any reason to hate her, other than whatever gossip they'd heard. This ought to be doable for someone warm and charismatic. And for someone shy and awkward with strangers... Well, she had cookies and an app.

Alas, neither would work on Olivia.

"I concede your point." From the street, Morgen couldn't tell if the familiars were still up on the gym roof, but if they saw her coming and alerted their witches, and if Olivia *was* in there, she'd never get a chance to make her case. "Wait here, please." She gripped her amulet. "I'll yell if I get in trouble and need your help."

"I trust I'll be able to tell that by the witches waving their wands and sprinting out the front door after you."

"Ha ha." Morgen whispered the invisibility incantation and patted Amar on the arm before squaring her shoulders and walking toward the gym. Was it odd that she would prefer being chased by angry women with wands to giving a speech? Or trying to sell someone on her app? "Do you have to ask?" she muttered.

There wasn't anyone new arriving, and the gym door was closed. The meeting had to be in full swing. Morgen hoped there wouldn't be anyone looking at the door when she walked inside while invisible. She also hoped the witches wouldn't easily see through the magic of her spell.

A squawk came from the rooftop as she approached the door. One of the ravens. Zeke?

The black bird peered straight down at her, making her doubt that her spell had worked. She should have asked Amar before leaving. When she glanced back, looking for him, she didn't spot him by the truck. A werewolf could skulk around stealthily even without a spell.

When she looked back up at Zeke, he was still peering down at her. She didn't see any of the other bird familiars that had landed when Zorro had been up there, but they could be nearby. Zeke, if that truly was Phoebe's crow, hadn't raised an alarm yet. Maybe he was simply watching her and sharing a vision with Phoebe. Morgen hoped she was in the meeting so she would have at least one semi-ally.

She crept closer to the door, waiting to see if Zeke would object, but he lifted his head and scanned the parking lot, as if he'd lost interest in her.

Fine with Morgen. She eased the door open, relieved that it wasn't locked, and eased inside. A woman was speaking, but bleachers and stands holding quilts kept Morgen from seeing out to the middle of the floor. Off to one side, two women were unpacking boxes and setting up more stands. Maybe this *was* the meeting for the quilt show.

"...have three thousand eight-hundred and forty dollars left in our coffers," the woman was saying, "and I want to re-suggest that we lease a more adequate meeting room, now that Ellen no longer wishes to let us convene in her pottery studio."

"I wouldn't object to that, normally," another woman said, "but I'm sharing the lease with another artist now. He keeps late hours and doesn't believe in magic. He called the sheriff's department last month because of noise in the dumpster outside. It was Bella's familiar rummaging again."

"What's wrong with the school?" someone else asked. "This works fine, other than Doris unpacking quilts during our meeting."

"The bleachers are as comfortable as obsidian blocks, and there'll be more events here once the school year starts up again."

Morgen crept past the bleachers to look out at the speakers. She wasn't that confident in her invisibility spell and moved slowly, trying not to draw notice.

"We also can't *drink* here," another woman said. "Who wants to have a meeting without martinis and mimosas?"

"I do miss Stella's cocktail set and her ability to make a mean grasshopper."

About twenty women were gathered on the bleachers, most in their fifties and sixties or older, few carrying weapons or any obvious paraphernalia that would make Morgen believe they were witches, but there were exceptions. She spotted a couple of wands sticking out of purses or thrust through belts.

The lady who was standing with a paper that she was reading the numbers from leaned on a staff. It lacked antlers, but the glowing sphere attached to the top made Morgen think of the palantir in Lord of the Rings.

A clipboard on the bleachers not far from Morgen had a sign-in sheet with names, numbers, and email addresses. Was it a list of people who would present their work at the quilt show? Or had the witches written their names down when they'd come in? If the latter, Morgen could grab the email addresses and *send* them her app. The thought of being able to do that without speaking to the group or awkwardly introducing herself was appealing, but she doubted they would try some app sent by email from a stranger. Besides, the witches knew each other and probably already had each other's addresses. This had to be something else.

Despite the thought, Morgen slipped out her phone to take a picture of the information. As she did so, she noticed a familiar name on the sheet. Judith Farina. Maybe these *were* the witches. Gathering information for a roster update?

As she put her phone away, one of the witches looked in her direction. Morgen froze, waiting for a cry of accusation and trying to figure out what she would say when it came. If she'd wanted to talk to these women, she should have walked in openly, not skulked about and spied on them.

The woman looked back to her meeting without giving any indication that she'd seen anyone. Morgen let out a slow breath. The spell had to be working. Either that, or the woman thought Morgen was a part of the quilt-show set-up crew and hadn't believed her presence there was odd.

A cool breeze came from behind her. The door opening.

Morgen spun as someone she'd hoped to never see again walked in. Calista.

14

BETWEEN THE BLACK-PAINTED FINGERNAILS AND THE HAUGHTY SNEER on her lips, there was no mistaking the voluptuous woman's identity. Calista strode into the gymnasium, walking straight toward Morgen.

Morgen started to lunge behind the racks of quilts set up to the side of the door but remembered at the last second that sudden movement would allow people to see through her invisibility illusion. She crept to the side, angling toward stands that held patriotic red-white-and-blue quilts and crossing her fingers that Calista couldn't sense anything. Thus far, she hadn't seen Morgen—Morgen was certain Calista would have an extreme reaction if she did.

Calista did, however, frown in her direction when she reached the clipboard on the bleachers, as if she could tell that someone had been there taking a photo of people's information.

Morgen ducked fully behind one of the stands, though it was a silly hiding spot. If her spell wore off, all of the witches would be able to see her shoes under the quilt—it didn't fall all the way to the floor. Morgen resisted the urge to crouch down and peer under the gap. She also didn't poke her head around the stand.

The earlier conversations had fallen silent. Was everyone staring at Calista? Or at *Morgen*?

Another breeze whispered through the open door, and an animal with reddish-brown fur prowled past the stands. A fox.

Wait, that was Olivia's familiar, not Calista's. That had to mean both women were here.

The fox hopped onto the bleachers and out of Morgen's limited view. From her hiding spot, she could see other quilts, a fire extinguisher mounted on the wall, and a large scoreboard for basketball games.

"Your membership in the coven has been revoked, Calista," the woman with the staff said. "You've been asked not to attend our meetings anymore."

"And I had no intention of doing so," Calista answered, the sound of her voice triggering Morgen's memories of their fight in that garage, "but someone has to warn you women of the danger you're in from that Keller girl."

Uh.

"We're aware of her work."

Heels clacked on the wooden floor as Calista strode toward the group. Morgen couldn't resist peering around the stand. The witches were focused on Calista, not on her hiding spot.

A woman on a back bleacher stood up. Phoebe. Morgen hadn't been able to see her from her previous position.

Olivia walked in and stopped in front of Morgen's stand, blocking her view further. Her furry familiar hopped down from the bleachers and joined her by the door, and they faced the gathering.

Morgen knew she should slip out the door before someone discovered her—the fox had to be close enough to smell her already—but she wanted to see what happened.

"Are you *aware*," Calista said, "that she's putting together a werewolf army to use to take over the town?"

Morgen's jaw dropped. She was *what*?

"They're up there in Wolf Wood—at *Gwen's* house—every day, working for her, fortifying that farmhouse to turn it into a castle."

Repairing the roof and building a deck hardly counted as fortifications. It wasn't as if the Lobos were adding turrets and arrow slits to the house. Morgen bit her lip hard to keep from shouting a denial. Would anyone here listen to her? Or would they turn their wands on her and blast her into oblivion without hearing her out?

"She's making them talismans," Olivia added, "so they can't be manipulated with magic. So the werewolf-control incantation won't work for anyone but *her*."

Uh, no. It wouldn't work for Morgen either.

"She turned the entire Loup pack on my *sister*." Olivia's voice broke on the word.

Morgen clenched a fist. She had no doubt that Olivia's loss and pain were real, but this wasn't fair. The sisters had attacked *her*. They'd been after her from the beginning, and she didn't even know why.

The women on the bleachers murmured to each other.

"Perhaps we should call her to our meeting and hear her side of the story," Phoebe said.

Morgen risked peeking out again, heartened by the defense, though it might fall on deaf ears.

"Her side of the story about how she *killed* my sister?" Olivia demanded in a high-pitched tone. "We should have all banded together by now to drive her out."

"That you want to take her side, Phoebe, speaks volumes," Calista said. "I believe she's ensorcelled you. I insist that you allow Belinda to examine you."

"I'm not ensorcelled, and you've been committing *crimes*, Calista. *Murder*." Phoebe's face twisted with anguish as she shook her head. "You shouldn't be here. What if someone calls the sheriff's department? That Deputy Franklin came to the Crystal Parlor asking where you are."

What if someone *did* call the sheriff's department? Their office wasn't far away, though Morgen doubted Franklin would be there this late at night. Still, if they had an arrest warrant out for Calista and recognized her voice...

"I know," Calista said. "I risk a great deal in coming here to deliver this message to you."

Careful not to make any noise, Morgen pulled out her phone. She cranked the volume to zero and thumbed through the contacts to find Franklin's number.

"But you haven't been *doing* anything about the Keller girl," Calista continued, "and she'll have her army of werewolves outfitted with talismans and ready to take over the town before you realize what's happening. You *know* how difficult it was to keep the Loup pack from turning more people and trying to claim all of Bellrock as their own. If the other pack hadn't come along, and if we hadn't managed to deflect their violent tendencies onto the Loups—you're welcome, by the way—we might have lost everything. By the end of the month, Nora might not be the *only* dead witch."

Morgen found the number and dialed Franklin, checking again to make sure the volume was off on the speaker. Would the voices in the gym carry to him, and would he listen long enough to identify the speakers? Maybe she should have texted him, but she didn't know if the number he'd given her was a cell phone or land line.

The fox rose to its feet and started prowling around. Morgen frowned as it headed under the quilt stands and sniffed at the floor. Following her tracks? Did it remember her scent?

Franklin or someone else answered the phone. With the volume cranked down, she couldn't hear what he said.

The witches were muttering to each other, and she couldn't hear what any of them were saying either. Calista had stopped talking and was waiting for them to discuss her argument. None of that would let Franklin know Calista was there.

As the fox stalked closer, sniffing at stands and the quilts, Morgen had to scoot to the side. It peered in her direction.

"We were already aware of the werewolves at the Keller house, Calista," Judith said.

Yes, she'd used Calista's name. Morgen glanced at her phone but had to stifle a groan. When nobody had spoken to him, Franklin had hung up.

"And are you aware that her sister is now in town?" Calista asked.

Morgen jolted in surprise—and horror. Who'd told her about Sian? Olivia? It had to be, but how had she known from that brief skirmish that Sian was Morgen's sister?

"She may be training as a witch as well," Calista said.

Yeah, right. Sian was more likely to train as a unicyclist for the circus.

"She's putting together an army, I tell you. We *must* stop her."

The fox crept closer to Morgen. Its path wasn't direct, so she couldn't be sure it was on her trail, but she had a feeling it knew someone was hiding back there, and that it was suspicious.

Morgen scooted out from behind the stands, again careful not to move quickly as she stepped into the open. Calista's back was to her. Maybe if she took a picture and texted it to Franklin? She would have to hope this was indeed a cell number.

The fox sniffed the floor where she'd been. Feeling vulnerable, and wondering how long her illusion would last, Morgen eased out into the middle of the gymnasium floor. If any of the witches wore a trinket that allowed them to see through such magic, Morgen was clearly in the open.

Meanwhile, the fox sauntered after her, cutting off her retreat back to the stands—and the door—if she needed it. This was nuts, but Morgen needed a picture of Calista's *face* to send to Franklin, not the back of her head.

She got as close as she dared, zoomed in, and took a photo. Ten feet away, the fox stopped abruptly and stared straight at Morgen.

Morgen glanced around for an open escape. With Olivia and the fox blocking the route to the other door, she couldn't go that way, not without risking crashing into them. She spotted an emergency-exit door, but a sign warned that an alarm would go off if she opened it. Great.

A screech sounded, and Morgen jumped. Had a familiar she hadn't noticed spotted her?

But the noise had come from outside. More screeches erupted, and something that sounded like a cranky cat wailed. The witches jumped to their feet.

"Someone's out there," Judith blurted.

"Spying on us!" another witch said.

Calista and several others ran for the door.

Amar? Was that who the familiars had found?

As most of the witches ran toward the exit, Morgen texted the photograph of Calista to Franklin. She took another picture of the bleachers and a bear mascot on the wall, hoping this was the only gymnasium in town and that he would know exactly where it was.

She was tempted to try calling him again, but not all of the witches had gone out the door. Most had, but a red-haired woman in her fifties, the person with the staff with the glowing sphere on the top, walked straight toward Morgen.

She almost dropped her phone. The witch was looking right at her.

The invisibility spell must have worn off.

15

Morgen tried to whirl and sprint toward the emergency-exit door, but the witch with the staff held up her hand. The woman didn't speak an incantation or do anything else obvious, but a tingle ran through Morgen's nerves, and her feet rooted to the floor.

"I'm not a threat," Morgen blurted, lifting her hands, her phone still gripped in her fingers. Had Franklin seen her message? Would he send men to come check the gymnasium? "But I have to help my friend."

And her sister. What if Calista and Olivia knew where Sian was staying and had already done something to her? Damn it, why had Morgen asked Sian to come here? She should have agreed with Sian's plan to stay at her apartment in the city, the nice, safe, witch-free city.

"Your command of the invisibility illusion is impressive." The woman squinted at Morgen—or at where she didn't see Morgen but believed her to be? "Calista is right. You *are* dangerous."

"No, I'm not. I don't even know what I'm doing." Morgen glanced around, but every other person in the room, except for the two ladies setting up quilts, had run out into the parking area. To chase Amar? Just because they couldn't control him any longer didn't mean they couldn't hurt him. Or worse. Morgen tried to yank her feet off the floor, but the magic still held her. "Calista and the sisters are the ones who attacked me. Ever since I got up here, they've been trying to take over Wolf Wood and drive me away from Bellrock. They keep lighting the house and the barn on fire."

"Without provocation?" The woman had a calm, even voice. It wasn't full of accusation, but it wasn't warm and friendly either.

"*Yes*, without provocation. I've been trying to mind my own business."

"While hoarding the resources in Wolf Wood?"

"I'm not hoarding anything. *They* came in and stole all the moss and who knows what else."

"Your wolf drives witches away."

"He's not my wolf, and it's private property."

That wasn't the right thing to say, for the woman's eyes closed to slits. There was the accusation that hadn't been there earlier.

"You *do* seek to keep it for yourself," she said.

"No, I don't. It should be left alone for everyone." The amulet started to warm against Morgen's chest.

"I am Belinda, elected leader of the coven, and I will have your thoughts." The woman tilted the staff toward Morgen's head.

With her feet locked to the floor, Morgen couldn't dodge effectively. She tried to whisper the incantation that would let her see the woman's weaknesses, but Belinda pressed the sphere to Morgen's forehead, and a buzz jolted through her. She fumbled the incantation.

Morgen eyed the sphere, yellow, green, and blue colors swirling within it. This woman couldn't *truly* read her thoughts, could she? That was the stuff of science-fiction novels.

Beside the sphere, Morgen's phone was visible, still gripped in her raised hand. A text message had come back, the words *Who is this?* on the screen.

Morgen groaned. Franklin must not have put her number into his address book, and he didn't recognize it now. And here she'd thought she was a notable and annoying person that he wanted to keep track of.

As the cool kiss of the sphere pressed against her forehead, Morgen thumbed through apps on her phone. She spotted an alarm icon. She'd once downloaded the app in case someone tried to mug her in a dark parking lot. Oh, how she wished muggers were the only threat she had to deal with now.

She tapped the alarm icon with her thumb, and the phone blared in Belinda's ear. It startled her, and she stumbled back, the staff pulling away from Morgen's head.

Morgen took advantage by stomping on Belinda's instep and sprinting for the emergency exit. It only took a few seconds to reach, but she kept expecting an attack to strike between her shoulder blades and send her sprawling. Amazingly, she reached the door without trouble, shoved it open, and sprinted out into the night.

As promised by the sign, an alarm sounded. Well, that was one way to get the deputies to come…

Since she'd come out on another side of the building, Morgen could only see part of the parking lot, but she glimpsed women in that direction. Some remained near their cars and shouted instructions, while others ran toward dark trees at the edge of the lot. If Amar was out there in human or wolf form, Morgen couldn't see him.

Two cats raced past her. Familiars? Strays startled by the noise?

A siren wailed from Main Street, and Morgen jumped. She had no idea if that was Franklin bringing men to the school because he'd realized Calista was there, if someone was responding to the alarm, or if the witches had called the sheriff's department to complain about *Morgen*.

The emergency door opened behind her. Without looking back, Morgen sprinted for the street. If Belinda rooted her to the ground again, she would be stuck until the authorities arrived. As Amar had often pointed out, the witches were citizens of Bellrock and far more likely to be trusted and believed than strangers who'd recently arrived in town.

Morgen lunged around the corner and spotted Amar's truck still parked alongside the street. She *also* spotted vehicles from the sheriff's department speeding in her direction with their lights flashing. Suspecting her earlier spell had worn off, Morgen gripped the still-warm amulet and whispered the invisibility incantation again.

Overhead, an owl screeched. Several birds flew past. The ravens.

Three sheriff's department SUVs sped past Morgen, not slowing except to turn into the parking lot. Hoping that meant they hadn't seen her, she raced toward Amar's truck. By now, he might be miles away and in wolf form, running from familiars chasing him and heading deep into the woods.

Morgen rushed to the driver-side door and peered through the window. The cab was empty.

As she was debating whether to hide inside and hope nobody came to check the parked cars on the street, a thump sounded behind her. She spun as Amar rose from a crouch.

"Where'd you come from?" she blurted over the wail of the sirens.

"Heaven," he said, though he glanced at the flat rooftop of a building behind him.

"Shouldn't you have wings, then?"

"Get in. There's a raven following me. The witches won't be far behind. They tried to control me, and they failed." His eyes lit with triumph, and he touched his talisman.

"Good." Morgen ran around to the passenger side and climbed in.

"Yes. But I'm surprised they figured out I was out here." Amar slid into the truck and turned the key in the ignition. "I think I triggered a magical alarm that I wasn't expecting."

"While sitting in your truck?"

"I was in the parking lot."

"I thought you didn't approve of snooping."

"It wasn't snooping. It was scouting."

"What's the difference?"

"How many legs you have when you do it." Amar waited until the SUVs were out of sight in the school's parking lot before pulling into the street. "I brushed one of the cars," he admitted reluctantly, as if he'd failed in some grievous manner.

"It's worth it if you learned something. I approve of snooping—scouting—you know."

"Even though I alerted the entire coven that I was there?"

"Yeah, because I'm not sure I would have gotten out of that gym if you hadn't. The leader, a Belinda Somebody with a big staff, knew I was there. Why were you scouting?" She hoped he'd found out something useful, especially since all Morgen had accomplished was taking a picture of a roster and learning that her sister might be in danger. "And can you stop at the Wild Trout before leaving town?"

Morgen lifted her phone and bypassed more messages that had come in from Franklin to dial her sister's number.

"I smelled Calista's scent," Amar said, "and located the car I believe she drove to the meeting."

"Yeah, she was in there. She made a bunch of accusations about me and told them all that I'm raising a wolf army to sic on them."

"An interesting interpretation of having contractors build you a new deck."

"I didn't even ask for that deck."

"Regardless, the witches cast incantations and sent their familiars after me. *All* of them." Amar touched the top of his head, as if in memory of ravens and owls pecking at his skull. "I had to run out of their range and circle back. One of the witches almost lit my fur on fire twice. It was *not* a pleasant evening."

"I'm sorry."

Morgen's call dropped to voicemail, and she frowned at the glowing screen. It was possible her sister was jet-lagged and had silenced her phone and gone to bed early, but fresh concern hollowed out a pit in Morgen's stomach.

"The hotel?" She pointed to the turn up ahead.

From the way Amar was accelerating, she feared he hadn't heard her request—or was ignoring it.

He glanced in the rearview mirror. "We're only a few blocks from the school. If we loiter in town, the witches may be able to locate us."

"Breaking news, Amar. They know where we live."

He grunted and swung the truck into the hotel parking lot. Since Morgen had stayed there, she was familiar with the layout. She jumped out of the truck and started toward the little reception area up front, hoping the clerk would be willing to give her Sian's room number.

"Morgen." Amar stopped her with his voice, pointing at an open door toward the back of the building. "Is that her room?"

All of the doors opened onto the parking lot or a small courtyard on the far side. It had been convenient for taking the dog out to do his business, but it was also convenient for strangers to walk right up and knock. Or... force the door open?

"I don't know." Morgen shifted her route and headed for the room.

Any semi-contemporary hotel would have had doors that automatically closed and locked after being opened, but this place used old-fashioned metal keys and had few modern amenities. She peeked through the open door, an excuse on her lips in case it was a stranger's room and he or she caught Morgen peering in. But it wasn't. Sian's suitcase was on the bed, the lid open and clothing strewn about. A pair of pale-blue cartoon underwear dangled from a lampshade.

Morgen swore and ran in to check the bathroom, horror filling her as she imagined Sian's body on the floor with her skull caved in. Would the witches have done such a thing? Calista had murdered her own lover. Why would she pause at killing a stranger?

The bathroom was empty, save for an upended toiletries bag in the sink and toothpaste and deodorant on the floor. Someone had stepped on the toothpaste tube, the label written in a Southeast Asian language, and half the gel was squeezed out on the faded vinyl.

"I recognize Calista's and Olivia's scents again," Amar said from the doorway.

"Did they kidnap Sian? *Worse?*"

"I can't tell that simply from lingering scents. I don't smell any blood."

"Small relief." Morgen pushed a hand through her hair. "If they had kidnapped her, where would they have put her while they crashed the coven's meeting? And why wouldn't they have mentioned that they had her?"

Amar stepped in, eyed the panties on the lampshade, and shook his head. "I can't tell that either. Or why they would have rooted through her belongings."

"To find souvenirs from Borneo, obviously." Morgen tried dialing her sister's number again.

A phone rang in the room. She groaned.

Amar knelt and dug between the nightstand and the bed, then lifted a phone with a jungle-themed case from the floor, a gorilla peering out from the back. The screen was lit with an alert for Morgen's incoming call.

She slumped against the wall. Her sister was gone, and she had no way to track her down.

16

"If Mom were still alive, she would kill me for losing my sister," Morgen said numbly, staring at the clothes strewn around the hotel room and trying to figure out what to do next. Call Franklin? Who might even now be on a wild goose chase after Calista and irritated with Morgen for instigating it? She didn't have much of a choice, unless... "Do you think Olivia would have taken Sian back to their tree house and locked her up there? Stuck one of those rubies around her neck to hypnotize her and keep her quiet?"

"You lodged the big control ruby in the wall like a home-run hitter," Amar said.

"Yeah, but I don't think that broke it. Olivia probably righted that pedestal and set the ruby right back on it. Let's—"

Her phone rang. Franklin.

"Deputy Franklin," Morgen answered. "I've got a problem, and I need your help."

Judging by the pause, that wasn't how Franklin had expected her to answer.

"My sister is missing," Morgen added.

"You have a sister?"

"Yeah, she just got back from working overseas and is in town visiting. She's staying at the Wild Trout, but her room has been ransacked, and she's gone."

"Ms. Keller, I'm still working on the *last* problem you so cryptically alerted me to."

"I didn't think a picture of a wanted woman addressing the coven in the local school gym was that cryptic. Do you have someone who can help me find my sister?"

"Most people who want help from the authorities call instead of texting a photo of the side of a woman's face."

"I know, but I couldn't talk. Deputy Franklin, *please*." Morgen shook her head. This was pointless. They ought to go straight to the tree house.

Amar stepped outside and sniffed the air. Maybe if he turned into his wolf form, he would be able to follow the women's trails. But if they'd gotten into a car, he wouldn't be able to track them beyond the parking lot.

"We're questioning some of the local women about Calista now," Franklin said. "You said you're at the Wild Trout? I'll be there as soon as possible. And then I have some questions for *you*."

Morgen grimaced, wondering if they were about Nora's death. Or the deaths of the two Loups who hadn't survived the battle with the Lobos on her property. A couple of weeks had passed since that night, but she kept expecting the sheriff's department to put two and two together and come to question her.

"I'll happily answer them," she made herself say, "as soon as we find my sister."

Franklin sighed and hung up.

"I'll look around." Amar stepped back into the doorway to hand her Sian's phone and remove his vest and jeans, ignoring a pizza-delivery car that had parked in front of a nearby room. He tossed them onto the bed alongside the clothing already draped there. "If I can't track her down, I'll check the tree house."

"Thank you."

Amar shifted into his wolf form and padded across the parking lot. A startled oath from the pizza-delivery person echoed from the building walls, followed by a car door slamming.

Morgen paced the room, trying to think of something intelligent to do, but all she managed was to worry about Sian and once more regret that she'd called her sister into the mess that her life had become. Sian had barely recovered from a terrible disease, and now she'd been thrust into the middle of this hell. Morgen didn't want to contemplate the possibility that the arch nemesis she'd never wanted might have already killed Sian. Surely, Calista would have kept her alive, if only to use as a handle on Morgen.

Sell Wolf Wood to me, or your sister gets it...

If Calista did make that demand, Morgen would have to agree to it. What other choice did she have?

Bleakly, she wondered what the father she hadn't seen since Mom's passing would think if he learned that one of his daughters was dead. Would he even care? He'd never understood Morgen and Sian, always preferring to spend time with their brothers instead. The rowdy, garrulous boys who had always been more like he was. More *normal*. The last Morgen had heard—the word coming from her brothers instead of directly from their father—he'd given up his US citizenship to save on taxes and was living in Singapore. Morgen didn't even have his phone number.

"What happened to my room?" a familiar voice asked from the doorway.

Morgen spun to find Sian standing on the threshold, her eyes wide and her jaw slack as she gaped around. Neither handcuffs nor magical rubies adorned her, and she didn't look like she'd just clawed her way out of a car trunk or anyplace else that kidnappers liked to stash kidnappees.

"Sian!" Morgen rushed over and hugged her.

"Ugh. *Morgen*." Sian only endured the embrace for a second before pushing her back. "What *is* going on?"

"I thought you were kidnapped or murdered. Where have you *been*? And why didn't you take your phone?" Morgen thrust it toward her.

"I walked to the vet's office. The battery was dead, so I left my phone here on the charger."

"It was on the floor under the bed when we came in."

"Why is my—" Scowling, Sian stalked in and grabbed the underwear off the lampshade. "You didn't do this, did you?"

"Of course not. You know my organizational paradigms don't employ light fixtures. Why were you at the vet's office at—" Morgen glanced at the time on her phone. "It's after ten-thirty."

"Because I couldn't find my inhaler. It flew out of my pocket when I was kicking your enemies, and my asthma has been aggravated since I got sick. I needed it." Sian held up the inhaler but only briefly. She walked around the room, scowling fiercely as she picked up her clothing. "People touched my belongings."

"Violently, yes."

Sian held up a T-shirt. "I need to find a laundry facility immediately."

"I don't think the hotel has one."

"That's inexcusable." Sian's eyes widened again when she spotted her pajama bottoms on the floor on the far side of the bed. She lunged around the corner, clipping her hip on the mattress, and plucked them up. "I need these *tonight*."

"I'm sure your skin will survive them having been on the floor briefly. How long were you at the vet's?"

"On the floor and *touched*. By grimy strangers with who knows what hygiene habits?" Sian whirled, holding the bottoms aloft. "This is unacceptable."

"People raided your room, possibly with the intent to kidnap, maim, or kill you, and the fact that they touched your pajamas is your biggest concern?"

"*And* my underwear." Sian pulled another pair of panties off the floor and looked from the growing collection of clothes in her arms to her suitcase and back, flummoxed about what to do with them. She finally grabbed the mesh laundry sack that the intruders hadn't molested. "People aren't allowed to touch my belongings."

"Yes, I remember that from our childhood. It's a wonder you survived years of working in a tropical jungle. I hear grime abounds there."

"It does, but nobody touches my belongings. I don't think I can stay here." Sian walked around the room, picking up clothing that still looked clean to Morgen's eye and stuffing it in her laundry bag.

"Because the people who want to kidnap you know where you're staying and might be back, or because you need to wash your pajamas before you can sleep in them?"

"I trust there are laundry facilities at Grandma's house."

"Yes, of course. And the roof above the washer and dryer doesn't even leak anymore." As Morgen helped her sister pick up clothing, she noticed Amar, still in wolf form, sitting on his haunches in the doorway.

She wondered if he'd followed Sian's trail up to the vet's office and back before returning here.

"What is *this*?" Sian picked up Amar's vest, exposing as little of her skin as possible to it by holding it between her thumb and forefinger.

"That's Amar's. He'll need it back soon." Morgen raised her eyebrows at him, wondering if he would change back into a human—a naked human—while Sian was in the room.

"Why is it on my *bed* and touching my *luggage*?" Sian eyed the corner of her suitcase, as if she was contemplating hunting for disinfectant, or perhaps buying a whole new suitcase. "And those." She curled a lip at his jeans, laid the vest on them, and rubbed her fingers together as if she could wipe off the germs—or werewolf pheromones. "I'll check out of the hotel as soon as I finish gathering my belongings."

"I look forward to having you join me at Grandma's house."

Sian lowered her voice to mutter, "No laundry facilities," as she walked into the bathroom.

As soon as she was out of sight, Amar padded into the room and shifted into human form.

"I found her," he said dryly.

"Good work," Morgen said.

He grabbed his jeans and underwear and started to dress. "She went to Dr. Valderas's office and took a different route on the way back; otherwise, I would have crossed paths with her."

"Bellrock is scenic at eleven pm on a Wednesday night."

"I spoke with Valderas for a minute. Apparently, after they pulled her inhaler out from under his shoe cubbies, and she inquired about *Ralph's* health, they immersed themselves in a conversation about the science behind werewolf shifting, including the law of conservation of mass and other physics and math things that I don't remember."

"That sounds right."

Sian walked out with her repacked toiletries bag. She must have heard them speaking, because she didn't bat an eye at Amar dressing in the middle of her hotel room.

"Does your discussion with Dr. Valderas mean you believe in werewolves now?" Morgen asked her.

"When the facts, as I'm aware of them, change, I have little choice but to reassess my convictions and ideologies about the world." Sian zipped her suitcase closed.

"She believes in you," Morgen told Amar.

Amar grunted, hefted Sian's suitcase over his shoulder, and

headed outside. Sian lifted a finger, as if she might object to him touching her luggage, but she sighed, slumped wearily, and trailed him out.

Morgen wondered if her sister was starting to regret coming back to the US. At least she hadn't been kidnapped.

Unfortunately, Morgen worried that after tonight, the entire witch coven would be after both of them.

17

WHEN THEY ARRIVED AT THE HOUSE, A WOLF WITH LUSH BLACK FUR was sitting in the driveway. At first, Morgen thought of the leader of the Loups, the only other black-furred wolf she'd seen thus far, but that one had been dull and scruffy in comparison to this fine creature. The rain had stopped, and a half moon was visible in the night sky, the silvery light gleaming on its thick fur.

On *her* thick fur, Morgen realized with a jolt.

Amar stopped the truck and stared at her—at Maria—through the windshield. Mesmerized by her beauty?

"I told her I wouldn't get back together with her," he stated.

"You did?" Morgen asked in surprise. "That was her howling to you earlier, wasn't it? Calling you away from, uhm, me?" She glanced at Sian, who sat between them on the bench seat.

"It was. I made myself clear, but I'll see what she wants. She may have another warning." Amar glanced at the dark house, but nothing appeared amiss.

"Like to stay away from troublesome witches?" Morgen asked.

"You're not troublesome. You get *into* trouble. That's something different."

"You've got a good grasp on the language for a non-native speaker."

"I just know all about trouble." Amar sounded a little exasperated—as if that mess at the school had been *her* fault—but he smiled at her.

Sian sighed. "Let me out so I can start my laundry."

"Do you want to borrow my pajamas?" Morgen opened the door and hopped out, though she kept an eye on the black wolf. "They're clean. I brought an extra pair up to Bellrock. One never knows when there'll be emergencies."

"Tell me about it," Sian muttered, not accepting the offer. She tugged out her luggage and strode past the wolf to the front door.

"If Lucky barks, just tell him he's a good boy." Morgen supposed she should have followed to show her sister around, since Sian hadn't been in the house in thirty years, but she was reluctant to leave Amar alone with Maria. Even if he *had* said he wasn't interested, Maria might be able to change his mind with that lush black fur and those intent dark eyes.

Sian waved a hand in acknowledgment without looking back. Her shoulders had a weary slump as she climbed the porch steps, and Morgen wished her first day back in the country hadn't been so eventful.

Amar asked Maria what she wanted, speaking in Spanish.

She shifted into her human form to stand naked before him in the moonlight.

"To see if you want to hunt tonight," she said, resting a hand on her hip and thrusting her chest toward him. She managed to smile seductively at him and frown with disapproval at Morgen at the same time.

"I told you I didn't," Amar said.

"And I told *you* what I heard. The Lobos aren't the only ones concerned that you're spending time with a witch. I care for you, Amar. I'm here to protect you. Return to the pack. Don't stand out as a target. Just because you have that bauble doesn't mean you're immune to everything those witches can throw at you." She prowled toward him, radiating sex appeal but also the power of a predator. She was the perfect blend of athleticism and feminine beauty, and Morgen couldn't help but resent her for that.

"I'm aware of that." Amar looked at Morgen. "Will you go help your sister with her laundry?"

"She's forty-two and capable of turning a dial and pushing a button."

The exasperation returned. The smile did not.

"Fine, fine. Let me know if you need anything." Reluctantly, Morgen headed toward the house. They switched back to Spanish, so she wouldn't have understood the rest of the conversation anyway. She told herself to feel reassured that he wasn't interested in hooking up with Maria again. Unless she succeeded in seducing him tonight.

Morgen glanced at the camper van before going inside, a little surprised that Wendy hadn't left yet. The glow of a TV—or that gaming computer—escaped the drawn curtains.

Morgen was half-tempted to veer in that direction and take another stab at getting Wendy to help make silver receptacles for werewolf talismans, but she was tired, and she'd failed to make any headway with the witches. Maybe in the morning when she was fresh, she would be able to come up with another way to sway the coven to her side.

After checking on her sister and pointing out a bedroom that wasn't in the middle of having the floors refinished, Morgen climbed up to her room. Lucky, who'd been sleeping on the living-room couch, gave up his spot to pad up to the second floor with her.

She intended to wash up and go to bed, but she couldn't keep from glancing out the window. She could make out Amar and Maria standing and facing each other as they spoke. They weren't kissing, but she feared Amar would lose his resolve, be overcome by her beauty, and lope off into the woods with her.

To keep her mind off that, Morgen opened her laptop and entered the witches' names, phone numbers, and email addresses into a spreadsheet. She opened her inbox, started a fresh message, addressed it to all of the witches, and attached the desktop version of her program. She thought about simply sending it as it was but found herself typing up instructions, details about what had prompted her to make it, and finally a long explanation about what had happened since she arrived in Wolf Wood and how she hadn't wanted to make enemies with anyone. She also wrote about how she wished they could start over and that she could find a place in the town.

Tears trickled down her cheeks as she realized how much she wanted that, and the email was far more emotional than she'd intended. Would it be a mistake to send something like that without rereading it first in the morning? It might be a mistake to send it *at all*. It revealed too many of her vulnerabilities. Someone might use the information against her.

She highlighted the entire message and held her finger over the delete key, but she didn't press it.

"Hell, how much worse can things get?" She sent the email.

Lucky had taken over the bed while she'd been working and didn't answer the question.

After it zipped away, Morgen closed her laptop. She couldn't resist peeking out to check on Maria and Amar. It wasn't spying, she told herself. If they hadn't wanted to be observed, they shouldn't have been standing in the driveway.

Maria stepped forward and rested a hand on Amar's chest. She gazed up at him with warm eyes, her voluptuous body scant inches from his.

He stepped back, putting distance between them, and pointed at the woods. She stared at him in disbelief for a long moment, but his face was hard with determination. Silently, Morgen cheered. It wasn't as if he'd chosen *her* either, but if he didn't get back together with Maria, Morgen still had hope.

Maria shifted back into a wolf and loped across the lawn. She paused before entering the woods and lifted her snout to howl at the night sky. The sorrow and distress in that long ululating note sent bleakness through Morgen. It sounded more like Maria was mourning the death of someone than being upset over not getting laid tonight. Maybe she truly worried that something bad would happen to Amar if he stayed in Morgen's orbit.

Was she so sure it wouldn't?

When Maria finally disappeared into the woods, Amar lifted his eyes toward the night sky. He didn't howl, but he seemed conflicted as he gazed upward.

Morgen didn't think she'd made any noise, but Amar turned to look up at her window, as if he'd known all along that she was watching. Her first instinct was to spring back and dive into bed, as if she'd been caught doing something wrong. But she made herself hold his gaze. She touched her chest, then pointed at the floor, and raised her eyebrows. Did he want to come in?

He also held *her* gaze, but his face was hard to read. There might have been indecision in his eyes, or she might have imagined it.

Ultimately, he shook his head and walked to the barn.

She sagged. Everyone's words, including his, about how witches and werewolves weren't friends and certainly didn't have *relationships* came to mind. The fact that he was apparently drawn to her, or her magic, only made things worse.

Reluctantly, Morgen got ready for bed. Shortly after she returned from brushing her teeth, a knock at the door made her lift her eyes in hope. Amar? Had he changed his mind?

More likely it was Sian.

"There's more detergent in the cupboard with the cleaning supplies," Morgen said, opening the door.

"That's good to know," Wendy said.

She stood in the hallway with two jars and a leather pouch in her hands. A familiar green glow came from the jars, emanating from the bioluminescent moss powder inside.

"Here." Wendy thrust out her arms in offering.

"Here?" Morgen accepted the items, thoughts of being able to pay the taxes on the house and the Lobos for their renovations coming to mind, but she was confused. "Why?"

"That's your moss, at least some of it. Nora cured it before..." Wendy shrugged, averting her eyes and blinking several times. "Before... you know. I took some of it when I left. I was going to give it to you earlier, but I forgot."

"Thank you." Morgen was about to ask what was in the pouch, but Wendy spoke first.

"I read your email."

"I... didn't send you an email."

Wendy smiled lopsidedly. "Tamara forwarded it as soon as she saw the jewelry-imbuing formulas."

"Ah." Morgen vaguely remembered entering that data. She'd scanned numerous formulas, recipes, and schematics from Grandma's book collection, but many of them had been too old, the handwriting too imprecise, for a computer to translate. She'd had to type those in by hand.

"Did you mean to put so much, uhm, rare information into that collection?" Wendy asked.

"Rare?"

"Yeah, like the dragon kitty in *Castle Crawler*. It's so rare that people pay fortunes in the real world to get one for their characters to ride."

"Maybe some of Grandma's grimoires were rare."

"I'll say. I don't know how the coven in general will react, or how many will even read emails from you, but..." Wendy shrugged again. "Maybe they'll be more likely to accept you now."

"Probably not after tonight."

Morgen wondered if Wendy's friend had also shared the details of how Amar and Morgen had shown up at their meeting and created chaos. She was surprised Franklin hadn't called her back yet. Maybe he'd ended up catching sight of Calista and was in the middle of a late-night, high-speed chase. Morgen hoped Calista ended up in a jail cell. A magic-proof jail cell.

"You'd actually make a good witch and be a good addition to the coven. You have all those powers of organization. That eludes a lot of us." Wendy smiled self-deprecatingly. "They *should* want you to join."

"It would be nice to be wanted, but Calista and Olivia..."

"Don't assume they'll succeed in changing everyone's minds," Wendy said, as if she knew what had happened at the meeting. "Calista was kicked out, and my sister... Well, like I was telling you before, she started caring a lot about money, and that's not supposed to be our way. The others might hear you out." Wendy shrugged. "They'll be even *more* likely to hear you out and want you if you don't make talismans for all of the werewolves."

"Since the only jeweler I know has refused to make more receptacles for that project, it's not going to happen." Morgen had no idea how she would break the news to the Lobos. She imagined them angrily ripping out all of the upgrades to the house that they'd made.

"Actually, she hasn't." Wendy pointed at the pouch.

Morgen raised her eyebrows and hefted it. Whatever was inside made faint clinking noises, like metal against metal. She unfastened the tie holding the pouch shut and peered into it. At least a dozen silver necklaces with receptacles for her resin concoction were nestled inside.

"I don't think you should do it," Wendy said, "but I won't stop you."

More than that, Wendy was *helping* her.

"Thank you," Morgen said again. "But will you get in trouble with your sister and the others?"

"Not if you tell them you bought those at Walmart."

"In which section there does one find enchanted silver necklaces?"

"Between Crafts and Fabric and Household Chemicals."

"Huh."

Wendy waved and left Morgen with her gifts.

Morgen didn't know how to fix her problems, but if she made talismans for the Lobos, at least her enemies wouldn't be able to turn them en masse against her.

"Guess I know what I'm working on tomorrow," she said, closing the door.

After she set the items on the dresser, the jars glowing like nightlights, she grabbed her pajamas, determined to finally get some sleep. She couldn't keep from pausing in front of the window to look over at the barn. To her surprise, Amar stood at one of *his* windows, gazing over at the house. At her.

Their eyes met, and emotion tightened her throat. He was in shadow, the same as she, but she felt certain that he wanted to come over. And also certain that he wouldn't. Because she was a witch, and he was a werewolf.

He smiled sadly, as if he could read her thoughts, and left the window.

Morgen went to bed, but she lay awake with her head on the pillow, staring up at the dark ceiling. Wendy had implied that if she turned her back on the werewolves, she might be accepted into the coven.

But if she did that, the Lobos would be disappointed. *Amar* would be disappointed.

She closed her eyes, but that didn't stop tears from forming again. A thought percolated into her mind, one so abhorrent at first glance that she almost punted it away and locked it in a closet.

But it lingered, forcing her to consider it. What if she gave up the witch thing and asked Amar to turn her into a werewolf? Like Pedro had apparently done to Maria years ago. He'd made her one of them, and then they'd become mates. She'd claimed him, and he'd *wanted* to be claimed. If werewolves were drawn to werewolves, it made sense. If Morgen was one of them... Amar wouldn't have a reason to object to being drawn to her. He wouldn't have a reason to object to her at all.

When he'd first mentioned bites on the neck during the full moon, and being permanently turned into a werewolf, she'd been repulsed. And maybe she still was, but if people cared about each other, they made sacrifices to make things work, to be with each other. Didn't they?

She'd never been the kind of girl who considered changing herself to better suit the needs of a man, and this was a damn big change, but as she lay there looking at the ceiling and waiting for sleep to claim her, she couldn't get the idea out of her mind.

18

Long before dawn, Morgen woke to heat on her chest. The amulet.

She prodded it with her finger, wondering if she would receive another vision. No sooner had the thought come than the corner of the room lit up. Imagery formed, Grandma once again at the table, writing a letter while the giant leather-bound tome rested by her elbow. It was as if the vision was picking up where it had left off.

As she watched the letter writing, Morgen wondered why she hadn't thought to ask Amar if he'd ever brought magical driftwood to Grandma's door. That would have been a way to find out if these events had happened or were merely a dream conjured by her subconscious mind.

A knock sounded in the vision, and Grandma lifted her head. She left the table to peer out the window, cursed, and grabbed the letter and tome. She folded the paper and stuck it inside the book, leaving the title page briefly visible: *Incantations of Power*.

Carrying the heavy tome in both arms, Grandma hurried up the stairs to the second-floor library. She stepped inside and tugged on a decorative gargoyle mounted on the side of a bookcase. The case swung open, revealing a metal safe embedded in the wall. Unlike most things in the old house, it appeared modern and sturdy.

The safe lacked a number pad or dial, but the door held a familiar star-shape indention. Grandma withdrew the same amulet that Morgen now wore from under her shirt and pressed the matching medallion into the indention. The safe opened, going back deeper into the wall than Morgen would have expected. Even so, Grandma struggled to fit the book inside and cursed like a drunken sailor. Someone knocked again at the front door. She cursed some more, finally levered the tome in there, and swung the safe shut and shifted the bookcase back into place.

She straightened her dress, tugged her knee-high striped socks up higher, made sure her amulet was hidden out of view, and strode out of the library. She favored her left leg as she navigated down the stairs, leaning heavily on the railing. Something about the proud expression on her face made Morgen think she wouldn't have let herself limp if anyone was watching. Maybe that was why Grandma had favored the motorcycle. It could go most places but didn't draw pitying stares the way a mobility scooter or motorized grocery cart might.

When Grandma opened the door, Morgen jerked upright in bed. She recognized the callers. Olivia and Nora. A third woman lurking farther back on the porch was looking at the garden. Wendy? No, it was an older lady. She turned slightly so that Morgen could see her face. Treasurer Judith Farina.

"Hello, Gwen," Olivia said, smiling.

It didn't look like a sincere smile. Grandma didn't seem to think so either. She glanced toward the barn, maybe hoping her werewolf tenant would come eat the unwelcome witches on her front porch.

"Didn't your parents teach you to call someone sixty years your elder *ma'am*? Or at least *missus*?"

"I don't think anyone teaches anyone to use the word *missus* anymore," Nora muttered.

Olivia elbowed her and kept her smile plastered to her face as she faced Grandma. "Sorry, Gwen—ma'am. I just don't think of you as an elder. You're still a young woman."

"Not according to my knees, ankles, back, and what is either a corn or a fungal growth on my big toe."

"Ew," Nora said.

Judith cleared her throat and turned, a clipboard full of forms under her arm. Had they come to collect *dues*?

"Right," Olivia said. "We don't want to waste your time. But Belinda said that when you two were riding your, uhm, *hogs* together that you were thinking of leaving Wolf Wood to the coven in your will. Something about fellow witches knowing how to appreciate it and care for it and the younger generation—" Olivia pointed at Nora and herself, "—being the ideal candidates since we have decades ahead of us and won't fall for the tricks of land developers trying to get their hands on it themselves."

"I said I'd *think* about leaving it to the coven," Grandma said. "Belinda added all that crap about the younger generation. I was busy trying to wipe bug guts off my visor and forgot to object."

"Ah, you're a quirky lady, Mrs. Keller." Olivia waved Judith forward.

"Gwen," Judith said, apparently old enough not to receive a reprimand for the lack of a *ma'am*, "this is some paperwork I had a lawyer draft up in case you are seriously considering it. It would be a shame if your property fell to someone who didn't care about it the way our kind do. I know you're in good health and won't have to worry about this for a long time, but we should get things in place, just in case. Especially given that you insist on riding that death trap along the foggy coastal roads of Washington."

"Uh huh. I'm touched by your concern *for my property*." Grandma took the clipboard and perused the forms. "I'll have *my* lawyer look at this mess."

"I assure you the forms are very tidy and thorough, as is all of my documentation. You'd know that if you still came to the meetings." Judith smiled sadly at her.

"I've got better things to do with the time I have left than watch Stella swill cosmos and grasshoppers. I'll get on the horn if I need you." Grandma waved and closed the door. Inside the house, she scowled at the clipboard and tossed it on the sofa. "Might use those papers the next time I need to clean my visor."

The vision shifted, leaving Grandma behind and following the three witches to their cars.

"Do you think she'll do it?" Nora asked. "Leave Wolf Wood to us?"

"To the *coven*?" Olivia corrected, though she was practically rubbing her hands together like a cartoon villain.

The two sisters looked at Judith.

She shrugged. "Maybe. I don't think she's close with her family."

"Good." The vision faded as Olivia skipped the rest of the way to the car.

Morgen flopped back onto the bed. She didn't know if these visions were true or if she was dreaming, but if this *was* what had happened... it could explain why the sisters resented her so much. Delusional or not, they'd expected to get Wolf Wood for themselves.

The first thing Morgen wanted to do when she woke the next morning was check Grandma's library to see if a hidden vault lay behind a moveable bookcase in there. But knocking on her door, hammering outside, and a blender running in the kitchen promised that she'd overslept and might not be able to skulk around the house right away.

"Morgen," came Sian's voice through the door. "I have a headache and require caffeine."

Morgen shambled to the door. "There's a coffee maker, grinder, and plenty of beans in the kitchen," she said as she opened it.

Sian stood in the hall in her pink socks, her brown hair tousled and hanging in her eyes as she clenched a fluffy blue robe shut at the chest. It was too big to have come out of her suitcase, so she must have found it in the house.

"There's a shirtless, sweaty man standing in front of the coffee maker," Sian said.

"Amar?"

The blender whirred again. Morgen couldn't remember Amar ever coming in to use her kitchen appliances.

"No. One of your workers." Sian waved toward the walls. "Don't they bring their own food? And eat outside, thus ensuring the homeowner has privacy?"

"Privacy has been elusive of late." Morgen didn't want to speak with any of the Lobos first thing in the morning, especially before she'd showered and dressed, but the crotchety expression on Sian's face suggested she would be insufferable until she got some coffee.

Morgen cast a longing look into the library as she passed it but headed downstairs to the kitchen. Sian trailed warily behind her, peering out windows at men working on the deck.

In the kitchen, Lucky sat on his haunches, his tail swishing back and forth on the floor as he gazed raptly at a man drinking a frothy orange concoction straight out of the blender pitcher. It was José Antonio, the elk-meatball chef.

The way Lucky stared hopefully at the pitcher as José Antonio's Adam's apple bobbed made Morgen suspect more than ice cubes and fruit had gone into the concoction.

"Don't you need to go out to pee?" Morgen muttered to the dog.

"Nah, I did that earlier." José Antonio lowered the pitcher and winked at her. "Hope you don't mind, ma'am. Pedro rousted us out of the den early, and I didn't get a chance to have my power smoothie. But I needed to talk with you anyway." He set aside the empty pitcher and pulled a rolled-up catalog out of his back pocket. "Which barbecue do you want in your outdoor kitchen?"

"Which what in my what?"

Sian nudged her in the back. "Tell him to vacate the coffee station."

"Barbecue grill, ma'am." José Antonio ambled to the table and opened the catalog. Lucky, apparently his new best friend, leaned against his leg. "We're setting you up with a hookup to the propane tank so you can grill outside. We're even putting in a little fridge and plate warmer. Got a sweet deal from Vic at the home center. He always gives us wholesale prices on appliances on account of being afraid of werewolves. Don't know why. It's not like we're going to eat him. The fixings in that smoker he's always got cooking out back, now they're a different story." He winked again.

"Uhm." Morgen joined José Antonio at the table as Sian beelined for the coffee maker.

Someone had already made a pot that morning, leaving the power on with the last drops scorching and the soggy grounds still inside. Sian hissed with displeasure as she cleaned the coffee maker.

"I appreciate everything you guys are doing," Morgen said, "but I don't need an outdoor kitchen. Or for you to spend money on appliances. I can't pay…"

She paused, remembering the bioluminescent moss powder

glowing on her dresser. If Phoebe was still willing to link her to buyers for the valuable ingredient, maybe she *could* pay the Lobos for their work. She hated the idea that they were doing all this in exchange for the talismans she wasn't sure she could make. Yes, she had receptacles now, thanks to Wendy, but had she come to care enough for the Lobos for the formula to work?

"No need to pay, ma'am. Pedro said we're to give you anything you want, so you'll give us what *we* want." José Antonio grinned and thumped her on the back, then started flipping through the pages.

Sian frowned over her shoulder at them as she poured water into the coffee maker, probably thinking José Antonio's comment referred to sex. If only the werewolves wanted something so simple to supply. Not that Morgen would have cheerfully slept with the wolf pack in exchange for a plate warmer, but in theory, it was possible. The talismans were a more nebulous proposition.

"I'm certain I didn't request a grill," Morgen murmured as José Antonio pointed out promising prospects in the catalog.

"Yeah, but you'll love it once you've got it. Everyone does. Have you thought of putting a pool in up here? You've got plenty of room."

"A pool? In Bellrock? The average daily high in August is in the sixties."

"How about a hot tub?" José Antonio snapped his fingers at this fabulous idea. "I've got a catalog for those in the truck, and we already reinforced the deck for the outdoor kitchen, so it would be no problem to put in a hot tub. We could build a privacy screen out of latticework, though I suppose you don't need privacy up here."

Sian made a noise in her throat reminiscent of a cat preparing to hack up a hairball.

"Privacy is more elusive than you might think," Morgen murmured.

"Latticework it is. And how about this fifty-four-inch stainless steel bad boy, right here? Six burners, including an infrared in the back, a dual-position rotisserie, and halogen grill-surface lights. Look, an optional wind guard for those blustery days."

"It's, uhm, very nice." Morgen had no idea what she, as a vegetarian, would rotisserie. Zucchini kebabs?

"I'll tell Pedro." José Antonio rolled up the catalog and jammed it back into his pocket.

He ambled toward Sian, who saw him coming and skittered to the side while eyeing him as if he were a venomous snake. She'd been in the middle of pouring herself a cup of coffee and held the pot out like a shield.

José Antonio took the cup, saluted her with it, and said, "Thanks, ma'am," as he strolled out to the deck in progress. Lucky galloped outside after him.

Sian made another noise in her throat, this one impressively close to a werewolf growl. Maybe she'd learned to emulate animals during her time studying orangutans in the jungle.

"They seem to be decent guys," Morgen offered. "They're just not big on boundaries."

Sian shot her a dark look and found another mug. "Do you want a cup?"

"Yes, please." Morgen cast another longing look toward the staircase leading up to the library, but she supposed there was no hurry in going up there to look. Until she pushed that bookcase away from the wall, she could fantasize about the safe with that intriguing book and perhaps a letter from Grandma being in a vault back there. Once she moved the bookcase, she might learn that there was nothing there and she'd been dreaming, not receiving visions of the past from the amulet.

"Schrodinger's vault," she murmured.

"What?" Sian had two mugs in hand and gave her one.

"Nothing."

"I suppose you don't have any sausage, bacon, or eggs." Sian looked wistfully toward the refrigerator. "I miss American breakfasts."

"If I had those things, *all* of the werewolves would be in here." Morgen retrieved her bag of vegan granola from the pantry and set it on the table. "This is high protein and filling. I have oatmeal too if you want to cook."

Sian sighed dramatically and sat in a chair without touching the bag. "If your car hadn't been violated and abandoned in town, I could have driven to a restaurant. That Timber Wolf, perhaps. Such a place *must* serve meat."

"Yes, they probably even have a bacon trolley. But that restaurant is owned by werewolves, so I can't recommend it." Morgen pushed the bag toward her. "The granola is espresso flavored and there's caffeine in it. You might like it."

"Hm."

Morgen scooped out a handful for herself. She wouldn't mind a little extra caffeine fortification.

The chainsaw started up outside, making her think of Amar and what she'd been dwelling on the night before. By the light of day, volunteering to be turned into a werewolf seemed ludicrous, and yet... would it make it possible for them to be something? A couple?

His Lobo buddies wouldn't tease him about dating another *werewolf*, so he wouldn't have to hide that he had feelings for her. And if she were turned into one of them, she might not be considered a witch anymore—could one be both werewolf *and* witch?—so that wouldn't disgruntle him on a personal level. She wouldn't have any magical power over him, not that she truly believed she had that now.

Morgen shook her head, feeling silly and like she was betraying her inner self for contemplating such a thing. It wasn't as if Amar had asked for this or promised that he would promptly move in with her if she joined the werewolf realm.

Sian chewed gingerly on some of the granola.

"I know you're not that into guys," Morgen caught herself saying when the chainsaw noise paused. "Or girls. Or sex robots. But as someone who occasionally enjoys human companionship of some sort, could you see yourself ever... changing for someone else? To become a more... congruent half of a couple? In order to facilitate harmonious exchanges going forward?" Morgen rubbed her forehead. Why did she always feel compelled to use vocabulary words when she chatted with her sister? To prove she was as smart as Sian?

Sian, who'd been giving her an exceedingly unamused frown since the word *robots*, asked, "Are you contemplating a sartorial shift to thong underwear, spandex tights, and cleavage-revealing tops again?"

"No. Something more permanent."

"If you're not careful, thong underwear can be permanent."

"Ha ha. Did the orangutans appreciate your comedic talents?"

"They found me scintillating, yes. Though possibly because I plied them with durian fruit."

"Is that good?" Morgen had never heard of it.

"It's an acquired taste, though the scent keeps most people from rushing to try it. It's somewhere between raw sewage and smelly gym socks."

"I'm disappointed that you didn't bring back samples."

"Alas, transporting fresh fruit across borders is forbidden."

"Yes, alas." Morgen might have forgotten what she'd originally been asking, but the chainsaw started up outside. A reminder. "Amar and I have kind of contemplated dating each other. At least, we've kissed a few times, but werewolves hate witches, you see, so there's this wall between us."

"You're a witch now?" Sian's eyebrows twitched.

"I've learned a few incantations and made the talisman that Amar is wearing. It keeps other witches from controlling him."

Sian sipped from her mug, watching Morgen over the rim as if she were observing behavioral oddities from an animal in the jungle.

"You could become a witch too, I think," Morgen offered. "It's in the genes that we inherited from Grandma."

"Something handed down in the mitochondrial DNA from the mother, no doubt," Sian said, the words dripping sarcasm. The previous day's events might have forced her to acknowledge that werewolves existed, but maybe she wasn't ready for other kinds of magic. Or the idea that Grandma had been a witch and handed down that ability to her children and grandchildren.

"No doubt."

"Sustained change is tremendously difficult to maintain, and without proper motivation beyond some vague desire to please a mate—" Sian curled a lip, "—it is unlikely to last. If you insist, however, on contemplating such an action, you should study the Transtheoretical Model of Behavior Change and determine if you're ready to begin on such a journey. I will posit that a relationship that hinges on alteration of either of the principals is doomed to failure since the human ability to cultivate long-lasting change is so poor."

"In this case, the change would be physical and permanent. I'm pretty sure. I could ask Dr. Valderas."

"Are you contemplating surgery?"

"Something like that. Sort of a magical surgery."

Sian sighed again. "You're making me regret coming here."

"Do you wish you were back in a hospital room in Borneo with a deadly fever instead?" Morgen hoped her company wasn't *that* bad. It wasn't her fault that Sian hadn't experienced enough magic to believe it existed. Though Morgen admitted that her sister's comment about a relationship being doomed if it required an alteration to either of the principals was probably true.

What if Morgen let one of the werewolves turn her into a lycanthrope and then she didn't even get Amar? He might decide in the end that he preferred Maria or another woman. And then what? She'd be stuck turning furry at night and hunting down the poor innocent animals of the forests. Animals that she had turned vegetarian so she wouldn't have to eat.

She rubbed her forehead again, decided she'd been delusional to contemplate this, and took another sip of coffee.

"I don't miss the fever," Sian said after gazing out the window, "but I am distressed that I... won't be going back."

Morgen lowered her hand. "You're not going back to Borneo?"

"My supervisor is forbidding it. Not because of any failure on my part, she assured me, but because she doesn't want me to risk getting sick again, not when my body fights off tropical diseases so poorly." Sian grimaced and stared bleakly at the checkered tablecloth. "I'm not going to be able to continue doing field work. I can study captive primates in labs here, but... that's not the same. I told her as much. She suggested I go into teaching." The grimace deepened as her tone turned sarcastic again. "Because I'm such a natural with people and speaking to groups that the teaching profession would suffer a terrible loss without my contributions."

"I'm sorry." Morgen knew Sian was as much of an introvert as she and that field work was her passion.

Sian mumbled an indecipherable acknowledgment, refilled her coffee mug, and left.

19

Morgen started up the stairs to check the library, but a knock at the front door made her pause. Belatedly, her dog alarm went off, Lucky barking from the living room.

"You've gotten a little late and lax since so many people have been around," Morgen told him as she headed for the door. She wasn't sure who had put him back in the house. Maybe he'd been a pest as he *helped* the Lobos with the deck work.

With his paws on a windowsill, Lucky wagged as he barked at someone out front. A sheriff's department SUV was parked in the driveway.

Right, she'd asked for Franklin's help. She should have expected it. But she'd expected it much earlier, as in the night before. Fortunately, Sian hadn't been kidnapped, so it hadn't mattered that Franklin had never shown up at the hotel.

When she opened the door, he looked blearily at her, his eyes bloodshot with dark bags under them. Morgen realized she should have called back the night before to let him know she'd found her sister. She hoped he hadn't been searching for Sian.

"Hi, Deputy," Morgen said.

Franklin glowered at her, but his manners forced him to utter a polite, "Ma'am," and tip his hat.

Lucky pushed his way outside and sidled up to him, wagging his entire body, not just his tail. Franklin only managed to ignore him for a few seconds before Lucky leaned against his leg and gazed up at him with soulful brown eyes that ensured Franklin would feel like a heel if he withheld his attention. Franklin sighed and patted the dog.

"Did you find Calista?" Morgen asked.

"After questioning a number of members of the community, who claimed that you and a wolf crashed their quilt meeting—"

Morgen raised a finger and interrupted. "It was a witch meeting, not a quilt meeting, and those ladies are all in the local coven."

Surely, he had to know that.

Franklin kept glowering at her as he continued, "—they did give me a lead on Calista. At first, they were reluctant to admit that she'd been there, but their loyalty only lasted until I suggested that my jail cells had recently been modernized and that I was looking forward to locking some people up to try them out. They said she's hiding out in a cabin in the woods and won't leave the area until she's finalized some plans."

Plans such as slaying Morgen?

"We checked all of the known cabins in the area that are abandoned or only used for part of the year by their owners. Most were dead ends, but we did see one with the lights on as we were driving up to it. The lights went out, and the occupant disappeared in a hurry. There wasn't another road that she could have taken—if it was indeed Calista—but she disappeared without a trace." Franklin lowered his voice to a mutter. "Probably flew off on a broomstick."

Hah, so he *did* know these women were all witches.

"I haven't noticed any of them using brooms," Morgen said. "Just staffs."

"Yes, Belinda whapped me with hers when I suggested my men would frisk any uncooperative women for wands." Franklin pulled out a notepad. "I came to file your missing-person report. You said it was your sister?"

"Yes, but we found her. Her hotel room was ransacked last night, and I thought she'd been kidnapped. She's staying here now."

"It was a robbery?"

"She didn't mention noticing anything stolen, but she objected vehemently to strangers touching her undergarments—*all* of her garments—if you want to put that in your report."

Franklin closed the notepad. "I do not. You haven't seen Calista this morning?" He glanced to the side as two Lobos levered a huge stainless-steel grill out of their truck bed and carried it toward the back of the house.

Good grief, that had been fast. The guy that sold those truly had to be scared of the werewolves.

"No, I haven't," Morgen said.

"What about Nora Braybrooke?"

Morgen's insides clenched. For weeks, she'd been worried that Franklin or another deputy would come up to question her about that.

"Pardon?" she asked, her voice squeaking.

Lucky spotted a rabbit sneaking up on the carrots in the garden and sprang off the porch to chase it.

"She's missing too," Franklin said. "We've been trying to find her sisters to question them about it, but they've been elusive."

Morgen walked to the end of the porch to see if Wendy was there, but the camper van was gone. Had she delivered the gifts and then headed out of town? Morgen had hoped they might yet work together to improve the app.

"Ms. Keller?" Franklin prompted.

Did he sound suspicious? Morgen couldn't tell. She wrestled between wanting to tell him everything and worrying that she would be blamed—and thrown in jail—for Nora's death.

"Sorry, I was checking on something," Morgen said. "The last I saw Nora, she was in Calista's gyrocopter, flying in a storm." That was true. "I think she crashed. I heard from someone that she didn't make it." Also somewhat true. She hadn't gone to investigate the body herself. Pedro had told her Nora had died.

"She's *dead*?"

"That's what I heard."

Franklin swore. "What is happening in my town? And why are all of those werewolves working on your house?" he snapped as two more Lobos walked past with tools.

"They do construction, and I needed construction done."

"They're installing an outdoor kitchen."

"Yes."

"Are you settling in to stay in Bellrock?" Franklin frowned at her.

"Is that not okay?"

"I don't know. Will you be able to avoid illegally sneaking into people's houses to snoop around while you're here?"

Morgen thought of the Braybrooke tree house that she'd followed Wendy's ferret into. That hadn't technically been *snooping*. She'd needed to find Lucky and knock out the control device that had a hold on Dr. Valderas.

"Your silence is alarming," Franklin said.

"I was thinking."

"Alarmingly." He glanced to the side again. Two more werewolves were hefting the shell of a hot tub out of their truck bed.

Morgen gaped at them. She hadn't said yes to that. She hadn't said yes to *any* of this.

"I'd ask if you need anything else," Franklin said, "but you seem to be getting everything you could possibly want."

"And plenty of things I don't," she muttered.

"I'll be in touch if I hear anything else about Calista."

"There's one more thing," Morgen said as he started to turn away. "Calista threatened me and said if I didn't leave by the end of the week, the witches would force me out of the house, one way or another. I'm not planning to leave, so if you're around on... I guess it would be Saturday, maybe you'll get an opportunity to arrest her. Hopefully before she burns down the house."

"I'll keep that in mind." Franklin tipped his hat to her again and headed for his SUV.

Morgen closed the door, hoping she wasn't a suspect in the investigation into Nora's death that he might start next.

Enough delays. She headed up the stairs. It was time to look behind that bookcase.

Fortunately, nobody else interrupted her. She stepped into the library, nervous anticipation making her jittery—or maybe that was the coffee combined with the espresso granola.

After a quick glance around the book-filled room to make sure she was alone, she closed the door. She didn't want any witnesses.

She stepped up to the bookcase that she'd seen in the vision. Her palms were moist. The decorative gargoyle hanging on the side was exactly the same. That didn't necessarily mean anything, as she'd been in this room before.

Her fingers trembled as she lifted her hand to it.

"Here goes," she whispered and tugged on the gargoyle.

Nothing happened, and disappointment surged through her.

She tried twisting it to the left. Nothing. Then right. Nothing. She scowled and smacked it on its leering fang-filled snout.

To her surprise, a faint click sounded within the bookcase, and the gargoyle turned of its own accord. Hope replaced her disappointment as she pulled on the bookcase. It swung outward as easily as if it were a door.

"Who knew the secret to opening hidden passages was to brutalize them?"

Giddiness made Morgen grin. Even though she was now aware that magic existed, she hadn't expected the vision to show her the truth. But she soon found herself looking at the metal door of a safe embedded in the wall. A star-shaped indention identical to the one in the root-cellar door waited for a key.

Her fingers trembled even more as she lifted her matching amulet to it. As soon as she slotted it in, a soft *click-thunk* sounded, and the safe opened.

The hefty tome was wedged diagonally inside, along with a few gold coins, silver bars, and an envelope of cash. Huh. She'd sent poor Amar off on a quest for silver when there'd been bars in the house. Maybe later, she would offer some of the money to Sian so she could go buy pajamas that hadn't been molested by strangers, but for now...

She drew out the heavy book and took it to a table. The letter she'd seen in the vision was stuck inside. Morgen hesitated, not sure who Grandma had intended it for, but that didn't keep her from opening it to read.

To my heir, it started. Ah, Grandma hadn't known at the time who she would leave the house to. Maybe the witches of the coven *had* been a possibility in her mind.

Morgen shook her head, sad again that she hadn't visited her grandmother in recent years, that passing along her witch legacy had been a question mark for her. She probably hadn't known if Morgen or Sian would have any interest or would obey her wishes even if she detailed them in writing. Morgen wished there were some way that she could assure Grandma that she was doing her best to keep Wolf Wood safe and that she wouldn't let it fall into a developer's hands. Or the hands of ungrateful witches.

This grimoire contains powerful and potentially dangerous incantations and rituals, including those for raisings and banishings. Such information must not be given out to those who would use it for ill. In other words, this is some heavy shit. I regret having found the book, but better me for a keeper than someone corrupt who craves power. As your predecessor, I urge you to guard the secrets within with your life. Keep the ways of the sisterhood in your heart, and don't allow yourself vengeful thoughts or great desires, lest you be tempted to use this book for ill.

"Wow," Morgen murmured. "I'm guessing these are more than incantations to keep slugs out of the garden and mildew off the shower tiles."

She turned to a table of contents, and a shiver went down her spine at the first heading. *Summoning an Imp.*

"That is *not* on my to-do list."

At least item number two was *Banishing an Imp*. Others followed with titles such as, *Elixir of Seeing. Incantation of Authority. Empowering a Staff of Witchery.*

Morgen flipped to that one, wondering if Grandma had used it to make the antler staff. Amar had called it something else—a druidic Staff of Earth—but she hadn't been sure if he'd been telling the truth or teasing her.

"'Two witches of shared blood,'" she read aloud, "'must clasp the staff while incanting, *Under the moon's magic, infuse this rod of meager wood with power too great to be understood.* If their combined might is great enough, the finished tool may be used on worldly and otherworldly creatures to bereave them of their magic and restore—'"

Scratching at the window made Morgen jump. Black wings fluttered outside, and a raven struggled to find a perch on the small ledge.

"Damn it." She ran to the window, intending to sweep the curtains shut.

Before she could, she glimpsed something tied to the raven's leg. A note?

Was this Zeke? Or a spy? Or both?

The raven flew back into the air, cawing at her, then flapped its wings to alight on the roof of the porch below. Afraid it was Zeke—or some other witch's familiar—and that he had seen what she was doing, Morgen rushed back to the table. Before slamming the book shut, she pulled out her phone and snapped a picture of the empowering-a-staff page. Calista ought to count as a worldly or otherworldly creature—shouldn't everyone fall into one of those categories? Morgen would feel better if she had a weapon that she could use against her the next time they met. As much as she would prefer otherwise, another encounter seemed inevitable.

She locked away the tome in the vault, then slid the bookcase back into place. The idea that the raven might have been spying for several minutes and witnessed everything distressed her.

She jogged downstairs and out to the porch. The raven waited for her on the railing. All ravens looked alike to Morgen, but she suspected this was Zeke. He lifted a taloned foot, drawing attention to the note tied to his leg.

"Yeah, yeah, you're a regular carrier pigeon."

The raven stood still, letting her untie the note. Only when he sprang into the air and flew away did Morgen wonder if she should have tried to capture him to keep him from reporting back to Phoebe. That probably wouldn't have worked. When Zorro and Lucky shared visions with her, most of them were real-time. If Zeke had seen the secret vault and the book, Phoebe already knew about them.

"Wonderful." Morgen sank to her butt on the porch with her back to the wall, the bushes giving her some privacy to read.

Lucky, panting after his rabbit chase, clambered up the steps to sit beside her. The nefarious intruder had eluded him, as most things he hunted did. She gave him a pat as she perused the note.

Morgen, it read, *last night was chaotic, and I'm not sure how much you witnessed, but Calista is no longer respected or welcomed by the coven. Her words largely fell on deaf ears. Several of our sisters received your email and were intrigued by the software you included. Others wouldn't open it, but you can't win over everyone. We're convening another meeting tonight at ten at the graveyard behind the church, and we want to invite you to come. We'd like to talk to you and hear more about your project. If you wish the sisters to speak openly with you, please consider leaving your werewolf ally at home.*

It was signed Phoebe.

Morgen lowered the message to her lap.

"There's just one problem," she said.

Lucky swished his tail back and forth on the floorboards and looked at her.

"This isn't Phoebe's handwriting."

20

After staring at the raven-delivered note for a few more minutes, Morgen rose, intending to show it to Amar. One of the witches—presumably Calista or Olivia—was setting a trap for her.

The most obvious way to deal with a trap was not to step into it, but she wanted a second opinion on that. If she didn't show up for the meeting, would the witches attack her here? And what would they do? Send more Loups at her? Hurl more Molotov cocktails at the house? Something worse?

A few hours ago, Morgen would have assumed there was a limit to what witch magic could do, but the spells in that book dealing with summoning mythological creatures from another realm had chilled her. Imps couldn't truly be summoned... could they? What about worse things? Stories of demons and succubi and other supernatural creatures from what she'd *thought* was folklore came to mind.

As she stepped off the porch, Morgen paused to look at her garden hose. Instead of hanging in a coil from its usual holder, it stretched across the lawn and disappeared around the corner to the back of the house. For some reason, the water was turned on. She imagined the Lobos taking a break to drink out of the hose.

But when she walked around the house, they were huddled together, whispering and pointing to the new hot tub. They'd set it up on a corner of the deck with impressive speed. The hose snaked over the side, and the tub was already most of the way full. She assumed it would take some time to heat up, even if they'd set up the electrical already. What were they planning?

Two of them peered over at her, and the conversation paused.

"I'm looking for Amar," she said, feeling like an intruder.

In truth, she'd been curious about the hose. Amar was probably in the barn.

Instead of being annoyed by her spying, the Lobos smirked at her. One lifted a finger to his lips. They huddled and whispered a little more, and then two trotted past her and toward the barn door. Morgen clasped her chin as she waited to see what scheme they were enacting.

Lucky hopped onto the deck and inserted himself in the middle of the huddle. No fewer than four men petted him, and he wagged contentedly, alternating whose leg he leaned against.

An alarmed curse came from the barn. Amar.

"What are they doing to him?" Morgen asked.

The two Lobos reappeared, carrying Amar high over their heads, as if he were a log to be toted through an obstacle course. A squirming protesting log that had clearly been caught off guard. The Lobos picked up their pace as he bucked and twisted, on the verge of escape. Just before Amar would have freed himself, they threw him into the hot tub.

Water surged over the side, spattering the deck, the men, and Lucky. Lucky shot off the deck like a cannonball. The Lobos laughed uproariously at their former pack mate. Amar came up sputtering with his fists clenched.

Morgen wanted to protest the cruel joke, but the men threw up their arms and roared, "*Feliz cumpleaños!*"

She blinked. That was *happy birthday*, wasn't it?

As Amar sprang out of the water, his jeans, vest, and hair soaked, two of the guys opened the grill lid to pull out a bakery box and two bottles of tequila. It wasn't even lunchtime yet, but that didn't keep them from opening one of the bottles. Someone started singing, and the others chimed in.

José Antonio clapped Amar on the shoulder, and the vexed expression faded from his face as someone thrust a cupcake into his hand. It returned when someone else tried to shove a cupcake into his *mouth*, his mouth that wasn't open at the time.

Morgen watched with bemusement while wishing she'd known it was Amar's birthday. She would have gotten him something.

Maybe she could get him the gift he and all the other Lobos had been wanting for weeks. Talismans for the pack.

Before, she'd doubted she could muster the necessary caring to make the spell work, but as the men joked with Amar, she decided she felt less ambivalent toward them than she once had. They seemed to be treating him well now—at least what counted as well for a pack of werewolves—and they'd helped her and Amar survive the onslaught by the Loups. They'd also accompanied them to the Braybrooke tree house and would have helped invade it if the witches' booby traps hadn't kept them off the property. In addition to all that, they'd been fixing up her house for free.

She eyed the future outdoor kitchen and spa area. *More* than fixing it up. As she'd told her sister, they were decent guys.

Maybe she *did* care for them. At least a little. Huh.

Amar noticed her standing quietly in the corner. He shook the water out of his hair, grabbed two cupcakes, and walked toward her. He frowned down at the desserts, paused, and asked something in Spanish over his shoulder. José Antonio laughed and answered.

"*Sí, primo, la manteca de cerdo.*" He rubbed his stomach and licked the frosting off a cupcake. "*Delicioso!*"

Amar rolled his eyes and joined Morgen.

"I asked if they're vegetarian. Judging by his sarcastic response, I don't think he knows, but I highly doubt they're frosted in lard." Amar shot a dark look over his shoulder, and José Antonio laughed again and stuffed the rest of his cupcake in his mouth.

"That does seem unlikely." Morgen pointed at the box. "That's from the vegan bakery and coffee shop. Even if it weren't, lard isn't that typical in cupcakes these days."

"Good. You can eat it." Amar thrust one toward her.

"Thanks." Morgen juggled the note so that she could accept it. "Happy birthday," she said, reluctant to ruin the festive mood by bringing up the message.

But Amar noticed it and pointed. "What's that?"

"Zeke delivered it, but I don't think it's from Phoebe. Despite having her name on it." Morgen handed him the paper and took a bite of the cupcake. Sweets before lunch weren't on her diet these days, but one had to celebrate birthdays, right? Besides, these were extenuating circumstances. Witches were plotting against her on a daily basis, familiars were spying on her, and her sister had almost been kidnapped. She deserved cupcakes.

"It's not from her?" Amar asked after reading the note.

"No. I had plenty of chances to see Phoebe's penmanship when I was organizing her store. I'm also not positive that was Zeke. There were other ravens at that witch gathering, and they all looked alike to me. And they were all bullies who chased off Zorro." Morgen frowned toward the woods, realizing she hadn't seen the owl since he'd sent that vision. She hoped he wasn't injured again and hunkering miserable in a tree somewhere.

"Then it's another trap."

"That's what I'm afraid of. Even though I'd like a second chance to let the witch community of Bellrock know that I'm not a threat and that they should invite me in... showing up seems like a bad idea."

Amar scowled, either because water was dripping from his hair into his eyes or because he wasn't pleased to hear that she wanted to be a part of the witch community. Since frosting was stuck in his beard, it wasn't that intimidating of a scowl.

"I say we ignore the invitation and stay at the house and perform a ritual to create talismans," she said. "Wendy gave me some receptacles to use."

"Oh? Good. Do you think you can make the ritual work?"

"I hope so. Given the number of burly werewolves wandering around the property at any given hour, I'd prefer that witches *not* be able to turn them against me. Or you."

Morgen reached up and wiped the frosting off his face, eliciting another scowl, the indignant kind that kids gave to grandmothers who spat on napkins before using them to rub grime off their cheeks.

"Sorry," she said, "but your pogonotrophy efforts were being diminished by the frosting in your beard."

"My what?"

"Pogonotrophy. The cultivation of a beard. Having my vocabulary-loving sister nearby always turns me into a bit of..." Morgen paused as the frosting she'd wiped off threatened to fall to the new deck that had yet to be painted or stained.

"Know-it-all?" Amar's scowl turned into a smirk.

"Wisenheimer."

He nodded. "Know-it-all."

"Fortunately, you're not the type to be intimidated by women who won their grade-school spelling bees."

"I'm not. Especially since I've seen you stride willfully into warded vans and houses and be knocked on your ass."

"So, you're saying that I lack street smarts?"

"I'm saying that your idea to avoid the meeting is a good one. You wouldn't be able to resist walking straight up and being blunt with the witches who just finished laying traps for you. Of course... if all of the Lobos had talismans, we could be your bodyguards and protect you if you *do* want to go."

"I'll see what I can do, but I'm leaning toward emailing the witches again, now that I have their addresses, instead of speaking to them in person. It's what introverts prefer. Emails cut down on uncomfortable confrontations. And you can include cute puppy pictures to further soothe cross feelings."

Lucky chose that moment to bound back onto the deck. He beelined for her, sniffing at the frosting drooping from her finger. Morgen lifted it out of his reach, vowing to find a napkin.

Amar's eyelids drooped, and he fixed her frosting problem by leaning in and licking it off her finger. "We could also ignore the witches altogether and stay here tonight."

"That might be okay," she whispered, surprised by his open display of... frosting-licking in front of the others.

Chortles came from the Lobos, not the appalled glowers that Morgen might have expected, given that they'd apparently been telling Amar that witches and werewolves didn't hook up. Maybe the tequila and sugar were combining to make them cheerful.

Amar ignored them and straightened. "Let me know if you need me to help you with chores so you have more time to dedicate to the talismans. I still have the shop vacuum."

"The kitchen cutlery, utensils, washcloths, and other small items that aren't nailed down would prefer you stay out of the house with that."

"A shame." Amar touched her shoulder, then headed to the barn.

Morgen glanced at the Lobos. Most of them had gone back to joking with each other, noshing cupcakes, and sampling the tequila, but Maria had joined the group and was frowning at Morgen.

Morgen stifled a grimace. She hadn't realized Maria was there. Had Amar known? Would he have licked Morgen's finger in front of his old girlfriend if he had?

After waving a curt acknowledgment, Morgen hurried into the house. She would have to wait until dark to perform the talisman ritual. Today, she would grab Grandma's secret book, hole up in a room with no windows that avian familiars could spy on her through, and study some of the incantations. It was possible that the witches, when they realized Morgen hadn't fallen for their ruse, would bring their trap *here* to spring.

21

As twilight approached, Morgen laid out the twelve silver necklaces that Wendy had given her, each with a concave circle, oval, or moon-shaped receptacle sufficient to hold magical resin. The small cauldron and electric Bunsen burner were set up on the workbench, along with all of the ingredients.

Almost all of the ingredients. Morgen would have to cut herself and spill her blood when it was time.

She rubbed her fingers together, wincing at the thought of dripping out enough blood for twelve talismans. It would be more reasonable to do this over a couple of nights, but she worried that the witches would do something *tonight*. Outside, the Lobos were finishing up and would leave soon, so they wouldn't be near the house where they could easily be ensorcelled and turned against Morgen, but the coven surely knew where they lived. And where the Loups lived as well. If they wanted a werewolf army, they could find one.

"For now." Morgen turned up the burner and started measuring ingredients.

A knock sounded at the root-cellar doors. Amar?

Morgen hadn't yet taken her clothes off for the ritual, but she'd shut the doors anyway, wanting privacy. Even though she believed she cared enough about the Lobos now to make this work, she knew she would need peace and quiet so she could concentrate fully.

As soon as she opened one of the doors, she wished she hadn't. Maria stood there in a short-sleeved blouse with the hem tied up in a knot to reveal part of her flat stomach. As usual, her lush black hair tumbled around her shoulders, and she looked far more like a model than someone who'd been helping stain the deck all day.

"May I talk to you for a minute?" she asked.

Morgen peered past her, wondering if Amar was nearby. Maria's tone was neutral, not menacing, but it occurred to Morgen that if she wanted to get rid of the competition, she could turn into a wolf and attack. It was dark enough now for that.

Morgen reminded herself that she knew the werewolf-control incantation and ought to be able to keep Maria from hurting her.

"I won't bother you again after this," Maria said. "I just want to talk to you before I leave."

"Leave?"

It sounded like she meant permanently, not for the day.

"We're almost done, and there's another project over by Flicker Lake that some of us are starting tomorrow. I'll be working over there."

"Ah." Though it might be a bad idea, Morgen stepped aside so Maria could descend the stairs into the cellar. "What can I do for you?"

Maria leaned a hip against a workbench, folded her arms across her chest, and regarded Morgen frankly. "I need to know that you actually care for Amar, or I'm going to do my best to gnaw your head off."

"Of course I care for him." Morgen crossed her own arms over her chest. "Do *you* care for him? Or the guy you're supposedly mated to? What's the deal?"

"I care a great deal for him. And Pedro."

"So much that you think you get to have them both?"

Hell, she was pretty enough. Maybe she *could* have two men wrapped around her finger. But no. Amar had pushed her away. Good man.

"So much that I want to make sure Amar doesn't do something that could get him killed. Like falling into a witch's web."

"Why is everyone so convinced that I, a complete neophyte to magic and all of witchdom, have the power to spin such webs?"

"You've controlled our kind before." Her eyes closed to slits. "I believed you were controlling him as well, but since I've seen the talisman work, I'm less certain."

"I'm not controlling him." Morgen tried to keep her tone calm and reasonable, but frustration threatened to boil over. Why did she have to defend herself to this woman? "You're the one who's been trying to seduce him."

"To keep him from becoming some witch's *plaything*," Maria said in exasperation.

"Oh, sure. That's the only reason. It's not because you regret hooking up with a jerk who's full of himself and you've realized that leaving such a good guy was a mistake."

Maria's eyes narrowed even further, and she growled low in her throat.

Fear shot up Morgen's spine. She wanted to spring back and grab the closest weapon—the wicked athame knife that she intended to cut herself with—but she forced herself to stay put, lift her chin, and hold Maria's threatening gaze. At the same time, she rehearsed the werewolf incantation in her mind.

Long seconds passed as their stare continued, neither of them moving or looking away.

"Pedro's not a jerk," Maria finally said. "But you're right that

Amar is a good guy. And sometimes, I do regret my choice. But Amar having an interest in you is the reason I... tried to seduce him, yes. To get him out from under your spell. I'm afraid for him. I'm afraid you'll use him the way other witches have used our kind. And since you've cultivated so many enemies, that could be deadly for him. You could throw him away to save your own life."

Morgen clenched her jaw. It took a moment before she could unclench it enough to bite out, "As I said, he's protected by the talisman. It's great that you think so lowly of me, but even if I wanted to *throw him away,* I couldn't. And I *wouldn't*. I care about him. I wouldn't have been able to make his talisman if I didn't."

Maria's elegant eyebrows arched. "That's required for the ritual?"

"That and cutting open a finger and pouring my blood into the magical resin." All right, *pouring* was hyperbolic, but she *had* dripped several large drops into the concoction.

"Show me."

Morgen lifted the book and pointed out the passage, though she doubted it would prove anything. According to the recipe, a witch didn't *have* to care for someone to make a talisman; it just worked better if they did. But as Morgen had found when she'd tried to make the first one, she had to think positive, *caring* thoughts about the recipient for the magic to work.

"His talisman works very well," Maria mused. "That Nora was a strong witch, and she couldn't override it. I know she was strong because *I* couldn't override her magic on *me*." Her voice had turned growly again.

"I'm glad," Morgen said, though Maria was focused on the book and barely seemed to hear her.

Finally, Maria looked toward the ingredients on the table. Morgen braced herself, expecting Maria to ask her to make one for her. While she might be able to make talismans for José Antonio and the other werewolves who'd been working hard on the house these past weeks, she doubted she could summon feelings of *caring* for Maria, her rival for Amar's affection.

"You intend to make talismans for the others?" Maria asked.

"Yeah, as many as I can manage."

"You care for them?" Maria's eyebrows went up again.

"I'm about to find out."

Judging by her frown, that answer didn't satisfy Maria.

More seriously, Morgen said, "I'm going to try. I do appreciate the work they've done and that they've... seemed to accept Amar back into the pack. They're kind of asses, but he cares about them."

Maria snorted softly. "They can be asses, yes. That is true of every pack. Only those with strong personalities and a wild streak are drawn to the wolf way."

Morgen thought of her own musings about asking Amar to make her a werewolf. Did she have a strong personality and a wild streak? Not really. She was fairly certain she would regret that choice if she made it.

"I don't think he likes being a lone wolf as much as he says he does," Morgen added.

"No," Maria agreed. "I don't think so either."

Morgen took the book back and returned it to the workbench while groping for a way to ask Maria to leave her alone so she could start.

"All right," Maria said softly, as if she'd read Morgen's thoughts. "I withdraw my objection."

"To me in general or me with... him?"

"To you with him. I object to *all* witches in general." Maria smiled faintly. "But I believe now that even though he's still in danger from standing at your side... I don't think you'd sacrifice him."

"No." Morgen's throat tightened. "I wouldn't. I don't want him to be hurt because of me. Or because of anyone."

"Good," Maria said softly.

The doors rattled, making them both jump. The one she'd opened to let Maria in had fallen back shut, so they were locked to anyone without an amulet.

"Maria," Amar bellowed.

"It's for you," Morgen said, though the angry tone surprised her.

"It sounds like someone is having a—what is the expression?—conniption fit," Maria said.

"Nobody uses that term anymore, but yeah." Not sure what was wrong, Morgen jogged to the doors to let Amar in.

He leaped down the steps, pausing only to look her up and down, as if searching for injuries, before striding forward to face Maria.

"What are you doing in here?" he demanded. "Threatening her? I told you to respect my choice and stay away from her."

"It's okay," Morgen said, as Maria said something stern to him in Spanish. "We've arrived at an understanding."

Amar gave her a quelling you-don't-grasp-what's-going-on look and thrust a finger toward the doors. "Leave, Maria."

"Of course, *lobo gruñón*. Of course." She patted him on the cheek and sashayed up the stairs.

He bared his teeth at her before facing Morgen. "Are you all right? She didn't bother you, did she?"

"No, it's fine."

Amar looked her up and down again, as if he couldn't believe she wasn't bleeding from dozens of bite wounds.

"I'm not sure I'll be able to make her a talisman," Morgen said, "but it's fine."

"I'll be curious if you're able to make the *others* talismans."

"If people stop barging into my cellar, I'll be able to find out."

"I barge because I care."

"I'm glad." She smiled and kissed him on the cheek.

He rested his hand on her hip to keep her close and gazed at her as if he were contemplating kissing her back. And not on the cheek.

But a screech came from outside, and they both looked up. Another raven? It sounded more like an owl.

They climbed the stairs in time to spot Zorro flying out of the barn through one of the windows.

"I need to replace those so he can't go in and out," Amar said.

"You don't want him hunting in the barn and keeping the rodent population down?"

"I don't want him nesting in my projects and throwing up owl pellets all over the place."

Zorro alighted on the roof above them.

"I don't suppose you'd like to spy on another meeting for me?" Morgen called up, though she felt bad that he'd been driven away from the last one by witch familiars. "Down by the graveyard behind the church. I'll find out what owls like for treats and get some for you."

"A treat for an owl is a yard full of rats," Amar said. "They're carnivorous."

"So are ferrets, apparently, but that didn't keep Napoleon from ravaging my avocado crisps."

"That ferret's name is *Napoleon*?"

"It is."

"Maybe it's Nappy for short. You can't judge all carnivores by that ferret's actions. *I* would never eat avocado crisps."

"But Girl Scout cookies are okay?"

Amar squinted at her. "Are you teasing me?"

"Yeah, but my way of doing it has to be a lot better than being thrown into a tub full of cold water."

"Hm."

Zorro turned his head left and right, hooted a few times, and took to the air. He headed in the direction of town. To spy on the meeting?

"That's a good owl," Morgen said. "Maybe I could get him some toys. Do you think he'd like a stuffed weasel with squeakers? That's a favorite of Lucky's."

"I'm sure he'll let you know if he wants anything. Besides to defile my workspace."

"That's a reward in itself."

Laughter came from the deck, along with the rumble of jets—the hot tub being fired up. Someone called for Amar to join them.

"Is it typical for a construction crew to try out the homeowner's hot tub after installing it?" Morgen asked.

"I don't think so, but you're getting the special treatment."

"The special treatment? The opportunity to see them in their swimsuits?"

"Trust me. They didn't bring swimsuits."

Morgen wrinkled her nose. "Just don't let them turn into wolves in there. I hear fur is hard to get out of the filters."

"I imagine so. I'll boot them out and tell them to go home."

"Thanks. I'll get back to the talismans."

"Good. I'll see to it that you aren't interrupted again."

Amar had no sooner left the cellar than Zorro shared a vision. Anticipating queasiness, Morgen bent over and gripped her knees.

He was soaring out of the trees and over the buildings of town. Several large elms lined the graveyard behind the church, and he flew over a parking lot to land in one. From there, he eyed the rows of tombstones with a few old mausoleums interspersed here and there.

Though it was a couple of hours before the time the note had indicated, cars were arriving, several familiar from the meeting at the gymnasium. Morgen should have asked Amar what type of vehicle Calista drove. Though she had no proof, Morgen suspected she was the one who'd forged Phoebe's signature—and her raven—to send that message.

A few vans were among the arriving vehicles. Not Wendy's mural-covered camper but white vans without windows in the back. Two women opened the rear doors of one and hauled out a large cauldron and a tripod. Another grabbed a couple of skulls.

Whatever they were planning for the night, it was more than a friendly chat.

22

Morgen's cut fingers throbbed as she tipped her concoction into a sixth receptacle and thought caring thoughts for Arturo, the boy she and Amar had helped in town after he threw a rock through a window. The older Lobos made him dig ditches, run errands, and perform other grunt work, but Arturo usually managed a goofy grin while doing the tasks. He called her Ms. Morgen and respected Amar. It wasn't difficult for her to think caring thoughts about him, and the magical resin started glowing before it even entered the receptacle.

Five other resin-filled receptacles were stretched out on the workbench, hardening into talismans. Each one had glowed, though some had glowed more profoundly than others. The one she'd made for José Antonio still radiated a dark-red illumination. The one she'd made for Pedro had only glowed briefly and lowly before fading. She hoped it would still be effective.

Nothing in the book said that the amount of glow that emanated from the talismans mattered or would determine how much protective power they had, but she had a hunch it worked that way. It sounded like magic operated in degrees, not absolutes.

The werewolves kept referring to how some witches had more power—more ability to control them—than others.

Morgen set the cauldron down and grabbed a towel to wipe her face as she grabbed another bandage from the stack she'd brought down to the cellar. It would have been easier—and less devastating to her fingers—if she'd increased the amount of each ingredient she put in to make one big batch instead of creating each talisman individually, but her gut had told her that wouldn't work, that each piece should be made special for each wearer.

Alas for her fingers.

A knock sounded at the door.

"I'm not dressed," she called, assuming it was Amar again.

During the last hour that she'd been working on the talismans, she'd heard a lot of male laughter, so she assumed he hadn't been successful in shooing the Lobos out of the hot tub. He might even have joined them. She didn't mind, but she would feel safer once she hung these talismans around their necks.

Another vision came to her, and she gripped the edge of the workbench. The last one hadn't been too nausea-inducing, but if Zorro had to fly away at top speed and shared imagery of him careening through the trees, she would have to act quickly to ensure an inappropriate ingredient didn't end up in the cauldron.

But Zorro was still perched in the large elm, looking past branches and leaves and into the graveyard. The witches had moved from the parking lot to a circle outlined by a low wrought-iron fence. Fog was creeping in from the Strait, or was it creeping in from someone's spell book? Were there incantations to create weather phenomenon? Morgen well remembered the storm and the giant hailstones that had pummeled the house during the battle with the Loups.

The fenced circle was near the back of the graveyard and behind a mausoleum, so it wasn't visible from the church or the street. Several familiar women had gathered around it, though

Morgen didn't see Phoebe, Belinda, or Judith. This gathering was half the size of the one in the gym. Olivia was there, her face dark and sullen. She kept touching a knife in a scabbard that she'd thrust through her belt.

A new van arrived in the parking lot. One filled with more paraphernalia for whatever hell-inspired ceremony they were setting up?

No, Morgen realized with a start. That was Wendy's van.

Disappointment surged through her as Wendy parked, got out, and walked toward the graveyard. Had she agreed to be a part of this trap? Why, after giving Morgen the receptacles for the werewolf talismans? Had she believed that had been a mistake and confessed to her sister?

Olivia saw her and lifted a hand in beckoning. Wendy hesitated, a little uncertain, but after another wave, she walked into the graveyard.

A woman in a black robe stepped out of the mausoleum nearest the circle. Calista.

"Morgen?" Amar knocked on the door again.

Caught up in the vision, Morgen found that she couldn't answer.

Calista walked into the circle and pressed a baton to fine gravel on the ground, then started drawing in it. Whatever that baton was, it left an orange residue behind. That residue emitted a matching orange glow that infused the fog, turning the graveyard into a Halloween spectacle.

Morgen was growing more and more glad that she hadn't opted to go to that meeting. As the orange fog spread, blanketing the graveyard and seeping out into the parking lot, Zorro shifted on his tree branch, jostling the vision. No, he was swaying. Back and forth, as if he were being hypnotized.

Buddy, Morgen thought, the first twinges of nausea coming over her. *You may need to get out of there.*

Calista straightened. She'd drawn a circle within the circle, with dots and squiggles placed precisely here and there. Other witches were making a fire inside it and setting up the cauldron and tripod. One woman sat cross-legged with a book as old and large as the one Morgen had pulled from Grandma's safe.

Thoughts of raising imps and who knew what else came to mind. Hopefully, whatever they were trying to do wouldn't work when Morgen didn't show up. The witches deserved to spend the evening completely wasting their time.

Zorro tilted his head and looked toward the parking lot. An older witch stood there with a cat cradled in one arm. In the other, she held a wand pointed at Zorro. The cat was looking straight at him and hissing.

Definitely get out of there, Morgen silently urged, though she'd never seen evidence to suggest she could communicate from afar with her familiars.

Zorro must have reached that same decision on his own. He sprang from the branch and flew toward the top of the church. The witch disappeared from view as Zorro focused on the steeple, but something seemed to strike him.

The vision jolted, and a mental whiplash struck Morgen. She staggered back and hit one of the workbenches. The vision faltered like lights flickering in a storm. A wave of dizziness crashed into her, and her heart pounded erratically in her chest.

Could the other witches hurt her through her link to the owl? Fear for Zorro and for herself made everything worse.

She must have cried out or made some other alarming noise, for Amar shouted her name again, his voice thick with concern. The doors rattled as he tugged at them, only the magic infusing them keeping him from tearing them open with his raw strength.

Morgen's legs weakened, and her knees threatened to give out. She stumbled toward the stairs, wanting to let Amar in, in case she passed out. She felt like she would. The vision kept flickering as

Zorro landed on the steeple, putting it between him and the parking lot. She hoped he'd flown far enough and was safe.

The vision ended abruptly. The dizziness did not.

Morgen reached the doors, pushed them open, and dropped to her knees as she sucked in the night air. It didn't help to clear her head. She wobbled, and the cellar seemed to spin and flip upside down.

Amar lunged in and caught her before she toppled down the stairs.

"Morgen!" he called, but his voice seemed far away, just as his touch did. Just as her body did.

The dizziness turned to darkness, and she passed out.

23

Morgen woke in a bed she didn't recognize and stared up at a dark, unfamiliar ceiling. Something coarse and scratchy lay on her, the texture unpleasant against her bare skin. She slid her hand down to check—yes, she was still naked. Wherever she was.

"Amar?" she whispered, remembering that he'd kept her from falling.

How long ago had that been? Minutes? Hours? A week ago last Tuesday?

When she turned her head to look around, a faint twinge of dizziness reminded her of the witch's attack on Zorro—and somehow through Zorro to her. Morgen was surprised she didn't have a splitting headache.

"I'm here." His dark shadow appeared beside the bed. "Are you all right?"

He sat down on the edge of the mattress.

"I... don't know. Where am I?"

"My apartment."

"Your apartment... in the barn? I thought it burned." Ah, yes, those were the beams of the barn's ceiling.

"It did," Amar said. "We're in the loft. I've gradually been rebuilding it. So far, I've just got the floor done and the steps leading up to it."

"And a bed, and the scratchiest blanket in the world." Some kind of wool-wasp blend, as far as she could tell. She would have pushed it off, but that would have left her lying stark naked next to Amar. As a werewolf, he probably had no trouble seeing in the dark.

"It's a hide," he said dryly. "Bear."

"Ew."

"I didn't know your objection to animals went beyond consuming them."

"I'm not excited about being enrobed in their remains either. Remind me to get you a nice faux mink blanket for a belated birthday present. For when guests with sensitive skin sleep over."

"If you'll agree to sleep over, I'll find an all-night blanket store so I can wrap you in silk throws."

"Silk is made from the larval cocoons of the mulberry silkworm," she said reflexively, before his words fully registered. "The pupae are killed in the process."

"You're a difficult woman to date."

"I know. I'm encouraged that you want to." She reached out to him as it dawned on her that he *wanted* her to sleep over.

"I saw the talismans." Amar clasped her hand. "Did the magic work?"

"We'll have to test them, but I think so. There was glowing." Morgen started to smile, glad that she could give him good news, but then she remembered the glowing orange fog in the graveyard. She sat up, worried about Zorro and also worried about what the witches were doing. If she was lucky, nothing that would affect her or anyone else outside of the graveyard, but... she hadn't been lucky lately.

"Good." Amar squeezed her hand and leaned in to hug her, his lips brushing her cheek and sending a tingle through her. That was delightfully distracting and made her want to forget all about the other problems. "It means a lot to me that you're helping the pack," he added. "*My* pack."

Thoughts of the witches faded further from her mind as his warm bare arms wrapped around her.

"You care about us," he murmured, the words a contented growl.

"Mostly you." She pulled her hand free, but only so she could wrap her arms around him.

"You've gone against the wishes of your kind to protect us from them." He kissed her neck, and heat flushed her body, making her want to shed the hide for more reasons than prickliness. How wonderful it would be to lie in the bed with him, naked flesh pressed to naked flesh. "The others will see that they can trust you, that you're a friend to werewolves."

He nipped at her sensitive skin, a passionate growl rumbling from his chest, and her body tingled not only with delight but with heated anticipation and raw arousal. She remembered that he wasn't quite a man and that being with him could be different from being with her ex and the others she'd been intimate with before him. Maybe the idea should have scared her, but she found herself scooting closer and gripping him more tightly.

"Even if they don't," Amar whispered, inhaling deeply, as if her scent enticed him, "I no longer care what they think. I've realized… you're more important to me than their opinions. Than they are." He drew back but only enough to look into her eyes for a moment, and she remembered the eyes in the forest, watching her intently from the shadows. Drawn to her. "I want to be with you."

"Me too. I mean, I want that too."

His hungry mouth found hers in the dark, his muscled body sliding over her, powerful arms trapping her on his bed. In his lair. And she *wanted* to be trapped.

She ran her hands over the hard swells of his shoulders, then pushed her fingers through his hair. Pleasure raced along her nerves as he slid one of his hands down to stroke her bare side, nails grazing her skin, nails with a bite of sharpness, like the claws of the wolf he could become. Rough callouses caressed her skin, kneading her flesh, cupping her breast.

Morgen gasped and arched up toward him, blurting, "I was even thinking of asking you to turn me into a werewolf."

His hands stopped their exploration of her body, and he lifted his head to look at her. She couldn't see his expression in the dark, but she worried she'd said the wrong thing. Or the *right* thing, at least in his eyes, and that he would be eager to turn her words into reality.

A cold blast of fear drove the heat out of her body as she realized the possible ramifications. She'd said she was *thinking* about it, right? Not that she was positive she wanted him to do it. Would he be disappointed if her follow-up blurt was *never mind!* and she said it was a horrible idea?

"Those with witch blood may not be turned into werewolves," Amar said.

"Oh." She was relieved but a little surprised that the relief didn't come out in that syllable. It sounded muted to her ears. Maybe a part of her had actually wondered what it would be like to lope along on a moonlit night at his side.

"And it's definitely not recommended for those who don't like to hunt," he said.

"I guess it would be hard to be a vegetarian wolf."

"Very," he said dryly. "But I'm touched that you would consider making such a sacrifice for me." His tone shifted from dry to intent. "*More* than touched."

"I didn't want the witch thing to bother you, or for you to have to choose between me and your pack."

"They will see that having a witch as an ally is a good thing."

He pushed his fingers through her hair, nails grazing her scalp. "And even if they don't, I don't care. Like I said, I choose you over them. Over anyone." He leaned in close again, his eyes boring into hers, his lips scant inches from hers. "You're *my* witch."

The growled words rekindled the heat within her, and she pushed the hide aside and molded her body to his. "Yeah, I am."

He shrugged out of his vest and jeans and pulled her back into his arms, his hands rousing her to levels she hadn't experienced in ages. Or ever.

Strange that he'd ever thought she was the one with the potential to control him. As his hands and his mouth explored her body, she knew she would do anything he wished.

But she'd no sooner had the thought than he broke the kiss. His gaze swiveled toward the nearest window.

"*Amar*," she groaned in protest as his roaming hands paused.

"Someone's coming."

"I don't care." Breathless, she gripped his shoulders, trying to turn him back to her. At that moment, she wouldn't have cared if his whole pack was coming up to watch.

This time, the growl that emanated from Amar's chest was full of warning, not passion, and he slid her aside to prowl to the window.

"It's a *witch*," he snarled.

Of course it was.

Morgen slumped back to the bed, disappointment replacing the throbbing desire in her body. Why were these people so intent on ruining her life?

24

The grinding sound of a vehicle rolling up the gravel driveway reached Morgen's ears. A car door slammed.

Convinced that she and Amar weren't going to be able to finish what they'd started, she reluctantly slid off the bed. Memories of the ritual in the graveyard—and the attack on Zorro—returned to her mind, and guilt replaced some of her sexual frustration. She wasn't responsible for whatever those witches were doing, but she had sent her familiar to spy on them, and then she'd forgotten all about him, instead enjoying herself with Amar.

"Morgen?" someone called from the driveway. "Are you home?"

Amar growled again, his body tense as he looked through the window toward the driveway.

"That's Phoebe," Morgen said, recognizing the voice. "She shouldn't be a threat."

But it sounded like something was wrong. Something *else*.

When Morgen looked around for her clothes, she realized they were back in the root cellar. She'd been performing the talisman rituals naked, as all those grimoires demanded.

"Can I borrow something to wear?" she asked as another call came from the driveway.

It sounded like Phoebe was jogging to the front porch of the house. A knock came next, followed by Lucky's barking from the living room. If Sian had been sleeping, that would have woken her as effectively as a gunshot.

"My wardrobe is limited and wouldn't fit you." Amar wrapped the bear hide around her.

Morgen curled a repulsed lip, but if there was nothing else, there was nothing else. She gripped it closed like a robe and let Amar guide her to a set of stairs she'd never used before. Glad for his help, she reached the barn door and walked outside, only to be reminded of her lack of footwear as the gravel driveway stabbed her soles.

Phoebe was still knocking on the front door. A couple of lights were on in the house, and Lucky continued barking at this unannounced nocturnal visitor, but Sian hadn't made an appearance yet. Given that someone had wanted to kidnap her the night before, she might not open the door at all.

"I'm here," Morgen started to call, but a sharp rock jabbed her foot, and the words turned into a soft curse.

Though Amar was as naked and shoeless as she, he swept her into his arms and strode toward the porch. Phoebe noticed them coming and gaped.

"I hope she's not the kind to spread gossip," Morgen muttered.

"I hope she *is*." Amar smiled smugly down at her.

"Are you proud of yourself for snagging a witch?" Admittedly, she hadn't been fully *snagged* yet, but she hoped they could soon return to what they'd started.

"Once the rest of the town knows you are mine, they'll leave you alone. They'll know that if they *don't,* they will have to deal with *me.*"

Morgen didn't point out that the *rest of the town* hadn't been knocking down her door to ask her on dates. There was only one man she wanted that interest from, and she squeezed his shoulder to let him know.

Phoebe was still gaping when Amar set Morgen down on the porch. With the bear-fur hide wrapped around her, Morgen felt more like a cave woman than a witch.

"Hi," she said, since Phoebe was speechless as she looked back and forth between them.

Belatedly, Morgen realized that Amar hadn't put on clothes either. He was naked so often that it hardly seemed weird anymore. At least to her.

"I can go in and change if you have a minute." Morgen pointed at the door. She might have already darted in, but Phoebe stood in front of it, her fist still in the air from knocking.

Phoebe shook her head and recovered enough so speak. "I don't think there's time. My sister—" Phoebe pushed both hands through her graying hair. "I think she's gone insane. She's... raising something. It's forbidden magic. I don't even know where she found a grimoire with the ritual."

Morgen thought of the book from Grandma's safe. She hadn't skimmed through it all, but the chapter about raising imps came to mind.

"She got some of the other witches to help, the ones who have been denied access to Wolf Wood and were more inclined to go along with her." Phoebe frowned at Amar, though his nudity must have discombobulated her, for she quickly looked away. Morgen knew the feeling. "I need help," Phoebe continued. "She'll kill me if I work against her, but I'm terrified about what could happen to the town if I don't stop her."

"If it helps, I don't think she intends to use whatever it is against the town." Morgen squeezed past Phoebe and opened the front door. Whatever was happening, she wasn't going anywhere without shoes and clothes. Besides, her purse and the antler staff were in the living room. And maybe she should grab Grandma's book. There'd been a chapter on banishing imps too. "She's after me. Wendy is with her, so she probably knows about the talismans I started making. Oh, Amar." Morgen paused on the threshold. "Will you get those and give them to the pack in case anything happens to me? Did you leave the cellar door open after I, uh, passed out?"

"Yes, but I'm going with you. If she's summoning something dangerous, you'll need help. Those idiot witches could flatten all of Bellrock."

Lucky must have heard the door open, for he charged out, whacking Morgen with his tail on the way by, and ran into the yard. At least one of her familiars was safe.

"I think Calista is just after me," Morgen repeated.

"I don't want to see *you* flattened either," Amar said.

"I do appreciate that. Oh, will you grab my phone too?" Morgen almost blurted that she would call Franklin so that he could get some armed men to that graveyard, but with Phoebe standing there, she kept the thought to herself. Phoebe would want her sister kept safe, if possible, not caught in the middle of a gunfight. "It's in my jeans pocket."

Amar lifted a hand in acknowledgment and jogged toward the root cellar.

"I'll be right with you, Phoebe." Morgen didn't know what she could do, or why Phoebe had chosen her, out of all the witches in town who *weren't* at that graveyard, to help. But if Calista was doing all this to get to Morgen, or claim Wolf Wood for herself, Morgen had to do something. "Just need some clothes."

As she rushed across the living room, a vision came over her. She swore and tried to make it up the stairs, but she stumbled on the first step and had to catch herself against the wall.

This time, Zorro was flying high over town, the lights of Main Street visible far below, a few cars parked along the curb but nobody out on the sidewalks. Zorro was heading away from the graveyard, but she could still make out a few details. The strange orange fog that Morgen had seen earlier was visible. It glowed, lighting the tombstones in an eerie haze and showing people hunkered behind some of them. Calista was no longer in the circle she'd drawn, but something else was, something dark and huge.

Whatever it was, Morgen didn't think it was an imp. Nothing so small and relatively harmless. As black as the night, it was more shadow than a clearly defined body, but its amorphous outline reminded her of a T-rex with wings.

For now, the creature seemed contained by the circle, but would that last? Or was Calista even now preparing to release it, to encourage it to fly off and get Morgen?

It didn't bode well that the other witches were hiding from it. Calista strode into view, her huge book open and balanced in one arm. She held an amulet on a chain up in her left hand and was chanting.

Thanks, Zorro, Morgen thought. *You can let the vision go. We'll be down there as soon as we can.*

Down there to do *what*? She had no idea. Could a wolf bite a shadowy creature from another realm? Could she rap it with her staff?

Zorro alighted on a telephone pole. He wasn't going anywhere near the graveyard now. A good idea. But with his keen owl vision, he could still see it in the distance. Calista stumbled and bent over, as if someone had punched her in the gut—or a magical attack had overwhelmed her.

The creature stepped out of the circle, the orange fog swirling about its shadowy legs. Morgen knew next to nothing about summoning otherworldly beings, but even she knew they weren't supposed to attack their summoner and free themselves.

The other witches in the graveyard shrieked and ran. Calista rushed to the mausoleum and slammed the door shut, ensconcing herself inside.

Hell, who was controlling that creature now?

It marched ominously toward the mausoleum, red eyes burning in the amorphous outline of its dark head.

It battered at the cement structure, and the corners crumbled under its assault. That chilled Morgen even more than seeing the creature escape from confinement. If it could do damage, that meant it was far more than a shadow.

Zorro sprang from the telephone pole and flew away from the area. Morgen couldn't blame him, but that left her without a witness to relay what was happening.

The vision faded, and she straightened. She would have to go to the graveyard herself.

"Why are you naked with a fur rug at your feet?" Sian asked.

She stood a few steps up the staircase from Morgen, a book in her hand. A blessedly benign, cozy mystery book, not some grimoire. She must have finally come down to see what was going on with the knocking and barking. Her hair was damp. Maybe she'd been in the tub.

"I was using my witchly powers to make talismans in a nudity-requiring ritual, then was interrupted before I could have sex with a bear-hide-loving werewolf in the barn. Now, I need to get clothes and a grimoire that hopefully has instructions on how to banish a deadly supernatural creature from another realm."

"A deadly supernatural creature?" Apparently, Sian didn't object to any of the other details of Morgen's night.

"It could be an imp. But it seems largish for that. You better stay here." Reminded of the need for urgency, Morgen charged past her to run up the stairs.

"Stay here? Do you intend to thrust yourself into danger again?" Sian frowned and followed her to her room.

"All of the witches following Calista may be in trouble, as well as a young friend who may or may not be working with her, and—oh, yes—the entire town is also in danger."

"Why does any of that require *your* intervention?"

"The person raising the... *thing* has it out for me."

"That sounds like a good reason to stay away. What can you do? You're not a cape-wearing superhero. A second ago, you were naked on your knees on the stairs."

"Phoebe came to get me." Morgen tugged on clothing as she spoke. "She must believe I can help. I need you to stay here and let our brothers know if... something happens to me."

"*I* don't even know what's happening to you."

"A witch in a graveyard is raising something. I don't know what. Grandma's book spoke of imps, but imps are small, aren't they?" Morgen shoved her feet into her shoes without tying the laces.

"Imp has Old English origins from *impe* or *impa*, which means young shoot or graft and was originally linked to plants, though the sense of the word gradually shifted from plants to people, referring to children or offspring. The current definition, meaning 'little devil,' originated in the sixteenth century from a common pejorative phrase of the time: *imp of Satan*."

"The truly alarming part is that you're not reading that off your phone." Morgen grabbed a hoodie and ran into the hall.

"You know I enjoy etymology and have read numerous books on the subject." Sian leaned into her room and plucked out a jacket. "I'm going with you."

Morgen halted and gaped at her. "What? You don't know anything about imps."

"I believe I just demonstrated that I know more than you."

"I mean the real thing, not the etymological origins of the word."

"You're my younger sister. I'll go along in case I can keep you from endangering yourself. It's what Mom would have wanted."

"She *wouldn't* have wanted us *both* to endanger ourselves."

"Fear not. I'll do something rational, like staying in the car and calling the police." Sian raised her eyebrows. "Have you tried that yet?"

"We have a sheriff's department here, and Deputy Franklin *loves* hearing from me." Morgen would call him as soon as she got her phone.

She hurried into the library and opened the safe to pull out Grandma's book. Earlier, she'd memorized incantations about crafting magical staffs and moving silently while invisible. She'd thought *those* were the more practical spells to study, not the ones on raising and banishing imps. She would have to read about that on the car ride into town. Such things could surely be learned in ten minutes while navigating potholes, right?

"Has he heard from you tonight?" Sian asked.

"He will," Morgen said, though she feared she would only be endangering Franklin and his colleagues.

None of the novels she'd read suggested that devil-spawned creatures could be slain with bullets. For that matter, she had no idea how *she* would destroy that thing.

25

When Morgen and Sian ran out of the house, Phoebe was pacing in front of the porch. She lunged and grabbed Morgen's arm, almost dislodging Grandma's book and the antler staff from her grip.

"Zeke just sent me a vision," Phoebe said, her eyes wide with horror. "You won't believe the *thing* my sister has unleashed."

"I know." Morgen strode toward Amar's truck. He was waiting there with the talismans and her phone. Unfortunately, the rest of his pack seemed to have gone home for the night. "I saw," she added. "We'll do something."

Phoebe shook her head, defeat joining the horror in her eyes. "It's way beyond my knowledge. I don't know what we can..." She trailed off as she saw the book. "Is that one of the ancient grimoires of hidden power?"

"Sure, maybe."

"Does it have information on banishing demons?" Phoebe asked.

"On banishing imps." Morgen hefted the tome.

"What I saw is more than an imp. It's a full-fledged vile creature from the Ninth Circle of Hell."

"It's a punished sinner guilty of treachery against those with whom it had a special relationship?" Sian asked.

"What?" Phoebe's forehead crinkled in confusion. "No."

"Don't mind her." Morgen hugged Amar and accepted her phone. "She's very literal."

"I've simply read the source material," Sian murmured.

"It's a *demon*," Phoebe said.

"Ah," Sian said. "Perhaps a resident of the Eighth Circle then, there to eternally whip panderers and seducers."

"Just get in the truck if you're going." Morgen pointed her sister toward the passenger side, though she still wished Sian would stay at the house. But there was no guarantee that she would be safe if she did. If that thing—that *demon*—had escaped the summoning circle, who knew how far it could go? "We'll meet you there, Phoebe."

Morgen waved Phoebe to her own car, then threw the book and staff into Amar's cab and waved for Sian to get in. If she was going to battle a demon, she couldn't think of anyone she would rather have at her side.

Lucky ran up to the cab, tail wagging, clearly wanting to go along.

"Not this time, buddy." Morgen grabbed his collar to guide him back to the house. "It's going to be too dangerous."

Usually, when she had him by his collar, he went along meekly, but this time, he fought her, paws digging into the gravel driveway as he tried to surge back to the truck.

"*Lucky*," Morgen said sternly, pulling him toward the porch. "Knock it off. We don't have time for this."

She dug a treat out of her pocket and waved it in front of his nose. Usually, food made him eager to cooperate, but he kept whining and pulling.

Grunting and straining, she manhandled him up the stairs to the porch, opened the door, and thrust him inside. She tossed the treat in, hoping it would distract him, and shut the door. As she ran back to the truck, he barked from the window.

It was hard not to take that as a sign that he knew she was going into big trouble and wanted to protect her. But the last thing she wanted was for him to be hurt, or for her to be distracted during a crucial moment because she was worrying about him. It was bad enough she already had Zorro to worry about.

Phoebe drove off, gravel flying from her tires. Amar was waiting in the truck while Sian stood with the passenger door open, waving for Morgen to get in first. Maybe she didn't want to sit in the middle, pressed up against a werewolf. Since Morgen had no qualms about that, at least not when it involved *her* werewolf, she sprang inside.

"Do you know what we'll face?" Amar asked as Sian climbed in after her, shutting the door.

He must have heard and dismissed Phoebe's comment about demons.

"Zorro showed me something shadowy and huge escaping a summoning circle." Morgen dialed Franklin's number and dropped the big book in her sister's lap. "You took a speed-reading class, didn't you, Sian?"

"I taught myself to speed-read."

"Good enough. Find the parts related to imps and otherworldly creatures, specifically how we can get rid of them." Morgen frowned at the phone. Franklin hadn't picked up yet. Was he screening his calls? Sleeping? Ignoring it because he recognized her number? "Amar, we may need more help. Do you think the Lobos will come? At least the ones I made talismans for?"

She doubted those would do anything to protect werewolves against creatures from another realm, but the Lobos who received them might be appreciative and more willing to assist her.

"Come to help witches?" Amar navigated the truck down the driveway, Lucky's barks floating out of the house behind them.

"Yes, but like Phoebe said, the town might be in danger too." Morgen thought of the way Zorro had flown off at top speed. "You guys like living here, right? I'm sure your pack doesn't want to see Bellrock destroyed."

She *wasn't* that sure, especially when Amar didn't answer right away. Maybe he hoped the entire coven would end up getting itself killed, leaving Bellrock witch-free.

"If Calista regains control of the creature," Morgen added, "she'll send it after us. It could trash Wolf Wood, Grandma's house, and your barn. It would be a shame to lose your apartment before you've rebuilt the walls."

"And the bear hide that you adore."

"Yeah, its tragic demise would drive me to pen elegies."

Sian looked over at her.

"Did you find anything in there yet?" Morgen asked as the truck swung onto the paved road.

"Yes." Sian had turned on her phone's flashlight app and was flipping through the pages. "Blatherskite, bunkum, and balderdash."

"Alliterative. Let me rephrase. Did you find anything instructive when it comes to banishing demons?"

"I've marked pages on defending against supernatural apparitions and evil spirits. I've also marked your imp-banishing incantation."

"Good." After seeing the creature tearing into the mausoleum, Morgen doubted it qualified as merely an *apparition* or *spirit*, but hopefully, something would work. "Keep looking. See if there's anything on demons specifically."

She wrapped her hand around Grandma's staff, wishing that half the antlers hadn't been shorn off when she'd thrown it into the gyrocopter blades. That might have diminished its power.

"Even if it were undamaged and radiating power like plutonium, I wouldn't be that assured," she muttered.

It concerned Morgen that all of the witches had been running from the creature and that even Calista had flung herself into the mausoleum to escape it. Those women all had far more power and experience than Morgen. If they didn't know how to handle the creature, what could *she* do?

"Radiating power like plutonium?" Sian asked in a skeptical tone.

"Yeah. It's a simile. I was trying to think of an extremely radioactive substance."

"Polonium is widely considered the most radioactive element."

Morgen rolled her eyes. "Thank you."

"It's so radioactive that it glows blue." Sian missed the eye roll as she flipped a page. "It has no stable isotopes."

"*Thank* you."

"Though perhaps a comparison to the sun would be more apt, insofar as emitting energy goes."

"I'm so glad you're coming along to help," Morgen said.

"Naturally." Sian flipped another page.

Amar turned before reaching town.

Morgen glanced at him.

"I'm heading to pick up as many of the pack as will help," he said.

As they paralleled Main Street, Morgen glimpsed orange light coming from the core of town. Either the fog had spread... or something was on fire.

"We need to hurry," she whispered though he was going well over the speed limit.

Morgen dialed Franklin again. This time, when her call dropped to voice mail, she left a message, explaining the trouble at the graveyard and saying that Calista was there.

As she finished, the wail of a siren penetrated the truck's

windows. Maybe Franklin wasn't answering because he was already *dealing* with the trouble.

Amar turned again and drove up a bumpy dirt road without streetlamps. A few house lights were on, visible through the trees, but he kept driving until he reached the end of the road where a warning sign informed them that motorized vehicles weren't allowed on the trail that continued beyond a barrier.

A cabin, several manufactured homes, and an above-ground pool occupied a property to their left. The homeowners were outside and already in their furry wolf forms. Their eyes gleamed in the headlight beams as they looked at Amar's truck.

"We need help," Amar called out his window and jerked his thumb toward the back.

"We brought talismans," Morgen leaned past him to add. "For six of you." She called out the names. "The others are in the works."

The big wolves loped out of the woods and sprang into the truck bed, claws clattering on the steel floor. The vehicle trembled under their weight, and Sian gripped the door handle.

"If you're alarmed now, wait until they turn back into men and are all naked," Morgen said as Amar turned the truck around.

"Will that be more terrifying than your demon?" Sian asked.

"Given your aversion to werewolf sweat, possibly."

Amar glanced over at them, but it was hard to read his face. He might not have appreciated the joke, or he might be unenthused about risking the pack's lives for witches.

Morgen rested a hand on his forearm. "Thank you for the help."

She expected a mere grunt of acknowledgment—his version of *you're welcome*—but he surprised her by dropping his hand on top of hers and saying, "Someone has to keep an eye on you."

"As her older sister, that is my job," Sian said.

"Since when?" Morgen asked. "You've been living on the other side of the world for the last decade and barely came to visit when you *were* here."

"I've followed your work as much as feasible from afar. It's unfortunate that you've put your skills to use laboring for a mediocre company with little hope for advancement."

"Not everyone's job requires them to publish papers in academic journals that are read by seven people."

"Thanks to my research on primates and how they relate to humans," Sian said stiffly, "I've been published in the *Annual Review of Psychology* and *Frontiers of Neuroscience*. They're not only widely read by academics, but they're widely *cited*. Unlike this gargantuan tome of nonsense."

"Uh huh. Did you find the demon section yet?"

"Only imps are mentioned."

"That may not be good enough."

"You should have checked out a different book from the occult library."

Morgen's phone rang before she could explain that this huge tome had belonged to Grandma. It was Wendy.

Morgen almost didn't answer—the last she'd seen, Wendy had been joining the other witches in the graveyard, presumably there at her sister's behest to help them with their evil endeavor. But if nothing else, Wendy could be a source of information.

"Hello?" she answered.

"Morgen, it's Wendy," came a harsh whisper. "We're in a lot of trouble."

"I know." Morgen waited for the inevitable baiting of the trap. Olivia had to have ordered Wendy to convince Morgen to come to the graveyard.

"Calista said she was going to summon a demon to take care of everything," Wendy said, "and she *did*. I heard about her plans and came down here to try to talk Olivia out of helping, to try to get her to talk all the *other* witches out of helping. *Nobody* summons demons. It's crazy dangerous. But they wouldn't listen to me, and now it's out of control."

A cacophony of crashes boomed over the phone. It sounded like stone structures being knocked down—or completely obliterated.

Wendy swore. "Look, don't come down here. It's too dangerous."

"What?" Morgen had been certain Wendy would *ask* her to come down, whether she wanted to or not.

"It'll kill you." Wendy's voice turned squeaky. "It's going to kill *all* of us. The deputies can't do anything. We need the werewolves' help. Our magic isn't doing anything to stop the demon, but maybe their magic will be similar enough to its that they can slay it. Can you ask them to come? *Please*?"

Morgen glanced at the wolves in the truck bed. "I'll see what I can do."

"Hurry. There's not much—"

The call ended abruptly.

Amar glanced over. They were back on a paved road and heading toward the core of town—and the ominous orange glow. Even more sirens wailed now.

"They need werewolves," Morgen said.

"I heard," he said.

"Are your fangs magical enough to tear demon flesh to pieces?"

"I doubt it. Demons don't *have* flesh."

"What do they have?"

"A deadly incorporeal miasma of corrupted energy that resists blades, bows, and witchcraft." Sian pointed to a page. "I found a small entry on them."

"Anything on how to kill them?" Morgen asked.

"This just says not to summon them and woe to she who does."

"Helpful," Amar muttered.

As they swung onto Main Street, several fire engines and sheriff's department SUVs came into view, some parked near the church and others swinging into its parking lot. A building across the street was on fire, flames leaping from the rooftop. Shattered glass glinted all over the street in front of it.

"Are we going to be able to get close?" Morgen asked numbly.

As they passed a couple of tall buildings, the church came into view. Its steeple was also on fire, smoke pouring into the night sky.

"Do we *want* to get close?" Sian asked.

Morgen shook her head. Were they too late?

26

Two fire engines blocked the entrance to the church parking lot, so Amar had to park on the street. Phoebe's car was just ahead of theirs, but she wasn't in it.

Outside, the air stank of smoke and burning rubber. It turned Morgen's stomach even before Sian opened the door.

She, Morgen, and Amar slid out of the cab as the six wolves sprang from the truck bed. Amar distributed the talismans to his pack, hopefully the magic telling the werewolves which ones were meant for which person. Since they had no hands in their wolf form, he looped the silver chains over their heads for them.

Lastly, he tossed his clothing onto the hood of the truck and shifted into his large black wolf form. His blue eyes held hers throughout the transition, as if to let her know they were linked, that he was going into this battle for her.

"Thank you," she whispered, praying that he would survive and wishing that she'd kissed him before he'd changed.

She settled for resting a hand on his back, twining her fingers in his thick fur. Unlike Lucky, he didn't lean on her or wag his tail. He was a predator through and through, and he radiated power that would have scared her if he hadn't been on her side. Her protector.

The other wolves gathered around Amar, as if he were their pack leader. They bared their fangs, raised their hackles, and growled as they peered toward the orange fog, but they didn't charge ahead. They looked expectantly at Morgen, as if to say this was a witch problem, and she was in charge.

Wonderful.

She hefted her staff and headed down the sidewalk toward the church. Amar strode at her side, and Sian trailed after them, the book open to whichever page she'd deemed least full of balderdash and most likely to help.

As they walked, Morgen gripped her amulet, tempted to whisper the incantation that would make her invisible, but what was the point? She couldn't make Amar, Sian, and all the others invisible. Maybe the demon wouldn't notice them…

The sound of gunfire came from behind the burning church.

Morgen halted. Sian glanced at her.

"I didn't bring a bulletproof vest," Morgen whispered.

A burning tire rolled out of the parking area and into the street before flopping over.

"Perhaps we should return to the vehicle," Sian suggested.

Amar glanced at them, then continued on. Morgen resisted the urge to grab him, especially since he was moving quickly and she would only end up getting his tail, which he might not appreciate. But he'd told her that werewolves weren't impervious to bullets, silver or otherwise, and she also doubted they were impervious to demons.

The rest of the pack hesitated, then trotted after Amar.

Torn between wanting to help and not wanting to blunder into a gun battle and get shot, Morgen bit her lip and stood uselessly on the sidewalk. Just as she was about to creep closer, more gunshots rang out.

"What is that?" Sian pointed at what looked like roadkill on the sidewalk ahead, a dark-brown lump. The wolves had trotted by and a tire had rolled past it, and it hadn't stirred.

"Something dead," Morgen said.

The head of the animal—the *ferret*—lifted briefly before dropping back down.

Morgen swore. "That's Wendy's ferret."

"It appears injured." Sian started forward.

"Maybe, maybe not. He likes to play dead." Morgen reached for her sister, intending to stop her, but a woman's scream rang out from behind the church. It sounded like someone young. Wendy?

"Look out!" a man cried. Was that Franklin?

Morgen closed her eyes and marshaled her bravery. People she liked were in trouble, and she knew an incantation to banish an imp. She made herself continue forward while hoping that demons were close enough to imps that it would work.

When they reached the ferret, Sian gathered him in her arms. Napoleon cooed uncertainly. Since only Morgen had a weapon, she led the way, the staff raised in front of her.

"A lot of good it'll do against a bullet," she muttered.

They turned into the driveway, heading for the parking lot and graveyard in back. The church building blocked the view of both, but there was no missing the orange fog oozing across the pavement.

Something clattered into view. A gun.

"Find something that works!" a man yelled.

"Calista, banish it!" That sounded like Belinda. She hadn't been in Zorro's earlier visions, so she must have recently arrived.

Hopefully, the whole coven was back there helping. Not that it sounded like they were able to do much.

"I've lost control of it!" Calista yelled.

"No kidding!"

Morgen reached the back of the church and peered around the

corner. Above her, flames crackled as they burned more and more of the steeple.

More SUVs with lights flashing were parked in back. Their doors were open, and uniformed men crouched, using them for cover. A fire engine near the wrought-iron fence of the graveyard had been knocked over somehow, the metal warped, the tires flat. Another vehicle had exploded, leaving only burning wreckage behind.

In the fifteen minutes since Zorro had shared his last vision, the graveyard had changed vastly. Numerous tombstones lay flattened, and larger stone structures had been reduced to rubble. The mausoleum that Calista had been crouching in was similarly demolished.

Wait, she was *still* crouching there. The walls were gone, but she was taking cover from her foe behind a sarcophagus that reminded Morgen of something out of a European catacomb.

The great shadowy creature she'd seen in the vision towered over it and over Calista, far larger than it had appeared from a bird's-eye point of view. Some magic must have clung to the old sarcophagus, for when an amorphous limb swatted at it, it didn't topple over. Not like the fire engine had done.

An indistinct black tail as thick and large as that of a T-rex swished back and forth as the creature—the demon—attacked the coffin. The tail collided with one of the few tombstones still standing near it. It exploded as if a grenade had gone off.

"What *is* that thing?" Sian whispered, then cursed as Napoleon wriggled free from her arms and ran off.

"You read the demon entry," Morgen said, hardly blaming the familiar for bailing. She wished *she* could play dead. "You know as much as I do."

"Horrifying."

"Yeah."

Led by Amar, the wolves had reached the graveyard. They

leaped over the fence and charged together toward the demon. They were brave and powerful, but Morgen feared that if the witches' magic hadn't been enough to stop it, werewolf fangs also wouldn't be effective.

Belinda, with her staff in hand and the orb atop it flashing red, stepped onto a bench at the back of the graveyard. She gripped an amulet similar to Morgen's and chanted, her eyes focused on the demon as it snaked a shadowy arm over the coffin to reach for Calista.

Calista ducked and attempted to scramble away, but the demon caught her. Her terrified scream echoed from the tombstones.

Belinda raised her staff, and a brilliant white beam shot out of the orb. It struck the back of the demon with a blinding flash. Morgen held her breath and hoped that would stop it.

The creature hefted Calista into the air and hurled her across the graveyard. She flew over the back fence and landed in dried leaves under the elm trees where Zorro had perched earlier. Her scream ended abruptly. The orange fog seemed to swallow her, and she didn't appear again.

The beam coming from Belinda's staff flickered and went out, and the demon lumbered around to face her. It appeared unwounded.

The wolves surged in, snapping at its blurry borders. True to the description that Sian had read, it didn't have a solid body, not in any sense that Morgen was familiar with. The snapping of their jaws rang out. Morgen couldn't tell if their sharp fangs chomped into anything or if it was like they were biting at air.

Whatever they were doing, it did distract the demon. Its focus shifted to them, and Belinda was able to climb down from the bench and crouch behind it with two other women kneeling on the ground. Olivia and Wendy.

The demon's amorphous body shifted, and one of its arms

struck one of the smaller wolves. Arturo? His voice sounded younger than the others as he yelped in pain and flew through the air. He slammed into a half-toppled mausoleum.

An eerie wind moaned, swirling through the graveyard. Not born from nature, it seemed to originate with the demon.

Even though the hell creature remained focused on the wolves, swatting an arm at Amar this time, the wind was also an attack. It blasted into one of the SUVs where the deputies crouched. They barely had time to fling themselves to the pavement before the power hurled the vehicle end over end. It bounced across the parking lot, metal wrenching as it crunched in upon itself. Pieces of wreckage flew everywhere, even skittering past Morgen and Sian.

"This is suicidal," Sian muttered.

Amar ducked low and lunged in under the demon's blurry arms, his jaws snapping. He connected with the shadowy substance of the creature, but once again, the bite didn't appear to hurt their enemy. The demon kicked Amar, and he flew across the graveyard, just as Arturo had.

"Amar!" Morgen blurted in fear. She clenched the staff with determination. "I'm going to try the imp-banishing spell."

Sian gripped her shoulder as Morgen stepped away from the protection of the church. "You can't convince me that's an *imp*."

"No, but I'm hoping it's related to imps. And that the spell works on it."

"Morgen. It'll kill you." Sian flung a hand toward the groaning deputies. "If that wind strikes you…"

"I know, but Amar and the others are in danger. I have to try." Morgen pulled her shoulder free and strode closer to the graveyard.

She pointed her antler staff at the demon and whispered the incantation. To her surprise, white energy shot from the end of the weapon. It appeared identical to what Belinda had hurled, and it blasted into the back of the demon, flashing brilliantly before fading.

But just as with Belinda's attack, it did nothing to stop their enemy. Also, just as with Belinda's attack, it got the demon's attention.

It had been advancing on Amar, but now, it lumbered slowly around to focus on Morgen. For the first time since Zorro had shared the vision, she saw the burning red eyes in the shadows of its head. The rest of its inky form was so dark that she couldn't see through it, couldn't see anything but soul-swallowing blackness. Only the pair of glowing eyes were different as they bored into her with the promise of death.

"That's enough to make a girl wet herself," she breathed.

The demon shambled toward her, broken stone crunching under its mass, its supposedly incorporeal mass.

Morgen chanted the banishing incantation again, more loudly this time. Power surged through the staff, the shaft quivering in her grip, and another charge of white energy blasted the demon. This time, it struck it in the front, and the white light made its entire body disappear.

But only for an instant. The light faded, revealing the demon advancing ponderously but inexorably toward her.

Morgen hefted the staff over her shoulder, thinking of throwing it and hoping for the best, the way she had with the gyrocopter.

"You're just pissing it off," Sian whispered. Surprisingly, she'd run up to join Morgen. "Don't you know any other spells?"

"I might be able to find its secret weakness." Morgen scoffed, highly doubting that incantation would work on a demon.

"Do it, then."

The demon reached the edge of the graveyard and plowed straight through the fence, iron wrenching as it was warped and torn from the ground.

Amar and Arturo had recovered from being thrown. They howled and sprang after the demon, trying to hurt it or at least keep it from getting to Morgen and Sian.

"Under the moon's magic, allow me to sleuth and reveal thy silvery truth," Morgen blurted, hoping for the best, though it wasn't as if a demon would be afraid of growing old or being mauled by muggers.

To her surprise, an illusion formed in front of it. Tree branches and roots and green energy flowed up from a lush meadow and wrapped around the demon, binding it. Some kind of... nature magic?

Morgen glanced at the antler tips near the side of her head. When Amar had called the tool a druidic Staff of Earth, he'd said Grandma had used its magic on the garden. Maybe it *would* hurt the demon if she threw it at it.

"Wait," she said, though they *couldn't* wait. Despite the attacks from the wolves, the demon kept coming. "Grandma's book has another incantation, one that's supposed to give one's weapon power."

Technically, it had been to empower a staff of witchery, not a staff of *druidry*, but maybe it would work. Of course, the antler staff already *had* power. Was it possible to give it more?

"Say it," Sian said. "Especially if you're planning to club that Godzilla with your little stick."

"It's a *big* stick. One sec." Morgen dredged the words from memory—she hadn't cast that incantation before or spent much time memorizing it. "Under the moon's magic, infuse this rod of meager wood with power too great to be understood."

Sian pulled her farther back as she chanted. They were running out of parking lot, and the demon was still advancing.

Two of the deputies had recovered enough to kneel and shoot at it, but once again, the bullets did nothing. They went through the demon as if it weren't there and ricocheted off the side of the church. Sian swore as one whizzed past over their heads.

The wolves snapped at the demon's backside, but it didn't slow.

"Under the moon's magic," Morgen repeated, shouting this time, "infuse this rod of meager wood with power too great to be understood!"

The staff tingled and quivered, as it had before, but nothing happened, and the demon kept coming.

She pulled it from her shoulder and held it in both hands, aiming the antlers at the creature. If she had to, she would charge it like a knight with a lance, but the shadowy apparition and burning red eyes chilled her, making her want nothing more than to flee instead.

"Maybe a cleverer rhyme," Sian suggested.

"I didn't write them."

Frowning in concentration, Morgen willed the staff to take the energy she'd hopefully infused it with and launch it at the demon. A surge of power poured forth, and a green beam shot out. It struck the demon in the torso.

Morgen winced, expecting another flash of light indicating the uselessness of the attack, but the green energy burrowed into the creature. It *flowed* into it and swirled about, mingling with the shadows. The demon's advance halted.

"Did it work?" Morgen whispered.

Its blob of a head fell back, and a wail worse than the sirens spewed forth. Fire shot into the air, as if its mouth were an erupting volcano. The flames split a hundred ways and rained down on the parking lot and the roof of the already-burning church. One of the wolves yelped and sprang aside, his fur singed.

"You did *something* to piss it off," Sian said.

"Yeah." Morgen didn't know if she'd struck a deadly blow or only enraged the creature.

The wail ended, and the demon lowered its head and resumed shambling toward them. Even though the green beam kept flowing from the staff, the blackness of their enemy's torso solidified and drove out the intruding magic.

"Say it again," Sian said. "It did something. Can you put more power into it?"

"It's not a cordless drill with multiple settings. I—"

A vision blasted into Morgen's mind, and she gasped and bent forward, losing her grip on the staff.

27

Sian caught the staff, keeping it from hitting the pavement as the vision absorbed Morgen.

"Not now," Morgen panted as her owl familiar shared imagery of him navigating at top speed through the trees.

Except that he seemed to be running instead of flying, springing over logs and darting around firs and ferns. The vision had to be coming from Lucky, not Zorro, but she'd left him in the house. He must have found an open window or a door that wasn't shut all the way.

Damn it, where was he now? Wolf Wood?

Aware of the demon looming not twenty feet away, Morgen tried to drive the vision out of her mind. But it persisted.

Orange light was visible off to Lucky's side. Wait, was that the graveyard? Had he already run all the way down to Bellrock?

As Lucky charged through the woods, dodging around trees and leaping over obstacles, someone came into view ahead of him. Was that Calista? Yes, her face was visible when she glanced back at Lucky. She must have risen and run away when nobody was paying attention. And Lucky had to be tracking her through the trees between Main Street and Second Street, not some dense woods. A brick building off to another side looked like the back of the Back Alley Pub.

"*Morgen!*" Sian gripped her arm. "What are you doing? Godzilla is rejuvenating itself. Focus."

"Can't," Morgen said, though she tried again to push aside the vision and see the demon through it. "Help me."

A flash of insight came to her, and she blurted, "Wait, you *can* help me."

The book had said that two witches of shared blood had to grab the staff and say the incantation, that their combined power was what would infuse it with magic.

"How?" Sian asked.

As the demon started shambling toward them again, in the vision, Lucky caught up with Calista. She'd been running, but she wasn't as fast as Lucky. She glanced over her shoulder, hearing his heavy panting. Fear widened her eyes. Did she know it was only a dog and not a ferocious werewolf?

"*How?*" Sian repeated as the demon lumbered closer, towering high and blocking out the stars. The orange fog swirled all about its legs.

The Lobos were still harrying it from behind, but their bites didn't bother it. Amar sprang onto the hood of an SUV and toward the thing's shadowy back, as if with greater height, he might find its neck or another vulnerable spot. But he fell slowly through the demon instead of landing on something solid. Even though it destroyed tombstones and mausoleums with its blows, it was as if it existed only partially in this dimension.

"We both have to hold the staff. And here, hold my amulet too, but don't take it off me. We both have to say the incantation I just —" Morgen broke off. In the vision, Calista stopped and spun with a wand in hand. "No!"

As Calista opened her mouth and started chanting, pointing

the wand at Lucky, something swooped in from her side. An owl. Zorro.

He snatched the wand out of Calista's grip and flapped away as she shrieked in fury.

"Fight it, Morgen!" Sian urged. "I don't know what to do."

As Lucky bowled into Calista, driving her to the ground, Morgen managed to shift her focus from the vision. The demon was scant feet away, arms raised to smash them.

"We say the incantation together. *Now.*"

Morgen and Sian chanted, "Under the moon's magic, infuse this rod of meager wood with power too great to be understood."

Morgen focused all of her mental energy on the staff and willed it to blast the demon back where it had come from. This time, far more power surged into the weapon. It acted like a conduit for them, aiming their combined energy at the demon. No, more than a conduit. An *amplifier*.

The air crackled with electricity, and a visible blast of green power smashed into the demon. It blew a hole through its shadowy body and shot out the far side. The wolves scattered.

"Move it around," Morgen yelled, the energy humming so loudly in her ears that she could barely hear her own words. "Like a pencil eraser."

Sian glanced at her but didn't object. They shifted the staff toward the demon's blob of a head. Again, the green beam of power blew away the shadows. As Morgen and Sian shifted it lower, the entire body disappeared, even the parts they hadn't struck.

Morgen's sweaty palm slipped on the shaft. Sian's grip must have also been weakening, for the butt of the staff hit the pavement, and the beam lurched and took out a tombstone. The startling power shattered the stone and sent pieces flying all over the graveyard.

Morgen cursed and pointed the weapon skyward so it couldn't

hit anything else. Sian yanked her hand away as if the staff had bitten her.

With her touch gone, the beam disappeared, and the crackling energy faded. Morgen let the antler tips droop to the ground. The demon was gone, and the orange fog was dissipating.

"Well," Franklin's voice came from the side where he and one of his men crouched behind an SUV. "That was a lot more effective than our guns."

Morgen realized she was no longer getting the vision from Lucky. Had he succeeded in pinning Calista? Or had she pulled out some other weapon and attacked him?

"Round up these women," Franklin called to his men. "I want to talk to them, and we may all need medical treatment."

"Wait," Morgen blurted as Amar, still in his wolf form, trotted up to her side. "We need to find Lucky." She rested a hand on Amar's furry back, the words for him as much as the deputy. "He went after Calista. I think they're behind the pub." She flung a hand toward the woods behind the graveyard.

Franklin hesitated. Amar did not. He surged in that direction, leaping the wrought-iron fence of the graveyard as easily as if it were the curb on a street. Morgen started after him, realized she should thank her sister for helping, and paused long enough to squeeze Sian's shoulder.

"Thanks!"

As she rushed after Amar, Sian called, "You're welcome, but remember that touching isn't necessary to induce familial bonding."

Morgen issued a thumbs-up without looking back again.

She lost sight of Amar as his powerful legs carried him through the trees faster than she could run, but it was hard to get lost in the narrow greenbelt between two blocks. Footfalls behind her informed her that Franklin and another deputy were running after her. Good. If they caught up with Calista, Morgen wanted someone with handcuffs nearby.

Disgruntled feminine cursing came from up ahead, and when Morgen rounded a densely packed stand of evergreens, Calista came into view. Not threatening anyone with a wand or incantation but squirming and snarling on the ground. Lucky sat on her chest, a torn piece of fabric dangling from his jaws.

When he saw Morgen, he wagged his tail vigorously. As a further insult, it thwacked Calista in the face. He looked quite pleased with himself.

Amar was still in his wolf form and stood nearby, further ensuring that Calista wouldn't go anywhere.

The stirring of wings in a tree caught Morgen's eye. Zorro sat up there with Calista's wand clenched in his beak.

Morgen came to a stop beside Amar and rested her hand on his back again. "How come you don't have anything in your mouth?"

The noble look he gave her suggested he wouldn't deign to answer. At least it wasn't a *grumpy* noble look.

Franklin and the other deputy tramped into view.

"Your prisoner," Morgen offered magnanimously, extending a hand toward Calista.

"Yes, thank you, Ms. Keller." Franklin holstered his gun and pulled handcuffs off his belt.

Would they be sufficient for keeping a witch prisoner? Hopefully, Calista wouldn't be that formidable without her wand and whatever powders and hex ingredients she had stashed in her pockets. Presumably, the deputies would frisk her and remove those.

"Would you mind asking your fearsome canine to step aside?" Franklin added.

"Lucky." Morgen's treat pocket was mostly occupied by crumbs, the goodies having fallen out somewhere during the running and fighting, but she scrounged a piece and held it out. "Treat."

Lucky bounded over, dropped the torn fabric, and sat attentively for his reward.

As the deputies handcuffed the glowering Calista, Belinda came into view, picking her way through the undergrowth.

"Calista," she said, planting her staff in the ground. The men eyed the glowing sphere on top warily. "I will reiterate what I said before. You are officially cast out from the coven for dabbling in dark and forbidden arts and putting the entire town in danger. I'll be in touch with our sisters up and down the coast to make sure you're not welcome anywhere."

"Bite me," Calista said, though it was a weary retort, and there was a haunted look in her eyes. She had to know she'd lost control of that demon—and almost lost her life.

"Your repentant words won't change my mind," Belinda said dryly.

Calista looked at Morgen and Amar as the deputies led her away, but she only shook her head in exasperation, and perhaps defeat. Morgen hoped that meant she was going to give up on revenge, and also that she would rot in jail for the next twenty years.

"Let's hope," she murmured, having had more than enough of witches gunning for her.

Amar shifted into his human form. Morgen's hand had been on his back, and it ended up somewhat lower.

Instead of leering in appreciation, which she thought he might do, he winced and gripped his ribs. His nudity made it easy to see that bruises were already darkening his skin, and Morgen grimaced in sympathy, remembering how hard the demon had kicked him across the graveyard.

"Oh, my." Belinda looked at the nude Amar before she caught herself, then shifted her gaze up toward the trees.

Amar ignored her, wrapped an arm around Morgen's waist, and pulled her close to kiss her. He didn't let go of his ribs, and she vowed to send him to see Dr. Valderas soon, but she returned the kiss to show her appreciation—and that she longed to return to what they'd been doing before Phoebe interrupted them.

"I'll just... gather the ladies," Belinda said. "We should have a meeting. We've a few things to discuss."

Morgen was barely aware of her walking away. She might have kept kissing Amar for hours, but Zorro flew over and dropped something on her head.

"Ow," she blurted, breaking the kiss and catching it before it fell to the ground. Calista's wand.

"I see your owl is still irreverent," Amar said.

"It seems to be a permanent personality trait," Morgen said.

"Remind me to order new windows for the barn so I can keep him from leaving droppings on my projects and molting in my bed. I don't want my apartment to be unkempt now that I know I might be able to entice ladies to spend the night."

"Are you planning to entice a *lot* of ladies into spending the night?"

"Just one, but she's uptight about being covered in animal remains."

"Huh. She sounds high maintenance."

"Very much so." Amar grinned and kissed her again.

28

THOSE WHO WEREN'T IN NEED OF IMMEDIATE MEDICAL ATTENTION convened in the Crystal Parlor. The building was far enough from the graveyard that it hadn't been damaged, but the numerous bedraggled witches and familiars inside threatened the integrity of the display carousels.

Morgen stood in the back of the main room with Amar and Wendy—and Wendy's soot-covered ferret. Napoleon chattered from her shoulder, much livelier and more talkative now that there weren't any demons around. Morgen wouldn't have minded if Zorro had come into the shop riding on *her* shoulder, but she'd last seen him winging back toward Wolf Wood, clearly having had enough action for the night.

Amar stayed close to Morgen, clasping her hand and glowering at the crowd. After the battle, most of the other Lobos had disappeared, back to their home in the woods, or maybe up to Morgen's house to celebrate their victory in the hot tub. They'd sent Arturo, who had bruised ribs and an egg-sized lump on his head, to see Dr. Valderas. Morgen had gotten Amar to promise, however reluctantly, that he would also visit the vet, but he'd refused to leave her until he knew the witches wouldn't trouble her further.

Phoebe weaved through the crowd and display carousels, directing people where to stand and promising that if they broke anything, they would buy it.

Sian had walked as far as the front door, peered in at all the people, and said she would wait in the truck with Lucky. The fact that the other witches were curious about her and had questions had only cemented her determination to avoid the claustrophobic congregation.

As a fellow introvert, Morgen empathized.

Belinda stepped onto a chair—that earned a frown from Phoebe but not a comment about breaking and buying—so people could see her over the carousels and display cases. She raised her staff, and the murmurs of conversations halted.

"This has been a most unfortunate night," Belinda said, "driven by someone who was cast out of the coven and whom we shouldn't have been listening to or even speaking with anymore. Everyone knew that."

Belinda cast a baleful gaze around the shop but didn't let it linger long on anyone in particular. A number of women looked down at their feet. Phoebe frowned, but she didn't object.

"Now that Calista is in custody without her amulet, her wand, or any other tools to help her draw upon her powers, we shouldn't see more of her, but if she returns, she is *not* to be listened to," Belinda said. "People were hurt, and buildings and vehicles were destroyed because of her. We're lucky nobody *died*. We're also fortunate that someone was able to banish the demon."

Belinda looked at Morgen, as did everyone else, and she had to resist the urge to hide behind Amar. She'd longed to be accepted by the coven, but that didn't mean she wanted to be the center of attention.

"What if the demon had escaped Bellrock and ravaged the

entire Puget Sound area?" Belinda continued, returning her gaze to the gathering. "This is not what the powers of our ancestors were meant to be used for."

Nobody argued with her. Even if Calista had gathered supporters before, the night's events might have changed the minds of those who'd thrown in their lots with her.

"Now, we will discuss Morgen Keller's application to join the coven." Belinda turned on the chair to look at her again.

"Uhm." Morgen lifted a finger. "I didn't actually put in an application."

"Someone submitted one for you." Belinda quirked an eyebrow at Phoebe. "And assured us that you'd pay dues and share the continuing updates and additions to your software going forward."

Updates and additions? Morgen hadn't intended to make working on the witch database her entire career.

"We're going to make it great." Wendy waved her arms in excitement, prompting her ferret to chitter and run from shoulder to shoulder. "I'm already sketching artwork for it. There'll be a free version for everyone and then a paid version with the tutorials, right? I'm going to contribute a bunch of stuff on jewelry making. Of course, everyone in Bellrock should get the paid version for free, especially if they contribute, but we'll make enough from charging other witches in the world to pay the bills for the developers." Wendy lowered her voice to whisper to Morgen, "One day, I'll be able to get a house, right? With *broadband* internet." Her eyes gleamed with hope.

"Maybe you could start with an apartment," Morgen suggested, wondering when they'd firmed up their plans. Wendy must have been doing a lot of brainstorming out in her van. "A little one. I don't think we'll make a fortune from an app on such a niche subject."

"Are you sure? There are millions of witches around the world that need their ingredients, spells, and rituals better organized."

"*Millions*?" Morgen gaped at her.

"Sure. Not all of them have witch blood and can truly access magic, but that doesn't keep the hobbyists from trying."

"Huh. Well, if there's a market, maybe you could eventually earn enough to buy a house."

"Inexpensive real estate may be available in town after the demon attack," Amar said.

"Like the buildings across from the church that burned?" Morgen asked.

"*Very* inexpensive."

"I just need good internet," Wendy said. "You know, for uploading my work on the app."

"And conquering the world in *Castle Crawler*?" Morgen asked.

"Yes. And I'm conquering the *metaverse*, not just the world."

"Ambitious."

Belinda cleared her throat. "We'll take a vote now on the application."

All eyes turned toward Morgen again, making her wish she'd joined Sian in the truck. Several of the women's expressions were skeptical, but they weren't openly hostile. Only Olivia stared sullenly at Morgen. Most of the women simply looked weary and like they would do whatever it took to be allowed to go home.

"Raise your hand if you're in favor of Morgen joining the coven and sharing her software," Belinda said, keeping the two notions linked.

Morgen was glad she'd sent the alpha version around. If she hadn't, she might be receiving far more hostile and skeptical glares. Not every hand went up, but most did.

Morgen wondered if she should pander further by inviting them up to a hot tub party at the house, but given that it might be brimming with Lobos, that might not be a good idea. Besides, as long as Sian was visiting, she would frown sternly at anything resembling a party.

"That's the majority," Belinda said. "Welcome to the coven, Morgen. We'll send you an introductory packet on proper behavior for witches and what's expected from a member."

"Proper behavior?" Morgen mouthed.

"It mostly means you have to pay dues and come to the meetings," Wendy said. "And not do anything to embarrass the rest of the witches in town."

"Don't mention that you have two familiars, one of which is your *dog*," Phoebe whispered. "I only put the owl on the application. Zephyr."

"It's Zorro," Morgen said.

"That isn't a suitable name for a familiar."

"But—"

Phoebe lifted a hand. "I can only help you so much, Morgen. Go along with it."

"Are you *sure* you want to be one of them?" Amar rumbled. "Gwen was a lone witch."

"She also knew what she was doing." Morgen wondered who'd originally taught the witch ways to Grandma. *Her* mother or grandmother? Morgen might never know, but she hoped the amulet would give her more visions of the past so she could get to know Grandma better. Even if it was too late for them to have a relationship.

"Most of the time." Amar's eyes glinted, as if he'd seen a few notable exceptions during the years he'd known Grandma.

After the vote, the meeting broke up, and Amar accompanied Morgen back to the truck. He wrapped an arm around her as they walked, and she leaned into him before remembering his bruised ribs. He winced and hissed, though he quickly hid the hiss under a growl.

Apologizing, she pulled away from him, but he gripped her hand and kept her close.

"I'm fine," he said, issuing another growl as he gazed into her eyes, this one having more to do with desire than pain, or so she chose to interpret it.

It sent a little thrill down her spine, and she might have kissed him, but she spotted Sian waiting in the cab. Even though she was watching them indifferently—and might have been zoning out completely and unaware of their approach—it made Morgen self-conscious.

"Once Dr. Valderas patches you up, maybe we can return to what we were doing when this all started," Morgen whispered. "Somewhere private."

"Such as my apartment?" His eyelids drooped as he gazed at her through his lashes. "Or the woods?"

"I have a fondness for beds, but I guess I'd be amenable to either." Especially since *the woods* seemed to get him excited. Maybe that was natural for a werewolf. "As long as I can bring along some blankets made from soft and synthetic materials." And maybe an air mattress and Egyptian cotton sheets.

"Nothing gets a guy randy like talk of synthetic materials."

"I'm sure we can come up with other things to get you randy." She smirked at him.

"Yes."

They'd reached the truck, but before heading to the driver's side, Amar leaned in and kissed her.

Morgen thought about objecting, due to their nearby witness and his obvious injury, but the notion lasted only a second. She circled her arms around his shoulders and carefully returned the kiss, glad the night hadn't turned out as badly as she'd feared. They were both alive, and with luck, nobody would be out for her in the foreseeable future.

He nipped her gently, bringing to mind the powerful wolf

who'd sprung into battle with the demon, deadly fangs flashing. Maybe such things shouldn't have titillated her, but they did, and she hoped his ribs wouldn't take long to heal.

A knock on the window interrupted them.

"Please return me to the house before continuing your precoital stimulation," Sian said.

Amar snorted, swatted Morgen on the butt, and climbed gingerly into the driver's side. Given how tough he was, she worried that his ribs were *more* than bruised.

Morgen slid onto the bench seat beside her sister, giving her the irked glare that her interruption deserved.

"Did you have to change yourself to acquire your romantic partner?" Sian asked, unperturbed by the glare.

"I did not," Morgen admitted, smiling to think of Amar that way—and still vastly relieved that witches couldn't be turned into werewolves. Even if the thought had crossed her mind—*more* than crossed it—she was glad she hadn't had to give up anything about herself or succumb to a life of nocturnal hunting and meat eating to make Amar want to be with her. "I just made him some jewelry."

"I approve."

"Of men wearing jewelry?"

"Of gift-giving as a means of establishing a rapport. Fashion choices concern me little."

"Yes, I know. I've seen your socks."

"My socks provide ample cushioning, keep my feet warm, and dry quickly when dampened. They are practical and whimsical."

"Ideal."

"Yes."

EPILOGUE

Morgen brought two glasses of lemonade out to the porch and handed one to Sian. She sat on a wide swing made from a slab of cedar. It had appeared that morning without a word, but Morgen trusted the handsome craftsmanship was Amar's work.

His ribs had been *broken*, not merely bruised, and he'd been moving gingerly these past few days, but that hadn't kept him away from his projects. If anything, he'd been more dedicated than ever to his work.

Dr. Valderas had promised that werewolves healed quickly and that Amar would be back to his usual self in a week or two instead of the usual six, but he had forbidden Amar to shift into wolf form to run around and hunt at night. Not being able to answer the call of the wild had left Amar grumpy and irritable, and Morgen was a little surprised that the swing had appeared. When they'd first met, he *had* promised to make a piece of furniture for her, but she hadn't expected it after the fire, not when he was so behind on work for his paying clients. She would let him know that she appreciated it.

"Thank you," Sian said, accepting the glass.

Morgen sat beside her on the swing, wondering if this would prompt a lecture about her preferred *three feet of personal space,* but Sian was gazing out toward the lawn and the trees, her eyes unfocused. Lucky was nosing around out there, fortunately not sharing any visions of grass and gopher holes with Morgen today.

"Are you pondering how life has changed since you've discovered that werewolves exist, Grandma was a witch, and graveyard-demolishing demons can be summoned at any time?" Morgen asked.

"No. I'm pondering what I'm going to do with my life now that I can't partake in field work."

"You could retire and become a witch."

Sian gave her a don't-be-ridiculous look. "I'm forty-two. You don't retire at forty-two."

Morgen didn't point out that she'd been out of work long enough now that people might consider *her* retired. Oddly, she'd been so busy that it hadn't felt like retirement or even a vacation. In the kitchen, her laptop was open. She'd been adding information to her growing witch database all morning. Not, however, anything from *Incantations of Power.* She intended to keep that book's contents a secret, as Grandma had requested.

"I'll have to leave soon and return to the university. I'll see what kind of lab research opportunities are available." Sian's mouth twisted with displeasure.

"Can't stand the thought of hanging out here with me for a couple of weeks, huh?" Morgen said it lightly, but the thought stung. Her sister had been out of the country and working nonstop for years. Surely, she had some vacation time coming to her. Why did Sian have to rush off so soon? The Lobos had finished their work, so the property was a lot quieter. Even serene. "I guess you've never really liked..." *me,* Morgen almost finished, but she didn't truly believe that. She was just feeling hurt. "People," she said instead, forcing a smile.

"They can be unappealing."

"And siblings, as well."

Sian cocked her head. "What makes you think I feel that way? We're much more similar than we are to any of our brothers or cousins."

"I know, but the fact that you're already planning to leave suggests you don't want to be around me for extended periods of time."

"I don't want to be around anyone for extended periods of time. You know how I feel about crowds of people. Even with your werewolf construction workers gone, this property is still overflowing with inhabitants."

"Amar and Wendy are the only ones left, and they don't even live in the house."

Admittedly, Wendy came inside, but only to use the kitchen and the bathroom on the first floor. Morgen had offered her a room, but she preferred the privacy of her camper van. Or perhaps it was simply that she had her gaming computer set up in there and could blast the accompanying music without bothering anyone. Since Morgen had ordered the installation of a satellite dish for internet, Wendy hadn't hinted that she would be leaving soon.

"Your guests are around, and they make noise." Sian sent a baleful look toward Amar's chainsaw stump. "Last night, I woke to a ferret squeaking under my window."

"Serenading you with the dulcet notes of the Mustelidae family?"

"I think he was trying to catch a mouse."

"Dulcetly?"

"No."

"Your sense of humor is underdeveloped," Morgen said. "You should take a lab job at the university in Seattle so you can come up for frequent visits to enjoy country life and learn how to laugh a little."

"Frequent?"

"Occasional?"

"That might be acceptable."

"Your enthusiasm warms my soul."

Amar walked out of the barn carrying a wooden box with an opening cut into one side.

He stopped in front of them. "This is for your owl."

"You made him a nesting box?" Morgen didn't know if male owls used such things, but she beamed a smile at him, appreciating the thoughtful sentiment.

"I made an alternative home to my half-finished dressers, coat racks, and umbrella stands, the *current* places where he nests."

"That's unusual," Sian said. "Spotted owls generally prefer to nest in dense stands of old-growth forest where the tree canopy protects them from the sky."

"This one is special," Amar said in a flat tone.

"Especially irreverent," Morgen said.

She thought of the wand that Zorro had stolen. *Calista's* wand. Morgen had tried to give it to Phoebe, figuring it should go to a family member, but Phoebe hadn't wanted it. She didn't seem to want anything to do with her now-incarcerated sister.

Maybe Morgen could talk Sian into researching the wand with her and memorizing a few incantations. As long as Sian had witch blood too, she might as well learn how to protect herself. Especially if she was going to occasionally visit Bellrock. Morgen hoped things would settle down, but with a coven of witches and two packs of werewolves sharing the area, that wasn't a guarantee.

"Thank you for the gift, Amar. Do you have any suggestions on where to place it? On the side of the house? Or up in the trees?" Morgen looked at Sian, guessing she might know more about owls than Amar.

"They like to be near fields and wetlands for hunting," Sian said.

"We have a field here." Morgen waved to the sprawling lawn. "And, uh, does a new hot tub count as a wetland?"

"No."

Napoleon ran around the corner of the house, ducked between Amar's legs, and chattered at Morgen from the porch steps.

"Is there a problem?" she asked the ferret.

"Maybe there are mice under the porch," Sian grumbled.

Morgen shook her head as the ferret spun a circle, ran partway back to the corner of the house, then paused to wait.

"No... I think he wants help. Could Wendy be in trouble?"

"What kind of trouble could she have gotten into in her van?" Amar asked.

Napoleon ran back to the steps, rose on his hind legs, and chattered at Morgen again.

Amar reached down and plucked him up. "Maybe we should—" The ferret squeaked and went limp in his hand. Amar sighed. "Never mind."

"We better check the van." Morgen trotted down the steps, pausing only to take Napoleon from Amar's hand.

Once he was out of werewolf clutches, Napoleon came to life. He squirmed in Morgen's arms, then ran up to her shoulder, chattering and looking toward the back of the house.

Sian and Amar must have been curious, because they followed Morgen in that direction.

The van's side door was open, but Wendy wasn't inside. The sound of hot tub jets bubbling came from the deck.

Had some of the Lobos returned to use it? They were done with the construction, but several of them kept making excuses to stop by. They seemed to like that her home was smack in the middle of Wolf Wood, and the hot tub had been popular with them as well. Since they'd paid for it and done all the work to install it, Morgen hated to shoo them away, but if one of them was making Wendy uncomfortable, she would put a stop to that.

As she rounded the corner and the hot tub came into view, Napoleon ran down Morgen's back, sprinted up the stairs to the deck, and climbed up to the railing so he could see into the hot tub. The lid was open, and two occupants sat inside, Wendy and José Antonio. His arms were spread across the rim as he leaned back, clearly relaxed. Wendy, a little shyer, had her hands in her lap, though she was smiling at whatever he was saying—the noise of the bubbles made it hard to hear. She didn't appear to have been kidnapped or otherwise be in danger.

Nonetheless, Napoleon rose up on his hind quarters and chattered and squeaked.

"I'm *fine*," Wendy told him. "I'm not drowning. You didn't have to get help." She looked sheepishly at Morgen.

"What are you doing here?" Amar asked José Antonio.

"Preparing for the big barbecue party."

"Party?" Sian asked, her tone flat and unamused.

"You can hide in the house and read," Morgen told her.

"You knew about this?" Amar looked like he'd been about to chastise José Antonio.

"No, but if it's inevitable, I don't want my sister to flee the property."

"It's *supposed* to be a surprise," Wendy said. "I invited some of the ladies in the coven who are less… hate-filled when it comes to werewolves. And José Antonio invited some of the werewolves who aren't as hate-filled when it comes to witches."

"So, it's going to be a *small* party," Amar said.

José Antonio grinned and held up his thumb and forefinger with a tiny space between. "Only a few. But maybe more will come when the aromas from my talented cooking waft down the hill to Bellrock." He pointed to a pair of large coolers sitting by the new outdoor kitchen. "I'm going to make my famous elk balls in red-wine sauce. And I brought steaks, sausages, and hamburgers, and bacon to wrap around everything." He winked, brought his fingers to his lips, and kissed them. "Delicious. Oh, and don't worry. I brought eggplant to grill for the *señorita*."

"Or anyone else who'd like to continue to enjoy unimpeded arterial function in their body," Morgen murmured.

"I'll take a bacon burger," Sian said.

"I thought you were going to stay in the house and read," Morgen said.

"Not if there's bacon."

"All those years that our parents wondered how to get you out of your room, and they could have just fired up the grill?"

"As long as something good was on it. If they'd been barbecuing eggplant, I would have hidden under the bed and locked the door."

"Ha ha."

Napoleon kept running back and forth on the railing, chattering and peering at Wendy. He didn't seem to realize that she was unlikely to drown in the hot tub. José Antonio looked at him and growled. Napoleon flopped down, draped over the railing, and played dead again.

"The life of a familiar is fraught," Morgen said.

"That must be why they're so impertinent," Amar said.

"Maybe you could build him a nesting box, so he'd have a safe place to go."

"Ferrets enjoy climbing on cat trees," Wendy said. "I had one for him when I lived with my sisters."

"Oh, Amar is talented," Morgen said. "He could make an amazing cat—er, ferret tree."

Amar lifted his chin. "I *am* talented, and as such, I do not craft *ferret* trees. I create exquisite furnishings for highly discriminating clients with fine taste."

"You know you're holding an owl box, right?" Morgen pointed out.

"Only because I need to bribe someone's familiar not to molt on my belongings. I'm *not* making ferret furniture."

"You're still kind of a grumpy werewolf, you know." Morgen patted his arm, then mouthed, "He'll make it," to Wendy.

She beamed a smile at her.

Amar opened his mouth, as if to object further, but something out in the woods caught his attention.

Pedro walked out of the trees, heading straight for them with a grim expression on his face.

Morgen lost her humor as she eyed Amar, afraid Pedro was still holding a grudge and had come to challenge the rival for Maria's affections to a duel. Amar's face grew masked and hard.

Ignoring Morgen and the others, Pedro stopped on the lawn. Why had he come on foot instead of driving?

"We need to talk, Amar," Pedro said.

Amar handed the owl box to Morgen.

"Don't let him goad you into a duel," she whispered, wishing he wouldn't speak with Pedro at all. "If Dr. Valderas doesn't want you hunting, he definitely wouldn't approve of you fighting." She grimaced at the thought of one of his broken ribs puncturing his lungs.

But Pedro didn't throw any punches or even appear that angry when Amar joined him. He switched to Spanish, and they moved off for a private conversation. Pedro gripped Amar's shoulder, as if they were still comrades and Pedro hadn't been furious about Maria choosing Amar over him. Was it a ruse? A *trap*?

"Do you have any idea what that's about?" Morgen asked José Antonio.

He shook his head. "Nah, I haven't seen Pedro in a few days. Looks like trouble though. No other reason someone would have such a grim face when such good food is about to be made."

Morgen hoped he was wrong.

Pedro pointed toward the trees, then released Amar's shoulder and called what sounded like a warning to José Antonio before walking back into Wolf Wood.

"What did he say?" Wendy asked when José Antonio's easygoing expression faltered.

José Antonio hesitated. "Nothing you need to worry about."

"Is it something *you* need to worry about?" Morgen asked.

Something *Amar* needed to worry about?

José Antonio sighed. Instead of answering, he sank below the surface of the bubbles, as if he wanted to hide.

Amar remained on the lawn, gazing out into the trees, though Pedro had disappeared from view. Morgen headed over to join him, clasping his hand and trying to smile encouragingly.

"José Antonio implied there might be trouble," she said.

"Someone from our homeland who hunted us long ago has been spotted in the area," Amar said quietly.

"Someone who's still hunting you?"

He never had told her how his pack came to be thousands of miles from where they'd been born.

"It's possible," Amar said.

"It's not someone that witches sent after you, is it?" She remembered the story he'd told her of the hunter with the silver bullets.

"No. Nothing to do with witches this time." Amar squeezed her hand, then released it and headed for the barn. "Witches," she barely heard him say, "would have been easier to deal with."

THE END

The adventure continues in *Moment of Tooth*. Coming early 2022!